Hunger twisted tightly in his stomach at the sight of her, insistently reminding him of his purpose here. The reason he was brought back. Sebastian closed his eyes and tried to absorb as much of the home's warmth as he could through the tips of his decaying fingers. He drifted in a dark reverie as he imagined what it would be like to go inside, getting to the girl, and having her tender flesh in his hands, her pliant musculature surrendering to his teeth; and all the while, the warmth of her blood flooding the desert of his tongue.

Hunger sidled closer and spoke to him then, as a conspirator might, and told him of a plan, a plan of just how to get at this sweet, tender thing behind the glass. Sebastian nodded as the voices growled to him from his belly, and a dark, understanding smile spread arthritically across his lips.

"Yesssss," he hissed to them. "I sssssee…"

Inside the house, the girl kneeling by the bed suddenly stood and, with big, bouncing hops, she crawled up onto the bed. Hunger, like an ever-present collaborator, silently spoke of what Sebastian must do next; else his prey might make its escape.

Slowly raising his hand up off the glass, he let it drop. The solitary rap echoed in the still, night air, reverberating off the side of the house. As his face tried to manage a rictus smile, he saw the little girl looked toward the window. Satisfaction swelled within him when her opened her mouth and squealed in delight.

"Daddy!!!"

He smiled and licked his lips in anticipation as he watched her jump down from the bed and run across the room to open the window.

–From "Homecoming"

ISBN 978-1-63789-924-3

For information address Crossroad Press at 141 Brayden Dr., Hertford, NC 27944
A Macabre Ink Production -Macabre Ink is an imprint of Crossroad Press.
www.crossroadpress.com

First Edition

HORROR BOOK

BY THOM CARNELL

MACABRE INK

CONTENTS

FAMILY MATTERS

This is a 'cut' chapter from the first No Flesh Shall Be Spared novel. I thought that there were a few loose ends in the story that needed some tidying up, so, I wrote this. For flow reasons, I went with the more John Ford ending that's in the book, but I like this piece and wish I could have included it. I like that it sort of puts a button on Monk's story and hints at the life he might have had if he'd only just gotten out in time. There's just a simple beauty to this one that I find appealing. Hopefully, you will, too.

A chill, November wind blew dried maple leaves across the wraparound porch of the old farmhouse that sat out at the end of old Severin Road. The building's paint was cracked and its eaves sagged just a little, but the sense of warmth and welcome it gave off was undeniable.

The brisk breeze blew across the back of Aileen Chaiken's neck as she sat in her favorite porch chair and it caused her to shiver. She pulled her worn, blue cardigan a little tighter around her thin shoulders and hugged herself, her black hair swirling about her head like a pinwheel in the breeze. She pinched her face and squinted to see across the wide meadow that separated her modest, two-story farmhouse from the fields of corn and soybeans she and her husband, Oren, owned and worked.

She got out of the chair slowly and walked over to the porch's railing which ran alongside the perimeter of the house. As she leaned against one of the posts that supported the overhanging bedrooms on the second floor, she tried to see where Oren had gotten to. Her view was obscured however by the rows of crops.

That man… he was always working too hard, she mused. Lord only knew from where he got his energy. He was always up before anyone on the farm, and the last to turn the lights out… even at his age, the man never stopped.

In the living room window, she caught a glimpse of herself and, realizing she was squinting again, instantly relaxed her features. The reflection she saw there reminded her of one of those little apple head dolls Susie Lynn Russet sold at the county fair every year; their crumpled, brown faces gaping out foolishly from behind the meticulously stitched-together costumes of felt and gingham that she'd made for them.

Aileen carefully stepped down from the porch and walked without hurry across the ankle-deep grass that made up the house's front yard. She turned at the flowerbed of roses thinking that if it didn't rain soon, she'd have to put some water on them. The blooms were looking sad and the leaves were wilting slightly.

Once passed the colorful flowers, she headed on across the meadow toward the main roadway. She'd initially come out of the house to fetch the day's mail from the box located out at the edge of the property but had gotten distracted by the splendor of the day and the comfort of her overstuffed chair.

Jessup Browning, who'd been their mailman for nearly a decade, always arrived with his deliveries right around noon each and every day. He was funny that way, punctual in the way only country folk could be, and he'd not been late or sick a day in all of the years they'd lived on the farm. It was unlikely he would be late today.

She glanced down at the watch clinging to her wrist and saw that Mickey's hands were straight up in what her father had always called 'the hostage position.' She chuckled briefly, but still felt the bite from the distant memory.

As she walked along, she was finally able to see Oren who was across the field, driving the tractor back toward the barn. She could see his dark hair shimmer like glass for a moment in the day's sun. It was easy for her to imagine the sweet smell of the day on him, on his clothes, in his hair, on his skin. As it was getting to be just about noon, he'd no doubt be more than ready for his lunch. She knew he'd be wanting something hot, something that would stick to his ribs, after a hard morning of toiling in the oftentimes unresponsive fields.

They were lucky though, she supposed, luckier than most. A lot of their neighbors had already had to sell their lots out. Or, at the very least, they were slowly being bled to death by the bank as they tried to stay in operation. Loans taken had a way of coming due at the worst possible times and the hard life of carving your existence from the earth could sometimes be fickle. Being a farmer had never been an easy thing. It meant that your life was either feast or it was famine, although usually more famine than feast. Still though, it was all Oren knew; all he'd *ever* known.

Only the good lord knew how many farms in other parts of the county were gone now, gobbled up by the big corporations after all that unpleasantness with the Dead a number of years back. Even though, folks around here had been fortunate in that regard. The population wasn't so dense in these parts. So, when the dead ones came back, the population here had been pretty spread out. It had been easy to track Them and put them all back down in short order.

Whatever the local police or militia couldn't send back to their graves, the deceased's own family were pressed into service. Farming and tending livestock meant that you soon became comfortable with the idea of death and dying. Animals were born, they lived, and then they died to serve out their respective roles in the cycle. It was just the way things worked.

So, it was usually a quick prayer and a load of buck shot that returned things back to the way God had intended them. It was another one of the good things about most farmers being hunters—they had access to guns, and they knew how to use them.

Far off, she heard a sudden yelp followed by a curse that only the devil could author come from the direction of the fields. It was a sound that she knew all too well. Oren had a way of getting himself hurt with the slightest of provocations. He was always stubbing his toe or jamming his finger on things. His mother used to say that he could cut himself in a roomful of pillows. She was gone now, but the saying survived. Over the years they were together, she'd heard that yelp—and the curses that always followed it—more times than she wished to remember. She made a mental note, though, to get the first aid kit out and have it ready for him with his lunch.

The two of them had been married for going on twenty years now and they'd been twenty good years at that. They'd met at a local market, each grabbing for the same ear of sweet corn. Their eyes met and that, as they say, was that. A swift courtship ensued and the two of them were married a short time after, just a few short months after she'd come to this place in the middle of nowhere, in the middle of Ohio. The children came along in their own time and were the apples of both their eyes.

Oren's family had been farmers as had their family before them. It was a vocation that had been handed down from father to son like an old, tattered coat, with each successive generation finding that the garment yielded less and less in the way of warmth. The farm had given them life, though. And it made for fertile ground for them to lay down roots.

The farm… was family.

As for her side of the family tree, they were not people with whom she regularly kept in contact, especially her father. What she knew about him was limited to the sporadic things she'd read in the newspapers about the very different life her father had chosen for himself.

Her mother died giving birth to her, so Aileen had never been able to know her. She'd only heard stories. Growing up as an only child, she'd been raised by her mother's elderly parents and had seen precious little of her father as she matured. He'd chosen a path that she could never understand and, once she was married and had become a parent herself, one which she would not have anywhere near the children. She still held out hope that she and her father would one day reconcile and had even extended an open invitation for him to come live with her should he ever decide to leave his old life behind.

Who knew? Life could be funny sometimes…

She looked back over her shoulders and saw that Oren was out of the field and had just reached the large double doors of the barn. It would take him another half an hour or so to put up the tractor and give the livestock their afternoon feeding. There was still plenty of time for her to fetch the day's mail and return to the kitchen to warm up some soup for the two of them. She might even slice up one of the loaves of bread she'd pulled from the oven that morning, knowing they would still be warm for dinner.

She sighed quietly to herself as she continued across the field. She was tired, but still felt content in the knowledge that their lives were simple ones and, despite the hardships and the loans and the worry, they were glad for it. She'd never been one for the lights and bustle of 'city life' and the existence she and her family had carved out for themselves here was a comforting juxtaposition to the life her father led.

Aileen approached the fence which ran along the property line and carefully stepped over one of the split railings. The soothing scent of wild petunias and yellow-fringed orchids rode on the breeze like aromatic hitchhikers and teased her sense of smell. Despite her caution, the hem of her dress got snagged on a sharp splinter of wood and it ripped slightly.

"Oh, dear…," she said aloud, her voice sounding like silk as it was caught on the midday's air. "Tsk, now I'll have to mend that."

She looked up at the road and thought that it looked like a thin, black ribbon that had been stretched out in either direction for as far as her eye could see. In other words, the way was as clear as it always was at this time of day. Neighbors were all undoubtedly still busy with their chores and had no time—much less an inclination—to travel anywhere, not with the weather being as fickle as it had been as of late. Off in the distance, she saw the gathering plumes of dark clouds amassing in the distant sky.

Looks like we'll have a bit of rain comin' tonight.

With a small hop, she leapt across the drainage ditch which ran between the road and the property line. It was dry now but it was choked with robust moth mullein weeds, their white flowers brightly reflecting back the sunlight. Once she was across, she walked over to the mailbox. It was an old rusting thing that Oren had nailed to one of the fence posts that splintered a year or so ago. They'd found the length of wood back when they were replacing the fence in what Oren always referred to as 'the back forty,' even though it was only a few anemic acres. They'd been meaning to replace the old thing with a new one from the Ace Hardware back in town but, what with the crops needing looking after and the daily care of the livestock, they simply hadn't gotten around to it as of yet.

She pulled down the front door of the mailbox, opening it, and smiled when she saw that Jessup Browning had not disappointed her. It was nice to have some things that you could still count on, she thought to herself. Pulling the envelopes and advertisements from inside, she looked them over one at a time. Bills... Bills... A flyer from the feed supply depot in town... More bills...

She moved to close the box but noticed the corner of another, larger envelope laying deep inside, hidden in the shadows of the mailbox's dark interior. She bent down in order to get a better look at it. Sure enough, there toward the back, lay a folded-over, manila envelope wrapped in two large rubber bands. She idly noticed that there was no postmark on it.

"Hmmm," she mused as she glanced around. "What on earth?"

Aileen reached inside and pulled the faded package out. It was heavy and felt like it had four thin, rectangular blocks inside. She pursed her lips and wondered who could have sent it... and who delivered it? Recently, and not for the first time, a man from the Purina company had been snooping around, asking questions of them and their neighbors about their solvency and whether they'd be interested in selling off their land.

It seemed that the vultures always circled when trouble was nearest.

And even though they were in debt up to their eyeballs and desperately needed a break, Aileen knew that Oren would never abandon the farm. However, she also knew that if something good didn't happen for them soon, they would have no choice but to sell out like all the rest. The subject was never anything Oren wanted to talk about, but she had quietly begun to take notice of the wear such thoughts had begun to exert on him. It would all work itself out, God willing, she silently reassured herself, but, deep in her heart, she wasn't so sure.

She tucked all of the letters, with the exception of the heavy manila envelope, under her arm, and began walking back toward a spot in the fence where she could more easily get back over.

Stepping back over the drainage ditch, she ducked under the uppermost rail of the fence this time. Lord knows she didn't want to snag her dress again. After all, it was one of the few pretty ones she still owned.

Once through, she stood up and headed back across the field toward the house, turning the thick, brown package over in her hands. She again noticed its lack of postmark, and now, saw that it had no return address. The only thing written on it was her name plainly printed in a simple, almost child-like script across the front.

She smirked suspiciously. "This *is* odd."

She stepped over a clump of flowering weeds and, as she did so, a peel of thunder growled across the sky. She took another glance back at the horizon, back toward the Cumulonimbus clouds that angrily loomed off in the distance.

Definitely rain on its way.

She returned her attention to the heavy envelope in her hands with a shrug of her shoulders. She was curious now, so she removed the rubber bands and wound them around her wrist out of habit. She then slid her thumbnail under the flap of the envelope and dragged it across. As she did, she continued to walk toward the house, the sound of her feet shishing through the tall grass being the only thing to be heard.

A chill wind suddenly came up and pushed the envelope's flap open, almost as if an unseen hand had gently tried to help her to see what was inside. Aileen opened the envelope fully and peered into the yellow-hued interior.

She stumbled to a halt, her mouth falling to an astonished gape. The letters, bills, and advertisements under her arm fluttered like autumn leaves to the dewy ground.

She took a step backward.

"Dear god..." she said in a breathy hiss, her voice barely able to contain her astonishment and confusion. She looked around nervously, as if the envelope in her hands held one of her deepest, darkest secrets and she feared someone coming up behind her and spying them over her shoulder.

Inside the package, filed in neat, regimental rows that were held together by two more of the thick rubber bands, were what appeared to be thin, banded stacks of currency; cash–and *lots* of it. The entire envelope was packed with it. Forcing herself to calm down, she blinked her eyes and tried to focus on the uppermost bill on the first stack. Grover Cleveland's face grinned back at her like the Mona Lisa.

Aileen excitedly looked toward the barn for Oren, but he was nowhere to be seen; still feeding the livestock, no doubt. She returned her gaze to the envelope in her hand and to President Cleveland's beautifully engraved face. Hesitantly, she slid her finger across the bills, pulling up the corner of one of the bundles. They were *all* thousand dollar bills! There must have been at least a hundred of them! Their total amount was more than she could count, much less imagine, at a glance!

Just to make sure she wasn't hallucinating, she once again slid her finger along the side of the stack, and the bills cascaded back into place. The flurry was like a flip book she'd seen at the library when she was young: single images rushing past, duplicating motion. As she stared at them, she was pretty sure that she saw President Cleveland wink at her.

Behind the bundles, she found a single sheet of tri-folded, bond paper. She could tell by looking at it that there was more of the same handwriting that had been scrawled on the front of the envelope on it. Almost afraid to do so, she pulled the paper free and anxiously unfurled it. The letter was held open by the wind as she read what was written there.

Mrs. Chaiken,

Please forgive the informality of this letter, but my current circumstances necessitate my contacting you in this covert manner rather than coming to see you directly.

First of all, I want you to know that I am a friend of your father's. I wish there was a more personal way for me to tell you this, but, unfortunately, there is not. Monk was injured during a training exercise and, as you know something of the nature of the work he was doing, an infection spread quickly through his system resulting in his death.

I humbly offer my condolences on your loss.

I wanted you to also know that your father trained me when I was first recruited into The League and, I am proud to say, we soon became good friends. He spoke often of you and of his desire to come to your farm to live out his years once he'd retired. When I saw him last, he was very excited about coming to visit with you and spoke to me often of his great love for you and for your family.

Please find enclosed a token that he wished to have passed along to you should something like this ever happen. Consider it an expression of his love for you and for your family. I know the two of you have had your differences, but it was his hope that you would be cared for. I hope that you will accept this small gesture and let it be of some comfort to you.

Your father was a good man and taught me a great many things. It was my honor to have known him and to be the recipient of a bit of his vast and varied knowledge. He was my friend, and, though I will never forget him, I will always miss him.

Be well.

Aileen looked up, directing her gaze toward the barn where Oren was still undoubtedly working and worrying for their future. As moisture spilled from her eyes, she quickly knelt down to gather up the mail she'd dropped. She stood, brushing the tears from her eyes, and then hurried off toward the barn to find her husband.

Far off across the Chaikens' corn fields, under an old, bent, and gnarled walnut tree, a silhouette sat atop an all-black Suzuki GSX1300R motorcycle as if in meditation. The man and his machine were both hidden from the view of passersby within the drapery of shadows. The rider idly watched the woman from a distance through a compact pair of binoculars as she hurried off toward the barn. Even from this far away, she looked like a nice lady, he thought, as he put the eyepiece away. Her features were a lot like Monk's, but softened by a dignified and natural beauty.

Monk did good.

With a flick of a switch, the bike's ignition caught and the engine roared to growling life. The rider slid a pair of ear buds into his ears and pulled a full-face helmet over his head. He then zipped his jacket up, pulling a cell phone from his pocket.

Looking down at the screen, he scrolled through the tracks on the phone's audio player until he found what he was looking for; a little something for the road. Hitting 'Play,' he tucked the phone back into his pocket. In the small earpieces, a piano began playing a soft counter rhythm within the auditorium in his head. A plaintive voice cried out for a love long lost as a guitar wailed in mournful sympathy.

The man took a quick glance down and patted the sword he'd secured to the side of the motorcycle, within easy reach, *always* now within easy reach. He looked back over toward where Monk's daughter and her husband were carving out their little slice of Heaven and a small, satisfied grin danced across his lips.

Yeah, Monk did real *good.*

Reaching out, he pulled in the clutch and kicked the bike into gear with a clunk. With a twist of his wrist, the motor growled, and the engine vibrated reassuringly beneath him. The guitar in his ear cried another plaintive note and the voice whispered its sorrowful confession and, for a second, all seemed right in the world. At least enough for him to call it a win.

He settled into the seat and let the clutch out slowly. The motorcycle's back tire bit into the dirt and the figure rode off into the distance, dark clouds reaching down from the heavens to embrace him.

THE PROMISE

This is another Carpe Noctem piece that's been reworked and retooled. The prose is admittedly purple, but… it was the '90s, it was for what was essentially a Goth magazine, and it was pretty early on in my writing career, so… mea culpa. I've done what I could to try and elevate the piece from its humble beginnings with these new rewrites, but it remains what it is. I like this piece, though. It reminds me of an exciting time in my life when we were hard at work making Carpe Noctem and had no idea what we were doing. All we had was chutzpah, a burning desire to share, and our raw creativity.

"Speak of me as I am…one that loved not too wisely but too well."

~ Shakespeare, *Othello*

It's been raining now for over an hour and I still can't bring myself to go back inside the house. *Our* house. Our *place*. I mean, how could I possibly face all of those artifacts of our time together? The things so ordinary, and yet utterly devastating, to me, like the sight of your old, worn chair. The chair that I know I will never see you sitting in again. I remember when we met and you were sitting all by yourself in the corner at Cliff's birthday party. The room was too loud and too crowded that night, the air too smoky. The crowd had been chattering away about things ranging from the benign to the ridiculous and I had grown bored and was about to leave. But, slowly, almost without much thought, I gravitated to a chair that was near yours and we started talking. The ensuing conversation was both natural and captivating. We both had so little in common with the other people flitting in and out of the rooms, laughing and carrying on. For one thing, we weren't drunk. For another, neither of us was looking to 'hookup.' But you were a delight, never once striking me as self-absorbed or stupid like most of the other girls that were there. It was a great relief when you invited me to leave and seek the warmth and solace of a nearby coffee shop where we talked for hours. I remember being overjoyed that we'd found one another. 'Don't you ever leave me," I remember saying to you in jest. You laughed and said you never would. And yet, here we are…

"Love does not consist in gazing at each other, but in looking together in the same direction."

~ Antoine de Saint-Exupéry

After that first night, I remained delighted by you and everything you had to say, the insight and worldliness with which you spoke was something I'd never encountered before; not in anyone. And it was *so* refreshing. Soon, when the time came to relax and unwind, the list of friends I wanted to spend time with dwindled down to you and you alone. There was just something that I couldn't put my finger on drawing me to you; like magnetic opposites that were inextricably drawn to one another. Where you were weak, I was strong. Where I felt unsure, you walked with such confidence. All too soon, our lives dove-tailed into a natural union and we became one other's best friends and loves. Which all seems sort of funny now, doesn't it?

"Two souls with but a single thought,Two hearts that beat as one."

~ Maria Lovell

I can still remember how scared I was when the idea that you move in came up. I had a little shoebox of an apartment up on 43rd Street and there was barely enough room for me and that cranky old Persian cat I had. I remember how we both nearly jumped out of our skins that first night when she leapt upon to get between us as we lay in bed, having just made love. You were so understanding, saying that she fearsome she-cat attempting to reclaim the spot she had always thought was hers. We were quite a trio in that tiny apartment until we found the loft on Main that was to be our Shangri-La. I got my degree and found a job that would support the two of us, but you insisted on continuing to work and I understood—even respected—the desire to make your own way. The years went by and each of us began to feel safer in the day-to-day machinations of our lives than we ever had. I look back on those days with such love, and they are some of my most precious memories.

"Oh, call back yesterday, bid time return."

~ Shakespeare *Richard II*

Then, about a year ago, I started to notice that you'd begun to grow more and more distant. Your work took on a new importance in your life, and you found reasons to stay away during what had become "our time," just after dinner, when we would shut out the world and find our tranquility in each other's arms. I remember the first time I noticed you averting your eyes during our conversations, and then, in our lovemaking, and how that perceived apathy had lacerated my heart. Were you dreaming of being in someone else's arms? Was there someplace else you'd rather have been? It was all something I couldn't admit, even to myself. But now that you've gone, I can finally see how the signs were there all along; the fire of our love having quietly burnt itself out while neither of us was looking. And there I was, still trying to desperately warm myself on its embers. It took a lot for me to realize that love is something that no one person can keep alive. And, as trite as it all sounded now, it really did take two to make it live and breathe.

"We have left undone those things which we ought to have done; and we have done those things which we ought not to have done, and there is no health for us."

~ Book of Common Prayer

And now, here I stand, watching the glow of your taillights receding as you drive out of my life forever without so much as a thought or regret for what might have been. Your future stretches out before you like a highway of infinite possibilities, while I am left to return to our home, to our memories, and to the ghosts of our happiness. I wonder if I will be able to sense those melancholic specters as they pace these desolate halls at night. Will I see any of the apparitions that are now destined to weep forever for a passion once granted, but now denied? The twin lights of your car fade into the dark, while the rain continues to pour down, the water mingling with my tears. I stand out in the driveway for some time, feeling as though I could lie down and just will myself to die. Instead, though, I methodically collect the pieces of my shattered heart and take my first steps back toward my home, and toward my own uncertain future.

"Little do men perceive what solitude is, and how far it extendeth. For a crowd is not company, and faces are but a gallery of pictures, and talk but a tinkling cymbal, where there is no love."

~ Francis Bacon

THE APPEAL

This is another Christmas mashup similar to "The Heart of Christmas" in my third short story collection, Tuxedo Junction. This time, I'll be honest, it was a few weeks before Christmas, and I was watching The Godfather… and I got to thinking (sound familiar). I love the way the opening scene rolls out in the film, and the way it slowly introduces the audience to its characters and the power dynamic between them with its masterful use of movement and dialog. As usual, I ran a few of my observations through my brain, and this is the story that came out.

Firelight washed like waves upon the shoreline across Beluar the Tinker's broad, flat face, its warm glow throwing the elf's features into a sharp relief. His skin was weathered and pockmarked from a bit of frostbite he'd had when he was a child, but his frame remained strong and a fierce pride burned within his elven eyes. His clothes were traditional and of the old school: green tunic, short brown pants, and the pair of heavy, wooden shoes his father had carved for him. The Tinker stood quietly, as still as stone, with his hands pressed firmly to his sides, as he composed his thoughts before daring to speak.

The room around him was warm and predictably comforting. Rich, polished wood lined the four walls, and a thick, braided rug covered the center of the floor. Two immense, double-paned windows dominated the front wall and overlooked a scene like something out of a holiday card. The snowy tableau spread out in all directions, and for as far as any eye could see.

A festively decorated tree stood proudly in one corner. Wrapped presents were piled haphazardly around its base, ornaments and tinsel gaily reflecting back the firelight. Above the mantel was hung a broad oil painting of the Matterhorn, the artist's individually-placed brush strokes accentuated by the fire's cantering light. Directly across the room was another painting of an Italian landscape featuring several dilapidated, marble columns looking out over a shining Sicilian sea.

At the head of the room, dominating the intimate space, sat a large, overstuffed leather chair. High-backed and comfortable-looking, its shape was like that of a monarchical throne. Sitting nearby was a small table on which sat an ornate container of Arabian tobacco, a long pipe, and a steaming cup of a dark, foamy liquid. Used primarily for the reception of guests and those seeking special counsel, the room exuded warmth, safety, and, of course… Christmas.

The rotund man in the chair stirred. Dressed in red felt with white, furry accents, his weight pressed the chair's clawed feet deep into the rug's pile. The fat man finally looked up to give his full attention to the small elf standing before him.

"I believe in Christmas," Beluar began once he'd found his courage. "I believe in Christmas and I raised my family in the Christmas traditions. I worked as a Tinker and a fixer of things. I married and was blessed with a daughter whom I dearly loved. She was strong-willed and beautiful; the light of my life. My sin was the sin of most fathers: I was too kindhearted and gave her the freedom to choose how she wished to live her life, how she wanted to serve The Workshop… how to be happy. And to serve as I have served—as my father and his father before him served—for lo these many years."

He shifted nervously from one foot to the other as he spoke.

"I taught her though… to never dishonor The Traditions… or the sanctity of the Season. But, as young people so often do, she strayed, found a boyfriend somehow—a *human*—and left us and The Workshop, so that she could be with him."

The elf absentmindedly wiped at his running nose with the back of his hand.

"Two months ago, though, my ever-suffering wife, Gaylia, and I received a letter… from America. My daughter…"

He broke off, his voice choked by a raw emotion.

A larger than average elf—one of the Pole's security detail who had been standing invisibly at the edge of the room—stepped from the shadows and handed him a small glass of brandy from a decanter that was sitting on a cart made of silver in one corner of the room. Beluar drank from it welcomingly as he closed his eyes. A warm flush blossomed in his cheeks and spread across his face to redden the tips of his pointed ears. Once he had his emotions more in control, he opened his eyes and continued his story.

"I'm sorry…" he apologized softly. "The letter, picked up by our team during one of their supply runs, was from the police. Apparently, this human…" He swallowed. "He took her to one of their parties and introduced her to a group of his friends. They made her drink Bjorta, forced her eat Jolly Berries. And then, when they thought that she could no longer protest, they tried to take advantage of her." A tear broke free from his left eye and raced like a slalom skier down his cheek. The elf was so incensed, and held rapt by his own tale, that he no longer noticed. "But, she resisted. She *kept* her honor."

He gulped down the last of his brandy and the elf standing nearby took the empty glass from him, setting it gently back on the tray. Without a word, he retreated back to his place in the shadows.

"They beat her," Beluar's face contorted malignantly from the pain of having to say the words out loud as he continued talking, "like an animal. When we were finally able to see her at the hospital, her nose had been broken, her jaw… shattered and held together by wire."

He sighed deeply.

"My daughter…" his voice trailed off again like a lost child at a carnival. "She couldn't even weep because of the pain she was in. But *I* wept."

Beluar shifted his feet on the rug, his tears flowing freely now.

"I spoke with the police like you were supposed to do in that world, but…" He shrugged resignedly. "When they finally brought these *men* to trial, the judge sentenced them each to three years of probation. *Probation?!?*" He scoffed. "They went to their homes that very same day even while my angel still lay in her hospital bed. I remember standing there in the courtroom and feeling like *such* a fool. And those two bastards… they *smiled* at me," the elf sneered. "I told my wife… there was only one place for our kind to find true justice, only one place we could seek reprisal… and so, I came to see you."

"Why did you go to their police and not to me first?" a deep, bass voice rumbled from the chair.

A match suddenly flared at the table by the chair and its illumination lit up the speaker's face in a soft glow. Bright blue eyes shone like diamonds over the snowfall that covered the lower half of the man's face. Red cheeks blushed with warmth as the man's full, pink lips poked out from the arctic depths of his long, white beard. He carefully lit the long-handled pipe and rich-smelling smoke rose from his mouth as he did.

Beluar the Elf shrugged in guilty resignation at the posed question.

"What can I ever say to you? I am but an old worker who has tried to provide for his family, and to keep them safe in a thankless world. Please tell me… How might I now pay tribute? How might I show my everlasting loyalty? Ask of me anything but do what it is that I beg you to do."

The stout man in the chair by the fire looked up over his pipe, a deep concern spreading over his face.

"And what is it that you wish to be done?"

The Tinker hesitantly approached the large man, all the while keeping one eye on the elf in the corner. When he was close, he stood up on tiptoes and whispered something into the old man's ear. The longer the brownie spoke, the more the old man's expression darkened. When his request had been made, the elf slowly returned to his spot on the rug.

The man in the chair drew from his pipe once more and blew a large, cottony plume of smoke into the room. The vapor hung above their heads like a fog bank. Pouting his lips, the seated man shook his head forlornly.

"That… I cannot do."

The elf looked crestfallen. "I will give you *anything*, anything I have."

The man in the red suit sighed deeply, placing his pipe back onto its stand. He sat forward and leaned his face into the firelight. His icy eyes appeared sad and his expression seemed disappointed.

"You've been with us for how many years, Beluar? How many Seasons? And your family, how many generations have served? And yet… this is the first time you have come to me for help, much less sought my counsel." The big man shook his head. "And even though my wife is godmother to this your only child, you never truly wanted my friendship, never really needed my help." He shrugged as he leaned back into his seat, scratching at his hairy chin. "You were always afraid to be in my debt."

"As I've said…" the elf replied, looking at the floor despondently. "I didn't want to get into trouble. I wished only to serve."

"I understand," the man in red said. "You found your place in The Workshop, found a good trade, made a good living, the others of your kind protected you, and they had their own courts of law. You didn't need a friend like me.

"But," he shrugged, "now you come to me and you say, 'give me justice.' But you don't ask with humility… much less with any demonstrable respect. You don't come offering me your friendship, only your worth. You don't even think to have respect enough to call me by my rightful name. Instead, you come into my house on the day before the most important date on The Schedule, and you ask me to do what, *murder*?" He waved his hand as if to erase the idea's existence from the air.

"I merely ask you for the justice I was denied by these *humans*…" his voice rose as he became impassioned. "The very humans who we have *all* served so diligently for eons?"

"You do not ask for justice; your child still lives."

"Then, you must make them suffer, as she has suffered," the elf whispered, lowering his head as if ashamed by the request and its brutality.

The fat man picked up his pipe and, seeing that it had gone out, he set it aside. After a few moments of silent consideration, he stood up from the chair, grunting softly as he did.

"Beluar…" the old, fat man said. "What have I done to make

you treat me so disrespectfully? Had you but come to me… in friendship… then, these sons of Adam that shamed your family would be suffering this very day. And then, if by chance, an honest worker such as you should make enemies in the future, then they would become *my* enemies." He held up a round finger as if in warning. "And then, they would fear you."

The elf looked up at him sheepishly, understanding his meaning all too well.

"Please, help me…" he said as he bowed his head reverently. "Santa."

A smile spread like cheer across the fat man's face.

"Good." He shook his corpulent finger in warning before lowering it. "But, one day, and that day may never come, I may call upon you to do a thing for me. I will call… and you will answer, yes?" His stern expression faded and brightened. "But, until that day…" he held out his hand, "accept this gift of justice on the eve of the holiest of all days."

Beluar reach out and took Santa's offered hand, pressing his lips to the back of it.

"Thank you, Santa… Thank you!"

Santa placed his other hand on Beluar's shoulder, patting him gently on the back and guiding him from the room. When he was gone and the door had closed, the fat man ambled back to his chair and reflectively began refilling his pipe.

"Give this to… the troll, Vaegon," he said to the silent figure still standing in the shadows. "I believe he knows his way around the human world. I want reliable people to handle this; people who won't be seen and who aren't going to be carried away. I mean, we're not murderers, despite of what this *Tinker* says."

The elf standing at the periphery of the room nodded, and then, abruptly reached up to touch an earpiece in his right ear. After a moment of silent listening, he looked to Santa.

"Sir," he said, and his voice was deep and strong, "you are needed in The Barn. There are some details that need to be finalized before Launch."

Santa nodded, but was already looking tired and they hadn't even really gotten started yet. He stood up, setting his freshly-filled pipe aside for later. He stepped over to the hearth, holding out his hands to absorb some last-minute warmth before heading back out into the frigid cold. After a minute, he nodded to the silent elf, clapping him on the arm, and the two of them reluctantly left the glow of the still-smoldering fire.

HOMECOMING

This story was first drafted a long time ago… maybe 1992, and a version of it was later used in one of the early issues of Carpe Noctem. I tried my damnedest to make it fit into the first No Flesh Shall Be Spared, but, again… it fell by the wayside due to Context. After that, it just sort of languished in a drawer until recently, when I decided to take another look at it and its Rashomon-like structure. Ultimately, I decided that the book you now hold in your hands was the perfect place for it.

Erin Connor walked through her bedroom door, pulling the green wool sweater she was wearing over her head. She tossed it half-heartedly at the battered, wicker clothes hamper that sat by the window on the far side of the room. As she stretched her arms wide, happy to be free of the garment, she suddenly felt how tired she was from the day and sighed out loud.

And even that felt like it took too much effort.

Her day had not gone well. First, there was the doldrums of her part-time job at the stationery store. Then, there was the mad dash across town to pick up her daughter, Monique, at her mother's. And it had all culminated in her spending a thrilling evening of cooking dinner, watching a little TV, and paying bills. She sighed sadly. These days, her paychecks never seemed to stretch far enough to cover anything else, much less everything it was expected to. Her rent had been increased recently and, boy… was the pinch ever being felt.

Although it was hard for her to admit it, life was proving to be a lot more difficult without her husband, Sebastian, around than she'd thought it was going to be. He had been gone (she still couldn't quite bring herself to use the word 'dead') for only a few months, but his help in times like these was already sorely missed.

And, if she were being completely honest, so was his touch.

At first, Erin had tried to hold it together by working extra shifts at the store in order to make some extra money. She figured that she wouldn't miss him as much if she just kept herself busy. But the extra hours added to the day-to-day care of a six-year-old dynamo had been more than she could handle.

And then, there was Monique herself…

First there had been the always painful, but never-ending, questions regarding her Daddy's absence. 'Where was he? When would he be coming back?' And then, there was the onslaught of questions about the normal things kids her age had about the workings of the world. 'How is this made? How was that made? Did God make the flowers? Why is there air? Why? Why? Why?' and on and on and on.

To *all* of these inquiries Erin always felt like she'd always come up ridiculously short. She knew that children could be inquisitive, but Monique was just *so* smart. Sebastian always had just the right words to quiet the child's concerns. It was like he instinctively knew how to give the exact right answer to her questions.

Sadly, Erin did not.

Thank God her mother had been there to help when day care had to be put off due to its exorbitant cost. *Everything* was just *so* expensive. She'd done what she could to make ends meet, but continually felt as though she were on a very slippery slope. It all felt very 'one step forward, two steps back' to her. She knew that the money would one day not add up, and that financial problems were coming. She just wasn't sure when they'd get here, or what to do when they did. Life had suddenly become so *hard*.

But it was in the quiet hours such as these, when Monique was already in bed and asleep and the house was still, that were the worst for her. The night would stretch out in front of her like a long, dark, lonely road, and, in its silence, Erin would listen to her own heart break.

Night after night, she would find herself like this, here in the bedroom. And there, waiting for her, were all of the things—all of *his* things—that she could not yet bear to get rid of.

His side of the bed.

His side of the closet.

His clothes.

His shelves full of books.

His guitar.

His. His. His.

They were all there waiting for her, like silent monuments to a love that now lay black and bloated in a grave at the back of the nearby cemetery.

Erin thought back to a time when Monique was just learning to walk and the three of them danced around the room as the Rufus song, "Sweet Thing," played on the radio. They'd whirled around the room together, the baby tucked tightly into the crook of his one arm while the other was wrapped strongly around Erin's waist. She smiled as she thought of how happy she'd felt that day… and how safe. They'd all laughed until they weren't able to laugh any more, and, with time and a lot of repetition, the song's title soon became a pet name for their little girl.

Erin sat down on the bed, finally succumbing to the weight of the day, and the tears came unbidden, tracing their familiar paths down her face. The small, pearlescent drops fell like raindrops from her cheeks, making tiny, wet circles on the thighs of her black stretch pants.

She smiled at herself and wiped away the mucus running out of her nose.

It looked as if tonight was going to be another one of those nights, like every other night had been since Sebastian passed. She would cry for a little while, pick through some old photographs, cry some more, and then go to the closet and press her face into some of his clothes just so she would never, ever forget how he smelled.

Finally, exhausted, she'd collapse onto the bed and cry herself to sleep.

"Sebastian," she whispered to the empty ceiling, "I miss you so much."

Then, the tears began in earnest.

"Dear God. Please bless Mommy and Gramma and Spot and Smokey and..." Monique prayed into her tightly clasped hands with the sincerity of a newly-reformed 12-Stepper, "please let my Daddy know that I love him and that I said hello."

The child knelt beside her bed with her eyes clenched tightly shut. Softly, she whispered into 'God's ear' and hoped beyond hope that He was listening. Stuffed animals sat along one side of the room, perched like spectators on a shelf, each bearing silent witness to the child's quiet confessional.

"Mommy says that Daddy is there with you in Heaven. I hope so. I hope he is happy and having lots of fun. Does he still have my bear with him? I gave him to Daddy at his fumeral so that he would have some company. Mr. Jiggs, that's what his name is: Mr. Jiggs. He was my favorite bear." She paused, and then, "I guess both of my friends went away that day, huh? Daddy, and then, Mr. Jiggs. But... I guess you already knew that."

The little girl's eyes opened slightly and her gaze roamed the room aimlessly as she spoke. "I really miss both of them, God, but I'm not sad. Mommy says that, someday, I can see them again. She says that someday all of us will be together and we will live happy forever like the people in my storybooks. I hope that that day comes pretty soon." She sniffed back an unfamiliar emotion. "I really miss my daddy."

She scratched her nose with her one hand as she adjusted the thin, purple, ribbon that held her hair in place with the other. She thought a bit about whether there was anything left for her to say to the Lord of all Creation, anything she should let Him know. Finding nothing further, she concluded her prayer, "So... I think that's about all for now, God. I... I'm getting kinda sleepy, so, a-men."

The thing that had once been a man named Sebastian Connor slowly shambled up to the lace-curtained window outside of the small house on Portiere Road. His polished, but muddy wing-tip shoes crushed the rows of carefully-planted peonies as he strained to get a look into the glass. He raised an arthritic hand, now streaked by the black of decomposition, to touch the window. He rested his fingertips on the surface of the cold glass, feeling the warmth coming from inside the room through the clear pane; a dim sensation filtered through Death's dusty screen.

His dull, listless eyes caught a glimpse of his reflection in the glass and it was a decimated caricature that stared back. One half of his face draped from his skull like a flag on a windless day. The other was drawn and haggard-looking, its skin having been leeched of its hue, his complexion as bloodless as the exposed belly of a fish.

He'd looked better.

He sure as hell couldn't have looked much worse.

Through the glass, he saw a familiar-looking girl with bound, dark hair kneeling by a bed. His fetid brain could not immediately recall from where he recognized her, but he was very sure that he'd known her, once upon a time. Her face flitted across his mind's weathered screen as he worked to recall, but it was her eyes, so similar to his own, that caught and held his attention.

Hunger twisted tightly in his stomach at the sight of her, insistently reminding him of his purpose here. The reason he was brought back. Sebastian closed his eyes and tried to absorb as much of the home's warmth as he could through the tips of his decaying fingers. He drifted in a dark reverie as he imagined what it would be like to go inside, getting to the girl, and having her tender flesh in his hands, her pliant musculature surrendering to his teeth; and all the while, the warmth of her blood flooding the desert of his tongue.

Hunger sidled closer and spoke to him then, as a conspirator might, and told him of a plan, a plan of just how to get at this sweet, tender thing behind the glass. Sebastian nodded as the voices growled to him from his belly, and a dark, understanding smile spread arthritically across his lips.

"Yesssss," he hissed to them. "I sssssee…"

Inside the house, the girl kneeling by the bed suddenly stood and, with big, bouncing hops, she crawled up onto the bed. Hunger, like an ever-present collaborator, silently spoke of what Sebastian must do next; else his prey might make its escape.

Slowly raising his hand up off the glass, he let it drop. The solitary rap echoed in the still, night air, reverberating off the side of the house. As his face tried to manage a rictus smile, he saw the little girl looked toward the window. Satisfaction swelled within him when her opened her mouth and squealed in delight.

"Daddy!!!"

He smiled and licked his lips in anticipation as he watched her jump down from the bed and run across the room to open the window.

Erin's eyes snapped open and she knew immediately that something was wrong. Mother's intuition rang in her head, hot and fierce, like a fire alarm. She bolted upright in her bed, her hair mashed wetly to one side of her face. She held her breath and listened intently for any sound, any sound at all, that might tell her what was happening in the rest of the house. Her heart seized in her chest and she gasped out loud when she heard a low, muffled groaning drift through the wall.

Rising from beneath a blanket of scattered photos and tear-stained love letters, she got to her feet and pulled her nightshirt back down over her pants. Her mouth still tasted like toothpaste from when she'd brushed her teeth, so she knew she hadn't been asleep for very long. Distractedly, she brushed errant strands of hair from her face as she stumbled toward the bedroom door, heading in the direction of her daughter's room.

The hallway was dark as she came out of her bedroom. It took a second for her eyes to adjust to the almost non-existent light. The moon was a brilliant shaft of silver coming in through the bathroom window. Its light fell coldly across the carpeting, selflessly adding whatever it could to the small amount of illumination in the hall.

She hurriedly padded down the charcoal-colored carpeting that led to her daughter's room, to where she prayed her baby lay sleeping unawares. She paused momentarily considering that whatever she'd heard could very well have been nothing, but she still felt like she should go and check it out—just to be sure.

Outside of Monique's door, Erin was brought up short by the suffocating smell of wintergreen and flowers left past their bloom. The syrupy stench seeped from under the door like an aromatic tentacle, wrapping itself like a cat around her ankles. Erin ignored the momentary urge to draw her feet back as she slowly reached out her trembling hand for the doorknob. Gripping it tightly, she turned the handle.

From the other side of her daughter's bedroom door, through the crack, she suddenly heard a voice, softly whispering.

"Swee' t'ing."

Someone was *in there, in there with Monique!*

It seemed impossible but she was sure that the voice she heard sounded familiar. She wracked her brain trying to think of where she might have heard it before. Impossibly, the only thing that kept coming up was that it sounded exactly like... She dared not say his name. Her psychiatrist told her to expect certain things as a part of the grieving process, but audible hallucinations had not been one of them.

"Swee' t'ing," slithered the sound through the break between the door jam and the door.

A wet, smacking sound affirmed the sentiment.

"Swee' t'ing."

Erin carefully pushed the door open, peering inside the room hesitantly. She drew in a quick breath when she saw, sitting in a circle of moonlight, the figure of a man, bent over, and cuddling something in his arms.

Why hadn't she picked up something to use as a weapon along the way?

Within the close confines of the room, she was sure that the hiss of her breath was loud enough for whoever the man was to hear her, but, remarkably, he never turned his attention away from whatever it was that he had in his lap. She clasped her hands over her mouth and tried to keep from crying out. Despite her fear, though, she couldn't help herself from moving deeper into the room to get a better look. Finally, she was able to see more of his face in the dim light of the moon coming in through the window. She wasn't completely sure, not at first, but, in the half-light, she could swear that the man was Sebastian.

Her Sebastian!

She turned, reaching her hand back, and pressed it against the wall. She searched blindly for the light switch, her hand patting the drywall until it finally felt the nub of it under her fingers. She flicked the overhead light on and reality exploded in a blinding, disorienting splash of illumination.

As her vision cleared, she saw her husband, sitting on the floor before her, looking out of the window as if transfixed by the incoming lunar radiance. His face was splattered with a slick, dark fluid that looked like motor oil in the moonlight. His tongue—bloated and black—slowly dragged itself across his lips like the body of a wounded man crawling across the desert. The swollen muscle flesh caught bits of the material on his lips and pulled them toward his forever-chewing mouth.

Through one of his torn cheeks, Erin saw his blackened tongue manipulate a small bit of mashed flesh and push it toward the back of his mouth to be swallowed. Erin noticed that Sebastian's face had the same sated look he always had after one of her mother's big Thanksgiving dinners.

She stared at him for the next few seconds, and, despite herself, quickly cataloged his appearance. There was the suit she'd agonized over to make sure he looked just right lying in his casket. The twisted, green-black face with too much makeup applied to too little flesh. The tie clasp her father had given him just before *he'd* died. The shoes that now looked muddied and moldy, as if they had been kept in a dark, damp place where spiders dwelt and maggots feasted.

Her eyes finally—regretfully—drifted down to the thing he held in his arms and as they focused upon it, her world came crashing in, crippling her into inaction.

Monique, her little girl, her little baby girl, lay draped across her father's lap staring, wide-eyed and open-mouthed, up toward the ceiling. The front of her nightie had been torn open, the tattered remnants of the cloth lying limply on each side of her chest. Something dark and crimson dribbled from her nose and mouth like an old, leaky faucet. Her hair was mussed and the headband she always wore lay crumpled and discarded by her side.

Sebastian sat quietly, his attention split between whatever song it was that the moon was singing and the task of drawing out portions of his daughter's intestines in thick, squiggling handfuls. The girl's chest lay open; flaps of skin lying limply by her side.

Erin's splintering mind insanely thought that she looked more like a flesh and bone picnic basket than she did her little girl. Then, for some reason, she thought of Yogi Bear and the way he said, 'Pic-a-nick,' and her world fractured like glazed glass. She pressed the heel of her hand against her lips and bit down to stifle the tidal wave of hysteria that threatened to explode from deep within her. She knew, deep in her heart, that if she fell completely apart now, she might not ever stop falling.

Coils of Monique's viscera lay in a pile to one side of Sebastian's crossed legs, half-chewed but ultimately discarded like ropes of spoiled sausage beside a butcher's block. The child's blood stained the carpeted floor beneath Sebastian and steam swirled up from the offal in smoky tendrils that danced with the cold air coming in from the open window.

Erin choked back a wave of rising bile as she felt her knees go suddenly weak. Her legs finally abandoned her and, leaning against the door jamb, she slid to the floor. All she could do was watch as her dead husband continued to obliviously pull their beloved daughter to pieces, bit by precious bit.

Another gasp escaped Erin's lips as she watched him tug determinedly at a particularly stubborn bit of meat. She clamped her hand tighter against her mouth and tried unsuccessfully to catch and crush any sound she might have made.

Finally, Sebastian took notice of her, lifting his head slowly to meet her horrified gaze. He sat motionless and smiled a fragile, rickety smile, as if doing so caused him a great amount of pain. He opened his mouth as if to speak, and the half-digested contents of his daughter's dinner slid wetly down his chin.

Erin made another muffled gagging sound from somewhere deep within her throat. She felt her bowels slip a little, her body reflexively abandoning any thought of either fight *or* flight.

Then, unbelievably, she saw *Monique's* head move.

Just a little. Then, a lot.

The little girl opened her eyes and, using her father's shoulder for support, laboriously pulled herself upright, turning herself in her daddy's arms. She cuddled him for a moment, just like she had when she was a baby and had awoken from a nap. Then, she turned and focused her now-clouded pupils upon her terrified mother.

Erin noted how Monique's eyes once again resembled her father's, and that she also had the same leering smile he had; a malevolent grin made up of teeth and of blood and of viscous bile.

"Mahmm-ee..." she whispered as she reached out her hands for her mother.

"Oh, Baby..." Erin wailed. "Oh, my sweet, sweet little baby..."

Erin's mind, being able to stand no more, buckled for good this time. The walls of her intellect involuntarily folded in upon themselves and became a perceptual origami. She stared straight ahead; mouth agape, her expression now gone catatonic.

Sebastian looked at her and smiled. He cuddled their daughter closer to his breast; feeling the little girl as she completed her return to New Life. The two of them then sat together, connected by a gastronomic umbilical cord, both now looking hungrily up at Erin. Sebastian hugged his daughter and he pulled on a length of pink membrane with his teeth, snapping himself off another scrap.

He let Monique up, helping her to her feet, and gently pushing her toward her mother. As the little girl started coming over to Erin, she stumbled and fell to her knees, like when she was a toddler and was just learning to walk. Sebastian looked over her and into his wife's horrified gaze.

Softly, he spoke through his ghoulish repast, "Swee' t'ing."

Erin finally found her voice and, as the two most important people in her life started crawling malignantly toward her, her screams echoed into the cold night's sky.

ESURIENCE

In a weird way, this... is a story about food. See, in 2018, I made, for me, some pretty drastic changes to my diet. I went from being a pretty devoted carnivore to someone whose eating is now solely plant-based. My doctor was concerned about age stuff (like my cholesterol) and was talking about putting me on medication. After some consideration, I decided that it would probably be better for me overall to remove all meat from my diet and it's been that way ever since. I don't know if you've ever done something like that but, if you didn't grow up eating a lot of vegetables like I did, not eating soon becomes a very real option. This event, in a really roundabout way, led to me to looking into the concept of "intermittent fasting" (i.e., limiting your caloric intake to the equivalent of one meal a day). My naturally morbid curiosity then led me down a rabbit hole to something else that was being referred to as "extreme fasting" which is basically ingesting nothing but water for anywhere from eight to ten days. Of course, that set my mind racing... and here we are.

John Speakman climbed out of his 2017 Nissan Sentra and his shoes crunched on the loose soil of the parking lot. The space wasn't large, the lot having only a dozen or so spaces, and it was open and exposed. There were some cars sitting in a few sporadic spaces, looking like chess pieces left abandoned on a board but, other than that, it was pretty much just the flat, asphalt plane.

Next door to the lot was an aging, twenty-room apartment building that was rapidly falling into a stylized state of disrepair. Priced affordably, the building had become a haven for artist- and musician-types over the years; folks low on income who still needed both a place to ply their trades as well as a safe spot in which to lay their heads at night.

Speakman had long grown used to such places. There were a lot of his friends over the years that had lived in dwellings such as this all around the city. A writer himself, he understood all too well the motivations and financial woes of such folk and how they tended to end up in places like this. Where he lived wasn't much better. And he was one of the lucky ones who had stumbled into a place that not only met his needs but didn't break his wallet. But yeah… money was tight for everybody these days; especially for those who were bold enough to try and milk their livings from The Arts.

Speakman had come to The City right after graduating from college to start his career and to 'make a name for himself.' His teachers at the expensive university his parent's money paid for had filled his head with all sorts of delusions about how good his work was. They told him flat-out how well they thought he'd do 'out in the world.'

Somehow though, that promise never seemed to show itself. Instead, he did technical writing for a software company to meet his needs while his first novel—an existential sci-fi retooling of Conrad's LORD JIM—had been back-burnered by his physical exhaustion from having to work so many hours. Okay, that and a burgeoning sense of disdain for the literary world.

Speakman looked up at the three-story tenement towering up in front of him. With its paint cracking and its color fading, the place reminded him of an elderly man whose shoulders had been rounded by the weight of Life.

"Fuckin' Josh…" he sighed under his breath.

The Josh in question was Josh Murray, a friend of Speakman's from the previously discussed time in college. Josh had been a painter when they'd first met, but he'd soon gravitated toward his real love: sculpture. The subjects of his work tended to be big and his anatomies leaned toward the roundly corpulent—much like him—but the art itself was magnificent. Back when they used to hang out, Murray had been a heavy-set, plug of a kid who'd done a bit of Creative Design for a few local filmmakers right out of high school. He was a good guy and had been a good and valued friend once upon a time, back before they'd lost touch.

Speakman wound up drifting toward more writerly social circles after that and lost track of Murray and his work. He was never sure what had become of him over the years. All he knew was that the last time they'd talked, he'd been going on about some bold, new project he'd become interested: some kind of performance art, of all things.

The only reason Speakman was here now was at the request of Josh's mother who'd called him a few nights ago out of the blue saying that she'd not heard from Josh in nearly a month and she was starting to become concerned. She said she'd discovered an old phone book in some of the things Josh left behind at her place. She'd found Speakman's number and was just distraught enough to give him a call. After a lot of hysterical crying on her part, he'd finally agreed to drive out here and do a 'welfare check' on ol' Josh. He looked up toward the second floor where he thought he remembered his friend's place was and shook his head again sadly.

"Fuckin' Josh…"

Speakman tugged open the door that led to the second floor from the stairwell. The door was old, scarred, and made of metal plating fastened by screws over hard wood. The door shrieked like a frightened child when he pulled it open.

He wrinkled up his nose at the musty smell that came at him in a torrent, assaulting his senses with the scent of an unused attic. The smell was old and mildewed, and if it were ever a perfume, it would have had "Grandma" on the label.

After orienting himself, he finally found Josh's place at the end of the longest hall. He recognized it from a distance by the Pennzoil sticker that had been placed over the peephole. He dimly remembered sticking it there one night after a bit too much wine and some ridiculous chatter about whether or not the Artist had an obligation to his audience. Or some shit.

Shaking his head in nostalgic embarrassment, he reached out, knocking loudly on the door with his knuckle, and stood back to wait. A moment passed and its only accompaniment was the sound of someone's far off TV playing a game show coming through the walls.

He knocked again, louder and more forcefully this time.

From down the hall, a door suddenly burst open and a slight Asian woman poked her head out into the hallway. She was short and dressed in a long housecoat. Bug-eyed sunglasses sat perched on her nose like a vulture and she had a glass of iced tea gripped tightly in one fist. She looked down the hall toward Speakman, and then, in the other direction. Her expression was one of detectable annoyance.

"No one there!" she snapped, her English was clipped and machine gun-like. "He not answer door… not now, not for long time."

Speakman turned to look at her while doing his best to try and appear friendly. By the look on the woman's face, she probably thought he was a cop or a bill collector. Or worse, a process server.

"Um," he stammered, holding his hands up in appeasement. "I'm a friend of Mr. Murray's and…" He shuffled on his feet and glanced back over his shoulder at Josh's door. "His folks asked me to come by and check up on him."

The woman waved him away angrily.

"You go talk to Tony," she said as if it were the most obvious thing in the world.

"I'm, sorry… Tony?" he asked.

"He da Supah…" she replied curtly as she disappeared back inside her apartment. Evaporating like mist, she was gone from view as fast as she had appeared. The only thing that she left behind was the slamming of the door. From behind the barrier, he heard her shout, "1C… on firs' floor."

Twenty minutes later, Speakman was back outside Josh's door with the building's superintendent. Tony was exactly what you'd expect when someone said 'building super.' He was short and was lacking hair where he should have had it but had an abundance of it where he shouldn't. He looked like a cross between the Super Mario guy and the actor Joe Pesci.

"I don't usually open renters' doors for anyone but the cops," he explained matter-of-factly as he rifled through the impossibly large keyring that he kept clipped to his belt. "I mean, it's pretty irregular."

Speakman noted the mispronunciation and grinned surreptitiously. "Well, I appreciate you doin' this, man. His mom was pretty upset. Worried, y'know?"

Tony nodded wisely in response to both the question and to his finding the right key. "Yeah, I remember her when the kid rented the place. Nice lady."

He slid the key into the lock and turned the mechanism. The bolt clicked open and the door gently popped within its frame. Immediately, they were both struck by a sour, stomach-turning smell coming from inside the apartment. The odor stomped the musty smell in the corridor flat. It was a stench that was greasy and fatty and smelled like a bathtub full of dairy products gone bad.

Both of them stepped back and raised their hands to cover their noses.

"Goddammit!" Tony exclaimed as his cheeks bloomed a jade-colored tint. His expression changed and he looked suddenly irritated and angry, like he'd encountered this particular odor before and he knew that what he was going to find inside wasn't going to be pleasant.

He started back towards the stairs.

"You stay here and *don't* go inside," he called back over his shoulder as he moved back down the hall. "I gotta call 911."

Speakman waited outside Josh's apartment for a few minutes after Tony had gone like he was told. When he didn't come back right away, curiosity finally got the better of him, and he poked his head inside Josh's apartment.

Initially, Speakman wondered if the smell could possibly get any more intense inside, but he finally reasoned that it couldn't get much worse, so he ventured deeper into the apartment.

It did.

It took a second for his eyes to adjust to the lack of light since all of the windows had been papered over with newsprint. His first impression was that the place was a shithole. He could see stacks of yellowing newspapers and magazines that that had been piled like cord wood along the walls.

In one corner of the living room, he noticed a broad, wooden platform. On it, several half-finished sculptures cried out from their pedestals for attention. One—a demon-looking figure with wings that were bent and broken—had what looked like a human bite taken out of the clay shoulder. At least it *looked* human.

Around the room, Speakman saw dozens of Styrofoam cups, littered like leaves, which were half-filled with an unknown dark liquid; some of the cups having passed from 'something to drink' to 'sculpting tool wash receptacle' undetected.

Speakman wondered to himself as he gazed around the room how anyone could live like this. Just then, Tony the Super returned, entering the apartment like a man falling down a flight of stairs.

"Christ!" he grunted as he looked around with palpable disgust. "Well, I know *someone* who's not getting their fuckin' cleaning deposit back." He looked up at Speakman. "Amirite?"

Speakman grinned darkly and thought to himself that, while sorta cruel, the statement sounded pretty spot on to him. He wouldn't have returned it either.

"You find anything yet?" Tony inquired, looking around suspiciously.

Speakman just shook his head. "No, but… it's sort of a lot to take in."

Tony disappeared down the darkened hall, moving hesitantly, like he expected to see a ghost jump out or something. From somewhere toward the back of the apartment, Speakman could hear him as he continued to speak.

"Who fuckin' lives like this?" he asked the empty rooms, echoing Speakman's previous thoughts. There was a pause, then, "Shit! Goddammit! I found him! He's in the last bedroom on the right. Gooooooddammit!"

Speakman stepped away from the sculptures and tentatively followed the sound of Tony's voice down the hallway. He wasn't sure why he felt compelled to see exactly what happened to Josh, he just was. He rationalized to himself that he'd need *something* to say to his mother if she asked, right?

As he passed a small desk set near the wall by the hallway door, he noticed a thin, leather-bound journal or sketchbook sitting on top of some art magazines. Not even sure why he did so, he picked it up. Its binding opened like a blossom in his hand as if welcoming him to read it. Speakman recognized Josh's tight, draftsman-like penmanship, and absentmindedly slipped it into his pocket.

Heading down the hallway, that same odor he'd smelled before, the one that now seemed to be everywhere, intensified within his nostrils, demanding his attention. It was that same sour dairy smell as before, but it had now taken on the odor of meat having gone past its prime. Tony the Super came stumbling out of the bedroom looking even greener than he when he went in.

"I don't think you want to go in there, kid," he coughed out, and you could hear the bile bubbling at the back of his throat. "I'm gonna head out front to get some air; maybe meet the cops when they got here. You can stay if you want, but, for god's sake… don't *touch* anything."

And just like that, he disappeared back into the front of the apartment, leaving Speakman standing alone outside the room where the body of his friend lay.

He leaned his head into the bedroom hesitantly and the smell got even worse. It was as if the stench had centralized itself in just this room and the odor in the rest of the apartment was merely unintentional spill-over. It all made Speakman's empty stomach rollover and expose its vulnerable belly.

Finally, when he could stand it no longer, he strode over and cracked opened one of the papered-over windows. Fresh air poured in from outside like seawater and the room got immediately brighter once the fresh air and light could come in. Speakman turned away from the window, and it was then that he got his first look at the body of his friend lying on the bed.

The figure lay on his back, his rail-thin body fully supported by a multitude of thick pillows. His bones protruded from beneath his skin like too many wire hangers stuffed into a plastic garbage bag. His ribs were like girders that encircled his chest in a protective cage. The skin covering the rest of him looked sallow, and whatever tissue that had not gone yellow, had now gone gray, and lay stretched across his frame like a canvas.

As he expected, the stench around the body was where it was at its absolute worst. The smell got into your clothes and stayed there. And, all the while, carrying with it tales of the grave. There was some kind of black, coffee ground-looking material that was splashed across his lower face and the pillow under his head. Speakman noticed how the sheets beneath the body had been yellowed by Josh's sweat and expelled urine. The blotch reminded him of pictures he'd seen of auras.

It seemed impossible that the stick-thin creature before him had ever been alive, let alone the guy he'd once known. There was just no way that this was Josh. No way. The best he could remember, Josh weighed like two-ten… two-twenty if he weighed a pound. The body on the bed would be lucky if it came in at seventy or even eighty pounds. If that…

Speakman decided that Josh's mom definitely didn't need a full report on his condition, if this was what his condition was. He'd have to leave it at 'he looked thin,' if she ever did ask, and hope that would appease her curiosity.

"Christ, Josh," Speakman finally asked the corpse in front of him. "What the hell happened to you, man?"

When the cops finally got there, Speakman and Tony the Super each related their respective stories of how they'd come to find Josh's body. Speakman was still dumbfounded that this was the way his and Josh's friendship had ended. He shook his head as he waited for the cop in charge to finish up asking his questions and taking his notes. As they were finishing up, the Coroner's people arrived to cart Josh off, momentarily interrupting them.

"Well, it appears as if he died from extreme malnutrition and starvation," Speakman heard one of the techs tell the cops. "I mean, you saw the state of him…" He shook his head sadly. "They'll still do an autopsy, of course, but yeah… it's pretty obvious how this went down."

Speakman didn't really understand what he meant but felt like it was a bad idea to ask. Instead, he just stood there and tried to look appropriately aggrieved. The M.E. tech turned to look at Speakman.

"You found him?"

Speakman nodded. "Yes."

The tech nodded. "And the police have your information?"

Speakman nodded again. "Please feel free to call me if you need anything further."

The Medical Examiner tech nodded to him as he looked around the apartment. Speakman watched as the guy's eyes drifted from sculpture to sculpture. "It's sad… kid had some talent. I mean, it's kinda dark and sorta messed up but," the tech continued with a resigned shrug. "There's a kind of raw beauty to it, y'know?"

Speakman nodded.

He did.

After what turned out to be several more hours later, Speakman was back in his car, sitting for a bit, before heading home. He tried to relax and let the last few hours—and everything he'd gone through—go.

He thought back to how he'd begun his morning and how he'd set out from his place in *such* high spirits. He was just going to go do a good thing for an old friend after all; appease the worry of an elderly woman. It was supposed to just take a couple of hours, at the most. But now… as he sat in his car with the stink of his dead friend on him, he had a hard time finding good in any of this.

He closed his eyes and shook his head sadly.

His stomach made a sudden gurgling sound and he realized that he hadn't eaten anything since breakfast. He eyed the now slowly setting sun on the horizon and decided he'd have to look for a place to eat on the way back to his place. He'd call Josh's mom when he got home; maybe after he'd taken a shower.

He wasn't looking forward to it, though.

He wound up spying a Denny's sign fifteen or twenty miles up the highway. It rose up through the trees on the side of the road like a shimmering oasis of grease. When he pulled his car into the parking lot, he was already imagining how good the pancakes and coffee he'd decided to order on the drive over were going to taste.

He parked his car in one of the open spots in the parking lot and made his way inside. Walking up the sidewalk, the rich, bacony smell that hung over the place confirmed the wisdom of his stopping here.

As he was approaching the front door, he absentmindedly stuck his hand into one of his coat's pockets. His fingers encountered something unexpected, something that felt like a small notebook. He had a dim recollection of picking the thing up back at Josh's place, but so much had been going on at the time that putting it into his pocket must have slipped his mind. As he thought about it, he probably should have given it to the cops.

He pulled it out so that he could get a better look at it. The book was small—a little larger than a pocket phonebook—and it was bound in a tanned leather. The covers were without detail and were kept closed by a length of cord that wrapped around.

Speakman palmed the book as he pulled open the diner's door. Immediately, the smell of bacon and maple syrup washed over him in an aromatic wave. His stomach grumbled aloud and urged him to hurry inside. After being met by the hostess, a slim Hispanic girl with braces, he was soon seated in a small corner booth.

A black male waiter in his early twenties with a short-cropped head of hair and glasses showed up at his table after a minute to deliver a cup of coffee and to give him a menu. Speakman quickly ordered himself some breakfast and the waiter walked away. When he was gone, Speakman returned his attention to the book in his hands, turning it over and over, weighing it, and trying to get a sense of the thing before he finally opened it. Finally, his curiosity got the better of him and, hoping he would find some kind of window into Josh's frame of mind at the time of his death, he opened the cover.

The paper was thin; not 'family bible' thin, but thin enough so that you could see a bit of the writing on the pages underneath. The binding smelled of cigarettes and bourbon. And one of the first things he noticed were the paint drops spattering the edge of the pages.

He turned the book over and noticed a circular stain across the back cover. From the size of it, it could only be from a coffee cup. He flipped it back over and opened the front cover. Inside, on the first page, he saw only the words Kafka and A HUNGER ARTIST, written in Josh's handwriting.

He stopped reading long enough so that he could put two sugars into his coffee. He poured some cream into it next and watched the light tan plume of it dye the rest of the water in the cup. Taking a sip, he picked up his phone and went to Google to type the words, 'kafka hunger artist' into the search line. The results that came back were confusing.

'A Hunger Artist (German: "Ein Hungerkünstler") is a short story by Franz Kafka first published in 1922. The protagonist, a hunger artist—someone who starved themselves for money —who experiences a decline in appreciation of his craft, is characteristically Kafkaesque: an individual marginalized and victimized by society. The story explores themes such as death, art, isolation, asceticism, spiritual poverty, futility, personal failure, and the corruption of human relationships.'

Speakman looked up from reading and took another sip from his cup. The corners of his eyes grew tense as he considered what he'd read. It didn't make a whole lot of sense to him.

His sight wandered lazily around the small restaurant. The joint was sparsely occupied for that time of the day; just a few singles and one elderly couple in for dinner.

"Kafka?" he asked himself under his breath. He reread the page. "The fuckin' *cockroach* guy?"

He guessed he could see how the themes of the story might be of interest to an artist like Josh. Not feeling appreciated in his craft. It sounded about right.

Intrigued now, he turned the page.

On the next one, there was more of Josh's methodical penmanship. There were also some incredibly well-done doodles in the margins of small skulls, bones, and what looked like sticks that were tied in odd configurations. Then, in the center of the page…

```
Coptic Fasting
The Copts (Christians of Egypt 42 AD to present)
Coptic Orthodox Church of Alexandria
```

They fast according to the Coptic Calendar

Out of 365 days, they fast from 180–210 days

Like Lent on steroids?

Fast is usually planned *weeks* in advance

So… Josh was looking into Egyptian theology and fasting? That didn't seem *so* odd, he guessed. It wasn't like it was devil worship… or Amway. He shook his head and took another sip from his coffee cup. The warm liquid going down his throat felt good; rich and relaxing.

He looked back to the book and turned the page. On the next one, there were more of the same doodles he'd seen on the previous page. There was also more of Josh's handwriting which continued the previous train of thought.

Coptic Fasting = essentially being vegan (No meat, fish, eggs, dairy—basically all animal products). Through fasting, the Orthodox Christians attempted to recapture Paradise by refraining from carnal practices (like eating, sex, etc). They were seeking to get close to God through self-denial.

Next to that was written in smaller script,

'Get close to God?

Why would anyone want to do *that*?'

Then, in the side margin:

'the penitent comes face to face with the reality of his condition: the starting point of genuine repentance.'

The waiter came back to the table with a coffee warmup. He held a plate of ham and eggs in one hand, and steam rose like ghosts from the plate. In his other, he held his pot of coffee. His eyed the book Speakman was reading with a sort of amused interest. As he lifted the pot from pouring him the warm-up, his eyes briefly met Speakman's.

"So, uh… you a writer or something?"

Speakman shook his head, smiled, and closed the journal, making sure to leave his finger between the pages so he wouldn't lose his place. "No, I'm just reading something a friend of mine wrote."

The waiter nodded as his eyes continued roaming the room. It was clear that his interest in the book and its contents had already evaporated and he was just biding his time until his next order came up.

"Yeah, well… we get a lot of those types in here," he replied casually, catching the attention of a new customer coming in. He nodded to him as a greeting. "Especially late at night. They don't tip for shit, though."

"Is that mine?" Speakman asked, nodding to the plate.

The waiter shook his head. "No, yours will be up in a minute," and he smiled before heading over to another table where he set the plate down in front of a man in postman's uniform.

Speakman was silent as he watched the waiter walk silently away. Shaking his head, he took a sip of the fresh, hot brew in his cup and reopened the book. He returned to where he was and advanced to the next page. Predictably, there were more doodles. This time, they were of a school of happy fish floating amidst more of his notes.

Rules

`Vegan: Fish is okay (during Advent Fast (11/28–1/6), Apostles Fast (1/28–7/5), Fast of the Dormition of Mary (8/14–8/27)`

`Strict abstinence`

`Modern fasting: No food or drink from midnight to last sunset—some fasts end at noon (the hour Christ was placed on the cross)`

The waiter came by his table again, interrupting him, and gave his coffee another splash. "Your food will be up inna second, okay, man?" and his voice sounded tired and just a little bit bored.

Speakman nodded to him as he took another sip from the hot, steaming cup. He added a splash more cream and stirred it with his spoon. When he was done, he set the metal utensil aside.

Returning to Josh's diary, he turned to the next page where he found what looked like a schedule or some kind of comparative matrix that featured dates, duration, and derivations of same.

Fast of the Advent

Nativity (lasts for 40 days)

Fast of the Nineveh

3 days Repentance after the Prophet Jonah's call for them to repent

Fast of Great Lent

55 days lasts for the 40 days that Christ fasted + 15 days prep

Fast of the Holy Week—The Holy Pasch—Passion Week

Week preceding Easter

What the hell? What was up with this interest in religious rituals and not eating? He'd never mentioned any of it before. Although, admittedly, it *had* been a long time since they'd talked. Had this become a thing for him? And if it had, how long had it been going on?

He turned the page and continued reading.

Fast of the Apostles

15–49 days "begins Sunday after Pentecost

Feast day of St Peter & Paul the Apostle

Fast of the Dormition of the Mother of God

Precedes Feat of Dormition of the Mother of God

"fast is to ask for the intercession of Mary"

Wednesday / Friday Fasts

Wed: commemorates the betrayal of Judas

Fri: commemorates Judas' crucifixion

Strict Paramon Fasts

Day prior to Feast of Nativity / Feast of Theophany

Speakman looked up and gave the diner another once over as he tried to pull his head around what he'd just read. His attention was momentarily caught by the elderly lady in the couple a few tables away. He watched her for a second as she pushed a forkful of food past her dentures and into her mouth. The sound of her open-mouthed chewing was something he could hear from across the dining room. It sounded like someone was slapping a ham.

More to divert his attention than anything else, he flipped to the next page in the diary.

Health Benefits of Fasting

Promotes blood sugar control by reducing insulin resistance

Promotes better health by fighting and reducing systemic inflammation

May enhance heart health by improving blood pressure,

triglycerides, and cholesterol.

Found to boost brain function and prevent some neurogenerative diseases

Assists in weight loss by limiting caloric intake and ramping up the body's metabolism

Increases growth hormone secretion (vital for growth, metabolism, weight loss, and muscle strength)

Could help delay aging and extend longevity?

May aid in cancer prevention and increase the effectiveness of chemotherapy

So much of our social structure is based around food. It's hardwired into how we live our lives.

Speakman had never heard of any of this. All he knew of starvation was from the commercials he'd seen on late night television with that actress and the little kids on Africa. He looked to the bottom of the page:

Anorexia = "you just slowly stop eating"

"It's a suicide siren that continually whispers in the background"

A little dramatic, no?

So… he was looking into anorexia, then? Bulimia? And he somehow thought this was going to benefit him? How? It boggled the mind. He turned the page and kept reading.

Euphoria

"Being self-honest and having someone you trust with you during a fast is a huge deal because of the fact that the euphoria *will* lie to you."

"When starving, endorphins are released that make you feel more powerful so that you are willing to take more risks. What else do you have to lose? The body is already starving. But think… if you're successful, you eat. If not, well… you were already well on your way to dying anyway, so… Sometimes, when you finally *do* eat, those feelings go away, and the person is left feeling angry, sad, and dissatisfied with life

Beneath that was a small note that had been written in a different color ink; like an afterthought added later.

Endorphins are made in the hypothalamus / pituitary

Then, a return to form…

WORDS OF WARNING:

Getting yourself started eating again can be difficult

"had to stop fasts of any substantive length due to health reasons"

Then, written in black Sharpie in the margin was the word:

"Pussy"

The more Speakman read, the crazier it all seemed to get. Josh seemed to think that he could use fasting as a means to… what? Self-improvement? Something to improve his creative output? Really?!

It was all starting to read like the ravings of someone who'd lost their goddam mind.

To restart eating (increase sequentially)

Combine 2 tsp sugar w/ a shake of salt per qt. of water

¼ cup juice in quart of water

Broth or bouillon

Soups

Return to normal diet

Well, at least he had *something* that resembled a plan. It made good sense that not eating for a while and going to McDonalds would be a bad idea. Shit, it was a bad idea even when you weren't starving yourself. But, by starting with a liquid diet, it would ease his system back into gear; not give it any kind of sudden shock.

After that, the book looked like it was entries in Josh's personal diary or journal; page after page filled with more of his tight script. The doodles were gone now, replaced by an outpouring of his thoughts and emotions. It appeared as if he'd done his research and had now moved on to the 'active' phase of his experiment.

Okay, so… I'm told starting a journal is a good way to document important things that happen in your life; especially things that are monumental like I hope this project will be. My expectation is that, one day, someone will benefit from this experiment. Maybe even learn something important.

And so… I guess I begin.

As many of my friends will tell you, my weight has always been a bit of an issue for me. I remember my mom always saying that I had 'fatty blood' or that I was 'big-boned' when I was a kid.

As a teen, I developed a lifelong obsession with diet and with trying to lose weight. I kept it all a secret, but I guess it became obvious to the people who were around me. So, I've always tried to be healthy. I just was never able to get those last few pounds off.

And so, if the act of writing this journal is to have any validity, I feel like I should, at the very least, be honest… and so I have. I guess I can admit it now that my preoccupation with food has *always* been a distraction for me from my Work. And, if I am to ever take my Art (whatever *that* is) to the next level, I feel like it's important to get my weight finally under control. Once and for all.

I've been reading a lot online about something called 'intermittent fasting' and I've been doing a lot of research into the philosophy behind it. It seems like the most direct option. My notes (included previously in this journal) reflect that search. One thing I couldn't help notice when I first started looking into this topic was the connection between certain spiritualties and what we'll call 'caloric deprivation.'

My thinking… is that access to this feeling of spirituality can manifest itself into a 'kick in the pants' - artistically. Having undergone a bit of experimentation with going vegan and fasting from midnight to mid-day (effectively eating only once a day), I feel like my physical state improved and my mental acuity sharpened each time. I mean, I felt great and the Work seemed to improve.

Then, I read about The Coptics and what many would consider to be extreme food deprivation, and well… the gate of my mind was blown wide open.

And so, with all of this very much in mind, I feel pretty good as I embark on this journey; for my Art, for my health, and, mostly, for myself.

Speakman drew a long breath and took a sip of coffee before continuing to read. As he sat, letting the hot drink fill his belly, he noticed a man sitting on the other side of the diner. He had a sketch pad with him and he was hard at work on something, repeatedly gazing at his phone for reference.

Speakman shook his head and smiled. Then, he dove back into what Josh had written.

Day 1: Okay… not too bad. I mean, I'm hungry. I'm not even gonna lie. But, it's really only this dull ache in my belly. It's not anything I can't deal with. What's amazing though is how much time I have available to me now that I'm not always thinking about food: menu planning, grocery shopping, meal prep, waiting in restaurants, the eating of the actual food itself… I mean, I got *so much* done today. I'm really starting to feel like this is going to be a good thing.

Day 2: I'm man enough to admit when I'm wrong… and today, I feel like I was wrong. Today, I'm *hungry*. The words "fucking hungry" don't even remotely come close to what I'm feeling. I'm drinking a lot of water to compensate for the lack of food and to help make me feel full, but yeah… all I can think about is food. I keep imagining I can smell eggs and bacon cooking, but I know no one's here cooking. My research says it will pass, but…

The smell of bacon suddenly struck Speakman's nostrils. The rich, meaty odor made his stomach sit up and take sudden notice. He smiled at the synchronicity and returned to his reading.

Day 5: Decided to try the lemon juice and cayenne pepper thing I read about. People use them for cleanses and shit like that. Hey, it's at least *something* in my stomach, so… It's gotta be okay, right?

Sadly, I only ended up throwing it all up. And don't think it didn't taste like shit going down AND coming back up. From now on, I think I'll stick to just the water.

Speakman broke away again. He checked his watch, noticing how long his food was taking to arrive. He'd planned on stopping, grabbing a quick bite to eat, and being back on his way home before he knew it. He still had some things to do before he could call it a day.

Figuring he had no other choice than to wait, he went back to reading.

Day 6: Hunger's not too bad today; the pain in my gut is, at least, slacking off. Instead of those twisting aches and angry stomach growls, it's now more like a cat that's curled itself into a ball in the pit of my stomach. I find myself intimately aware of its constant purring, but I'm able to just let it be and the sensation soon passes. There's a weird contentment and calm that's come over me. I do indeed feel sharper; more mentally agile. And physically... it's like I am stronger and much more adept. I gotta admit... I could get used to this.

"Hey, as it turns out, there's some issue goin' on in the kitchen," the waiter interrupted. He was standing in front of Speakman's table with an ice cream sundae in one of his hands, and the ever--present coffee pot in the other. "It shouldn't take *too* much longer, but yeah... Sorry, man."

He refilled Speakman's cup as a consolation prize, and then, left before he could respond.

Day 9: Weird... woke up today and all of my feelings of hunger had pretty much disappeared. I opened my eyes only to find the cat in my stomach had vacated its spot. I knew I'd been keeping current on my water drinking, so I think I'm okay. I found a scale in an old box in the closet and weighed myself. I'm down 9 pounds. But again, and I can't stress this enough, I'm feeling fantastic. I even finished two sculptures that I'd back-burnered a few weeks ago. I couldn't sleep, and, of course, I felt hungry, so I went to get another drink of water. I wandered over to the pieces as they were sitting on their stands and started fussing around with them. I'm now feeling a lot more confident that I will be able to sell them both. By the time I'd finally collapsed into bed a few hours later, they were done. I emailed pictures to my agent and he wrote back in an hour or so later saying how much he'd dug them. So, there's *that*.

Still... I *am* noticing some light-headedness and 'whiting out' when I get up or move too fast. I've also caught myself holding onto things—counters, door frames, and the like–in Tarzan-like leaps from one stable surface to another as I make my way around the apartment. It only takes a second for me to get over the feeling, but again… the finished pieces–and the money they'll hopefully bring in –were welcome news. There may be something to all of this…

Speakman set the journal down for a second to once again try and think. He lowered his head, looking down at his paper placemat, and pressing his index finger against the center of his forehead. He was getting a headache and he knew that it was because he needed to eat.

He glanced back at the diary sitting on the table. From what he could tell by his writing, Josh seemed okay, focused, driven, but not any more out of his mind than usual. So, how the hell did he end up like… *that*?

He flipped back to where he was reading.

Day 14, I think: It appears that I'm making entries in this journal only sporadically as of late. At various times, I find myself too tired to write or I lose the book completely… sometimes, I'll be honest, I just forget. I'll try and be better. Hunger continues to be my absent guest… which, I'll admit, is unexpected. So much so, in fact, that I was watching a cooking show on television earlier and everything they were making looked absolutely disgusting to me. I even laughed when I heard one of the hosts giddily say how delicious it all tasted. All I could think of was how it was all glistening fat and slices of scorched animal flesh. It's weird (again, with the weird? so much is weird lately). I've never been someone that took issue with eating meat or even killing animals. It was just never a moral quandary for me. A week or two ago, I would have happily devoured any dead animal you put in front of me.

But now, once I stopped seeing animals as

a food source, it all just seems so damn *primal*, so much like what it is: eating another living creature. I don't know. I'm chalking up trains of thought such as these tc this goddam fast. On the plus side, though, I do continue to find myself energized by these great ideas I keep having on how to improve my life, my work, and how I can finally be healthier. I'm even down another seventeen pounds. Maybe this more Spartan approach to eating really *is* helping me. On thedownside, though... there continues to be the periodic spells of lightheadedness.

Speakman paused and, out of habit, took another sip of his coffee. He took a second to watch the elderly couple as they gathered up their things to leave the diner. He smiled when he noticed the man take extra care to help her on with her coat and hold the door for her. And as they walked out to their car, he saw them through the window reach out for one another and clasp hands.

Smiling, Speakman returned his attention to Josh.

Day 19?: Finished another sculpture today, but cleaning up, man... it took the rest of the day. I got tired again and kept having tc stop. Later, once I'd gotten up from a nap, I covered the windows with some newspapers to stop the sunlight from coming in and hurting my eyes. When I was done, I got back to work. I went back to sleep again though, right after I finished what I was doing. That's something that's been happening a lot lately: me getting tired and falling asleep wherever I am—like I have narcolepsy or something. Yesterday, I woke up on the floor in front of one of the easels. I keep losing time and when I *am* awake, everything seems surreal; like I'm watching it as it happens on a television screen behind a department store window. Weight loss to date: 35 pounds. Helloooo, Abs!

The sound of someone moving near his table prompted

Speakman look up. He'd hoped it was the waiter with his food, but saw it was another elderly couple coming into the diner through the front door. The hostess appeared to greet them and took them to the same table that the other couple had been at. Wordlessly, she directed them to sit there. Their clothes may have been different, Speakman thought, but they could well have been the same two people.

He shook his head and chuckled to himself as he went back to reading.

Day 22???: Two days past my goal of stopping this. I gotta say that I feel pretty good about how this experience went. For my own safety's sake, though, I've decided that I better start eating again. I've been 'whiting out' a *lot* more lately and I suspect I'm near the point where I either eat *something* or something bad is going to happen. In my notes, there's a recipe for sugar water or some shit that should help me to get going again. I remember from my reading that, when I start eating again, I need to start slowly. Otherwise, my system will reject anything I put in my stomach if it's too solid. I gotta proceed carefully and I need to keep focused on how dangerous this could all get... and how quickly.

Speakman noted how Josh's handwriting was getting sloppier with every entry. His typically tightly-packed markings were getting more and more loose and his sentences had developed the habit of moving across the page in an uneven line. Was his vision failing due to a lack of vitamins? Did he simply stop giving a shit as things slowly started spiraling out of his control?

Before he could continue with this line of thought though, the waiter came up to the table and, once again, refilled his coffee cup.

"Sorry, man... they're tellin' me now that one of the fryers went down and they're trying to get it working again." He shrugged impotently. "It won't be long, I promise."

Speakman nodded in lieu of answering. He had too much else on his mind. He watched plumes of steam come off the top of the freshly-filled cup as he turned to the next page.

Not gonna lie… I'm getting a little scared. I made the sugar water drink that my notes prescribed, but, of course, I threw it up immediately. AND, it burnt my throat like hell when I did. I tried it again a few hours later but had the same results. I know if I don't eat somethi..

Speakman turned to see if Josh finished his thought on the next page but found another entry there instead.

Christ! I must have fallen out while writing last time. I tried the drink again this morning and threw it up AGAIN. I freaked out a little and started frantically going through the fridge, thinking I could run whatever I found through the blender. But everything I had in there went bad over the past few weeks. After a bit of searching, I finally found my phone and tried to call my Mom, but she didn't pick up. Calling her ended up being exhausting and I hung up without leaving a message. I'll try again tomorrow…

"Christ, Josh," he said under his breath as he laid the book back onto the table. "Was there no one else he could reach out to? The old lady? Tony the Super? It all seemed like some kind of cruel joke. He momentarily imagined the panic that must have risen like a tidal wave in Josh's head as the days went by; wanting to eat, but being unable… It sounded like something out of a Poe story.

Speakman picked the book back up again and pushed on to the next entry.

I'm only going to take a few seconds to write something before heading back to bed. First off… No, I still haven't been able to eat anything yet. I can't. I tried, but I fucking can't. When the sugar water didn't work, I took a chance and tried to eat some sketchy cheese I found in the bottom of the fridge. I don't know what was worse: the sensation of swallowing it, the pain of having it in my stomach, or the feeling of it coming back up my throat. Anyway, I'm pretty fucking afraid. I decided to go down the hall later to get help from Mrs. Kwan who lives there. I realize now that I'm in WAY over my head and I'm beginning to think something is seriously going wrong here. Hopefully, she'll know what to do.

Speakman sat back and took another sip of coffee, considering all that he'd read. Cool, he thought, so he went to see the old lady down the hall. But then, he asked himself, why didn't she mention talking to him?

Day twenty-something: Okay, so... I tried to leave the apartment to go talk to Mrs. Kwan yesterday, but I ended up passing out on the floor by the front door. I'll be honest... it's all getting a little terrifying. I'm *so* tired all of the time, so goddam weak. I saw my reflection in the mirror and was pretty alarmed. I'm *so* thin. I look like those photos of World War Two concentration camp victims. My skin feels tight and I can't remember the last time I took a piss much less shit. I was gonna call my mom, but... I can't seem to find my fuckin' phone again. I'm such a goddam mess. Even the water is starting to taste awful again—tinny and sour-smelling—and I can't even seem to keep *that* down.

Speakman turned to the next page.

Tired. All I want to do now is stay in bed.

Damn it, I need to find my phone.

With the next entry, Speakman noticed that Josh's writing had degenerated even more. The lines were noticeably more erratic, the writing style more scrawling and child-like. Each individual letter *looked* like it had been a chore for him to write.

And as Speakman turned to the next page, he felt a dark sense of foreboding wash over him. Even though he knew how this story ended, he still felt a shimmer of apprehension as he read more of what Josh had written on the pages.

I don't want to die.

There was a large, empty space where it looked like small

drops of water had warped the paper. Then, at the bottom of the page...

Not like this.

"Fuck, Josh..." Speakman said aloud as he quickly turned to the next page.

Help me, mommy, was the only thing written there.

God.

He flipped through the last few pages in the book and found them empty.

As Speakman began to close the book's leather covers, a strip of four, small photographs, like the ones you get in a booth at the county fair, fell out of the back cover. The photos were of Josh and a girl Speakman didn't recognize. She was pretty with red hair and bright, clear, blue eyes. Her head rested on his shoulder and they both looked really happy. There was even a lipstick imprint of a pair of lips on one of Josh's cheeks. Speakman wondered who she was... and if she'd been around to maybe check on him.

Just then, the waiter came back to the table, interrupting his musings with a start. A second later, a plate of sunny side up eggs and hash browns slid across the laminated tabletop like a runner stealing home. Three strips of bacon corralled the contents of the meal on the plate. A second, smaller plate quickly joined the first bearing a stack of four fluffy, buttermilk pancakes. A small cup of maple syrup sat precariously perched on top of the pile.

"There ya go, Sir," he said agreeably. "And again, sorry for the delay."

Speakman closed the journal, slipping the strip of photos between the pages like a bookmark. He looked over the steaming feast that lay spread out in front of him. His attention momentarily focused on the two pats of butter that were sitting on top of the stack of pancakes, next to a small cup of syrup. He watched as the greasy squares slowly slid across the top of the stack and down the sides, leaving a thin snail-trail of fat behind them. Despite how hungry he was when he came in, Speakman blanched and felt his stomach roll over.

"Something wrong, man?" the waiter asked with a frown.

"No. No, it's fine. Just thinking about something I was reading."

The waiter smirked and shrugged. It had already been a long night for him… and it wasn't even nine yet. He still needed to get his roll-ups and side work done… The last thing he needed was a picky customer. He smiled at Speakman exhaustedly.

"Cool. You want any more coffee?"

Speakman shook his head. "No, I'm fine. Thanks."

The waiter nodded. "Well, this," and he held up the check before slipping it under the plate of pancakes, "is on us due to the long delay. Again, sorry 'bout that."

"It's fine, really," Speakman said with a tired grin. "It's just kinda how my day has been goin'."

"Oh, cool. Thanks. I'll check back to see if you end up needing any more coffee in a bit."

And with that, the kid turned on his heel and was gone.

Speakman looked down at the plates of food now sitting on the tabletop in front of him. The abundance of food seemed like an odd counterpoint to the leather-bound journal of his dead friend sitting next to it.

Suddenly… he didn't feel particularly like eating any more.

His thoughts couldn't help but return to what he'd read as he picked up his coffee cup, drained all but a last sip, and set it back in its saucer. He couldn't for the life of him imagine what it must have been like for Josh. Setting aside for a second the utter insanity of the project, the idea of wanting to eat, and physically not being able to, was absolutely heartbreaking. It's like his body went to war with itself. And, as he continued burning calories, there was no way for it to keep up. Soon, it would have had no choice but to start eating itself from the inside. At first burning fat, then, as those stores fell low, it would have had to turn to muscle. Soon, it would all come down to either him eating *something* or risk dying of malnutrition, which is exactly what happened.

Speakman picked up one of the slices of bacon and bit off one end; not particularly because he wanted to, but more because he felt an obligation to. As he chewed the salty, brittle morsel, it crumbled into unpalatable sand on his tongue. Choking, he took the last sip of his coffee in the cup to wash it down.

He set the plank of bacon back down onto the plate and reached for his fork. Oddly, his hand grabbed Josh's diary instead; raising it up as if to be read. As he flipped through the remaining empty pages, his imagination couldn't help but conjure an image of Josh as he painfully climbed into that bed where they found him for the final time, weak from hunger, and undoubtedly utterly terrified.

Christ.

He snapped the book shut and set it on the seat next to him. As his mind continued chewing over the idea of Josh's death, Speakman could only stare at the rapidly cooling—and slowly congealing—eggs on his plate. Absentmindedly, he stabbed one of the yolks with his index finger. The famous image from Luis Bunuel's AN ANDALUSIAN DOG of the eye being lanced flashed across his mind's eye. He dragged some of the thick, yellow fluid across the plate toward the toasted hay bale of hash browns with the tips of his finger.

Suddenly, the weight of the day bore down on him: the hours of driving, finding Josh, dealing with the cops, the prospect of talking with his mom when he got home, and now, learning of the fucked-up way his friend died. It all just pressed down onto his chest and made it hard for him to breathe.

He finally pushed his plate away from him and leaned back in his seat. Pressing his hand to his chest, he closed his eyes and worked to get his breathing back under control; doing what he could to reduce his heart rate. Despite the best of his efforts to remain composed, he felt a tear break free from his right eye and roll down his cheek. He wiped it away with his unused, paper napkin.

He sat for a few more moments, breathing in and out with his eyes closed. He felt his heart bumping rhythmically in his temples as he fought the urge to have a panic attack while he was in a Denny's.

After a minute, things seemed to settle down and he started to feel almost like normal again. He slowly opened his eyes and the first thing he saw was Josh's leather journal sitting on the seat near his leg. The edge of the book smiled up at him with hungry, white, papery teeth. He picked it back up and let the cover pull itself open to a random page.

`Help me, mommy.`

Jesus.

"This is stupid," he finally said out loud to himself, looking back down at the rapidly coagulating plates in front of him. None of this made any sense. The only thing he was convinced of was that he *needed* to get his ass home. He was exhausted and he'd pretty much just had the mother of all shitty days. He just wanted to go take a long, hot shower, and go to bed. He'd figure out what he was going to do next tomorrow.

He got up from his seat and picked up Josh's diary. He reached into his front pants pocket, and casually threw a ten-dollar bill onto the table as a tip.

"Hey, man…" the waiter said as he walked over to him. "You want me to box that up? Was there something wrong with the meal?"

Speakman shook his head. "No, it's fine. Everything was fine. I… I'm just tired and I'm just gonna head on home."

The waiter eyed him suspiciously but nodded. "Uh, okay."

Speakman smiled at him as best he could as he walked out of the restaurant. Walking to his car, he sighed sadly, knowing he'd be home and in bed soon.

And he could always find something to eat tomorrow.

Right?

HAPPY TOGETHER

This tale is my rumination on what many consider to be some of the most important things in Life, like Love and Marriage, Duty and Commitment. Love is a funny thing. When it's healthy, it can be the greatest thing in the world. When it's not, and when the dysfunction is codified by Faith, well… there's nothing quite as toxic. I mean, circumcision, scarification, genital mutilation, guilt, need, fear, and genocide. It's all there and on display… and all tightly bound in promises of forgiveness, social safety nets, and, ultimately, redemption. I will admit that there is a bit of writerly legerdemain involved within the workings of this story. I'm hopeful it will pass unobserved. "Pay no attention to the man behind the curtain," eh? Anyway, I really hope you enjoy this, my take on filial agreement.

"Let me know if that's too tight, okay?" Paul Sutton said his son, Nick, as he fiddled the boy's black bow tie. "I think I can tie it looser if it helps, so it's not choking you so badly."

The tie was one of those 'tie 'em yourself' jobs and, while he had a pretty good idea of how to tie one of the darn things, well, the fabric wasn't playing ball. Nick scrunched up his face like he'd just bitten into a lemon, and, while he was doing his best to stay put, he was still leaning as far away from his dad as he could. The boy angled his head in an attempt to give his dad more light in which to see.

"Stand still," Paul ordered his son even as he was chuckling. He remembered his dad doing this same thing for him once seemingly a lifetime ago, and he found himself growing nostalgic, and not for the first or last time today. "C'mon, Nick, quit foolin' around. We gotta get this done."

The room in which they stood was a small, wood-paneled anteroom off to the side of the main chapel of Marsden's Garden of the Roses. Located in the forests outside their town in a relatively isolated part of Pennsylvania, the church was one that the Suttons and a lot of their circle of friends had been a part of for years. Paul himself remembered growing up here, running up and down these hallways as a kid. He'd been born into this church, grew to manhood here, same as Nick.

Circle without end. God be praised.

As he continued looping the tie's fabric around itself with his fingers, he saw his son as he tried to get himself and his nervousness under control. When Paul looked up from finishing with his collar, he caught the boy gazing at himself in the full-length mirror that was hung on the wall. As he openly stared at his reflection, he slowly moved his head from side to side, appraising how he looked.

"I'm really doing this, aren't I, Dad?" he said, and his voice shook with emotion.

Paul braced his son's shoulders with his hands and stared earnestly his eyes. He felt a momentary lump rise like a buoy in his throat. He smiled at his son proudly.

"You're sure about this, aintcha, buddy?" Paul responded. "I mean, you love Lana, right?"

Nick nodded back eagerly, like one of those dogs that sat in the back of a car window. "You bet! She's… she's all I think about. All I *ever* think about."

Paul nodded knowingly. The two kids had been inseparable since they'd met back in grade school, spending virtually every moment either together or on the phone. They had always been the best of friends. The two of them getting married always seemed to the entire family like something destined to happen; just another thing in God's great plan that was meant to happen.

Lana had become like a part of their family when she'd lost her parents in that car crash in her sophomore year just a few short years ago. The kids both came to them and asked whether she could come and live with them since her parents and Nick's were close friends. It was only a short time later that she and Nick started talking seriously about marriage.

"And you want to be there for her, right, buddy? Provide for her. *Care* for her."

The boy nodded and lowered his head. "Yes."

"Forever, right? In this world and in the one that's to come?"

He looked up almost defiantly. "Absolutely."

"So much so, that you're willing to commit your life to her and to accept *all* of the responsibilities of being a husband, right?"

A tear broke free the corner of Nick's right eye and slid down his cheek. He looked up at his father and whispered solemnly, "Absolutely."

Paul smiled broadly and was never more proud of his son than he was right now.

"Well, then... your path is clear, then, right? Just always remember... our ways are not like the ways of others. Our covenant with God—and with each other—is special and it is forever. And, while our ways might seem different to those who do not worship as we do, there is a great and unabiding love to be found within it. A love... for God."

Nick nodded as if there was nothing that could shake his will from the decision he'd made. And, holding firm to his resolution, he stood a little taller.

Having observed the exchange between father and son, the two groomsmen, Jeffrey Gordon and Bob Smith, boys Nick had known since starting Elementary School, approached tentatively. They both put their arms around Nick and his dad's shoulders and the four men shared a hug and a moment of genuine tenderness.

"You've got this, man," Jeff Gordon said, running the flat of his palm reassuringly across the side of Nick's arm. He shook back a lock of his blonde hair from his eyes and smiled happily. "I mean, you guys were meant for each other. Everyone says so."

Bob Smith, who'd always been the sensitive one in their group, just stood there silently and looked like he was doing everything he could not to cry. All he was able to do without blubbering was to vigorously nod his head in agreement.

The three of them had always been friends since, and Nick

being the first to get married was clearly having an effect on all of them. It was interesting to observe their dynamic, Paul mused, as they faced what is, for most people, a defining rite of passage in Life.

"You're the first of us to find someone to care for, man," Jeff opined as he stepped away from the group to check how his suit was hanging yet again in the mirror. "This is going to be a beautiful thing."

Paul clapped Nick and Jeff affectionately on the back. He felt a wave of paternal affection for all of them rush over him. This was what it was all about: family, even if they weren't of your own blood. He smiled broadly as he felt waves of happiness, gratitude, and fulfillment all wash over him at the same time.

"Praise God," he said softly.

A young woman Paul recognized as Alice Montgomery, one of Lana's bridesmaids, suddenly poked her head into the room. He recognized her rich, brown eyes and blue taffeta dress through the crack in the door a moment before she stepped through.

"It's time," she said with a broad, nervous smile.

The chapel at Marsden's Garden of the Roses was essentially a large meeting room and auditorium that had been decorated in the style of a Seventies-era rumpus room: wood paneled walls, low shag pile carpeting, and furniture that looked like it had come from a few local estate and garage sales. The pews—long, backless benches, basically—were lined up in two columns with a wide aisle running through the middle of its rows.

Several large oval windows that overlooked a small, well-tended garden lined the outside wall. Several large paintings of nature landscapes adorned the other. At the head of the room was a slightly raised platform that had a podium and a low table with some items set on a white, linen drape at its center.

Friends and family sat together, holding hands and patiently waiting for the ceremony to begin. By the excited, anticipatory mood in the air, it was clear that everyone was anxious to get started. Finally, the gathered guests all politely began to douse their conversations and turn their focus toward the front altar.

Paul had, by now, returned to his seat in the front pew next to his wife, Katherine, who was waiting for him in her chair. They both sat and smiled at the Browns as they saw them enter the room. The Browns had been with the congregation forever and were trusted friends. Paul was happy to see that they could make it. Jonathan Brown was wearing a smart-looking brown suit and a beige tie. Claudia had on a lovely purple dress with her hair up in a bun. Jonathan wheeled her over to the far side of the room, near the back, and sat down in the pew beside her.

Katherine touched Paul on the arm and directed him to wave hello to the Knoxes who had just come up to them. Phillip Knox looked handsome in his dark blue suit and Audrey… Audrey was so lovely in her pale, yellow dress. It hung almost provocatively over her knees and, since it was short, there was never a chance for it to become caught in the wheels of her chair.

Paul looked up as he noticed the music being played by the speaker overhead fade and get abruptly shut off. Then, the sound of an organ gently playing took over. He turned his head to say something to Katherine, and saw Sam and Cynthia Bozeman also coming in. The black couple was a new addition to the congregation from San Francisco but seemed to be fitting in well.

Sam had on a dark suit and Cynthia wore a dark blue dress that had been gathered around her legs and secured to her chair's footpad. As Sam pushed Cynthia up the center aisle, they both smiled broadly as they greeted their friends one by one who were already in their seats.

"Everyone seems so happy," Katherine interrupted Paul's musings, as she moved her head from left to right, twisting as much as she was able in her seat. "I just love weddings… and to think, the one getting married is our little Nicky."

Paul chuckled and shook his head. "I remember when we first brought him home. Remember how much we worried about him?"

Katherine patted his hand lovingly. "Well, we both knew this day would come, right? That he'd one day grow to be a man and want obligations of his own…"

Paul nodded as he continued to look around the chapel,

smiling at guests and keeping an eye on the side door. His heart felt full as he quietly tried to put it all into perspective for himself.

His family was entering the next phase of its life. Soon, there would be grandbabies, then great-grandbabies. God willing. All coming to the church, to the church Reverend Davis now led and nurtured. He counted the many beaming faces around him and couldn't help but feel a sense of pride.

Paul took silent note of Jerry Soule and his girlfriend, Samantha, as they both walked to their seats in the middle of a pew. Then, he glanced over at Kevin Wood and Jordan who were scheduled to get married in June. Both couples were young, able-bodied, but not yet participating fully in the consecrations of the church. They would one day. He could tell by the focus and intent in their eyes that they—much like Nick and Lana—were the church's future, the next generation of their faith.

"God be praised," Paul whispered quietly.

Suddenly, the side door to the altar opened. Standing in the doorway, slowly rocking from one foot to the other and looking nervous were Nick, Jeff, and Bob in their tuxes. Nick's face was a little pale and had a looked like he was being led to a firing squad.

"Oh, my god," Katherine whispered, sounding amused. "Look! There's Nicky!"

They both smiled and she leaned over the handrail of her chair to excitedly kiss her husband on the cheek. There was some sudden movement by the door where the boys were, and Paul noticed Reverend Davis there, checking on them as he made his way to the podium.

He took a moment to give them each an appraising glance, stopping to pick something off one of Bob's lapels. When he finally came to Nick, he shook the boy's hand and, leaning in close, whispered something to him. Nick nodded as his eyes drifted over the crowd, looking for something. Paul caught his glance and nodded to him reassuringly. The boy smiled and nodded back resolutely. He then directed his attention back to Reverend Davis.

The preacher left the boys and walked to the center of the

dais. Smiling warmly, he extended his arms in greeting to the gathered crowd. As his gaze drifted over his congregation, he gave them, each in their turn, his most benevolent smile.

"Good afternoon, Brothers and Sisters," he said, and he let his voice expand to fill the wide room. "We are assembled here today for such a wonderful reason, aren't we?" His gaze drifted over the crowd like an errant balloon. "It appears that the firmament of our family is to grow ever stronger today; the bonds of our love of God to expand ever wider."

He took a couple of small steps back until he stood at the center of the stage. He shot a glance down and confirmed his placement, edging himself over until he stood on the small square of electrical tape he'd placed there back when they were setting up the chapel so many years ago. He looked out over the congregation and, again, smiled warmly.

"Stronger and stronger, larger and larger. So wonderful, isn't it? Praise God and glory to Him." He turned and extended his hand toward the boys. "Gentlemen, if you please…"

The trio snapped to attention and Paul was suddenly reminded of an old episode of the Three Stooges where The Boys went to a wedding. He chuckled at the memory and made a mental note to tell Katherine about it after the ceremony.

Nick stepped forward like he'd been shown at the rehearsal and the other boys dutifully came up behind him. They adopted Nick's stuttered pace, following along after him like stuttering puppies. The entire time, Nick's gaze remained focused on Reverend Davis as he slowly made his way across the stage. Paul noticed him biting his lower lip, much like he had when Paul had taken off the training wheels on his bike; scared but determined to take on this new challenge.

The other boys both had that look teenagers got when you put them in front of people, like they wished they could be someplace—*anyplace*—else. Paul remembered this kind of attention being hard when he was their age. He was proud that his son was behaving so maturely.

Once the boys had joined Reverend Davis in their places at the front of the altar, music began to quietly play from speakers set on each side of the stage. Paul immediately recognized it as

The Bridal March just as everyone who was able stood.

Paul saw Lana and her bridesmaids lining up in their powder blue dresses at the door at the far end of the chapel. The girls' hair was up and had been tied in place with ribbons of angel's breath. They all looked *so* pretty.

Reverend Davis nodded to the girls, giving them their cue to begin their Walk. Since Lana's parents weren't present, she'd decided during the rehearsal to make her Walk down the aisle unaccompanied. Paul had offered to act as a stand-in, but she'd just smiled and politely declined. Paul didn't mind. He knew she had her reasons. She was such a good girl and Nick was a lucky man. He nodded to himself, confident that they'd both become pillars of their little community.

Heather and Alice began walking down the aisle in the same slow, stuttered gait as the boys. Lana waited until they were both midway down the aisle as she'd been instructed before following them.

Paul glanced over and saw Katherine wiping a tear away from her eye with a crumpled tissue. Their eyes met and Paul patted her hand affectionately. The two of them had been together for as long as Paul could remember, and his heart swelled as he considered how they'd both lived up to their promises to one another.

"So beautiful," Katherine said quietly to herself.

As the Wedding March wound to its end, Lana and the girls arrived at their places on the dais in front of Reverence Davis. Jeff took Heather's hand and the two of them stepped to one side of the stage. Bob took hold of Alice's and they went to the other. Nick reached out and took Lana's hand into his own and she seemed to grasp for it gratefully. They smiled at one another and Nick's whole face bloomed a fiery red.

Now that the stage had been set, Reverend Davis once again smiled warmly, first at Nick, then at Lana, and then, back toward the congregation. With his hand, he invited the couple to come closer together for the ceremony. Paul took particular notice of Nick's hand as he continually caressed the back of Lana's with his thumb, reassuring her, already caring for her and making her feel safe. Paul looked over at Katherine and watched as she pulled another tissue from her purse.

"If everybody's ready?" Reverend Davis asked softly.

The wedding party chuckled nervously but nodded as one.

"Blessed be to you all," the Reverend began, pitching his voice so all could hear.

"Blessed be to you," the crowd responded.

"We come together today to join these two beautiful, young people in holy matrimony, to forge them together in pledge, in trust, and in holy obligation."

The crowd responded warmly, "Blessed be."

"And we, who gather together in God's name to worship Him in our most humble manner, are called to be the ones to bear witness to this joyous union. For it is we… who have stood by them for the whole of their lives, through their trials and their tribulations, their joys and sorrows. And it is we who will now witness and endorse this unification to one another. And it is also we who will support them in the ordeals that are still yet to be."

The crowd once again responded en masse, "Bless be."

Out of the corner of his eye, Paul recognized Jess Winters and his brother, Fred, as they stepped up onto the dais on the left side of the stage. They carried out a wide, wooden bench, similar to the ones on which the rest of the congregation now sat. They set the seat down in front of the altar and deftly draped a white linen cloth over it.

Reverend Davis took Lana's hand and led her to her seat. Paul noticed from where he was sitting how much her hand was shaking from nerves. And who could really blame her. He couldn't imagine how happy she must be: marrying the love of her life, taking an all-important step toward her future, and solidifying her place within the church. Katherine always said that getting married had been the happiest, most spiritual day of her life. Paul only remembered that he'd been nervous and that he needed to pee.

Lana allowed herself to be sat down onto the bench. She stretched both of her legs out in front of her like they were an offering. Fred reached behind a side curtain and brought out a small, wooden foot stool that matched the benches in its simplicity. He placed it on the ground before Lana and she set both of her feet down on top of it. Reverend Davis pulled a large cotton handkerchief from his breast pocket and covered both of her legs at the ankles.

"But what *is* marriage?" the preacher asked as he turned to face back to his congregation. "Marriage… is a bond, a duty, a promise, an obligation. A fealty, yes?"

"Blessed be," the crowd intoned, all nodding their agreement.

"But in this, our present-day society, godless and ultimately doomed, those things have been reduced to nothing more than words. By folks who stand before their brethren and God himself, promising a love that will be forever…" He scoffed and shook his head. Then, under his breath, he said, "Before God himself," as he sighed in disgust.

Paul looked over to Nick, a little worried for him because he knew what was to come next in the ceremony. This would be the critical moment, for both of them. They'd either commit to one another… or they wouldn't.

Paul watched Fred hand Nick The Sif, a long, thin, parcel covered in blue velvet cloth. He shook his head and grinned slightly, remembering the day when *he'd* been handed that very same talisman. Looking over at his wife, his heart again felt full of love for her, for Nick, and for all their friends and family in this congregation.

Nick carefully pulled open the flap at one end of the parcel. He carefully—reverently—pulled the contents out and handed the velvet bag to Bob. In his hands, he held a long, scabbarded sword. Its ornamental hardware glimmered in the light of the chapel.

Unsheathing the blade, he handed the scabbard off to Jeff Gordon who took it respectfully. Nick held the blade up for the congregation to see and they collectively oohed and aahed at the sight of it. To their minds, this was an honored and holy relic. Respect must be served. Nick turned the blade in his grip and handed it by the handle to Reverend Davis.

"Thank you, son," the Reverend said, smiling at him appreciatively.

Nick's eyes were wide from adrenaline as he stared first at

Reverend Davis, and then, at Lana. His gaze was fixed, and you could see, even at a distance that he was breathing fast.

"And this," Reverend Davis said, hefting the blade and showing it once again to the crowd, "is a powerful symbol of both our faith and of our personal integrity. It is a totem and a bond of what is never to be broken."

"Blessed be," responded the crowd.

Reverend Davis turned his back to the congregation and knelt down on one knee. He gently took Lana's ankles in his left hand, lifting them slightly. Paul saw Heather doing her part by putting a small flask of dark liquid, something to calm her nerves and settle her disposition, against Lana's lips. The bride drank from it eagerly, taking what was there in a single gulp. Almost instantly, her head slowly drifted to one side and Heather used her handkerchief to wipe any excess from her lips.

Reverend Davis took the opportunity to set the sword's blade into a small slot that had been carved into the top of the foot stool; edge pointing up. When all was ready and the blade was in its place, he gently set Lana's legs over the glimmering edge, covering them back up with the linen cloth. Checking her expression to make sure the contents of the flask were taking effect, he saw that she seemed to be relaxing.

The drink was a mild sedative and a pretty aggressive pain killer one of the parishioners who was a pharmacist came up with. It was designed to relieve the bride of anxiety and to buffer her from her pain.

Reverend Davis silently directed Nick to take his place, and the boy knelt down onto one knee near the stool. Once everyone was in their place, and he was where he was supposed to be, the boy looked up at his bride lovingly.

"And so, these two people make their promise, to one another, to us their family, and to the Lord God Himself." Reverend Davis continued, his eyes settling on Lana. He paused momentarily for effect, then, "Do you, Lana Rae Peterson take Nicholas Richard Sutton as your husband in Christ and community?"

Lana's head lolled a bit to the side and Heather reached over to help her better hold it still. "Ai… 'oo," Lana mumbled.

The assembled crowd smiled as one. "Blessed be."

"And you, sir," Reverend Davis said as he looked down at Nick kneeling at the feet of his bride. "Nicholas Richard Sutton, do you take Lana Rae Peterson as your bride in Christ and in community?"

Nick looked first up at Reverend Davis, then, at Jeff and Bob. Finally, his gaze found his parents and his resolute eyes met his dad's. A proud smile spread across his face as he firmly gripped the hilt of the sword.

"I do," he said as he pulled it out from the foot stool.

Lana winced as a dark, crimson stain blossomed over the linen that was draped over her feet. The fluid was almost black in the low light and it bloomed like a flower over the thin, bleached cloth. As soon as the blade of the sword came free of the stool, Jess and Fred ushered Nick aside, taking his place at Lana's feet. They quickly began administering surgical aid to Lana's wounds with a practiced hand.

The swords edge had, by design, severed the girl's Achilles Tendon at the back of her ankle. They packed the wound, each to a leg, with gauze, making sure to leave the parts of the muscle would remain separated, so that they would never heal.

Properly tended to, she would never walk again.

And it would be this moment that would be the glue that bound them together forever. And, as the Bible taught, the only way for either of them to find salvation and forgiveness for this, and for all carnal acts, was through the forgiveness of the almighty Christ.

Once Lana's ankles had been tended to and bound, a newly-purchased wheel chair with streamers and bright balloons tied to it was rolled out onto the stage. Nick had paid for it out of his own money and had opted for the top of the line. He'd saved all year to be able to afford it.

Fred and Jess were there to help lift the bride up and into what was now to be her primary way of getting around. When she was settled and looking pretty again, everyone on the stage stood back and Nick took his rightful place behind her as her husband. He proudly pushed her forward in order to present her to the congregation for the first time as his lawfully wedded wife. The congregation all applauded with joy for the couple.

"Brothers and Sisters," Reverend Davis said, raising his voice just a little in order to be heard, and stepping to the front of the stage. "May I now present to you, Mister and Missus Nicholas Sutton."

Paul looked over at Katherine and saw that she was openly weeping now. He leaned over and whispered to her, "I thought you said weren't going to cry?"

She glared up at him playfully, slapping at his hand. "Oh, shut it, you."

Later, at the reception, everyone was gathered in one of the chapel's two banquet halls. The rooms were normally only used for Sunday school classes, a few AA meetings twice a week, and as a meeting place for a small local Tai Chi group. Sparsely decorated and bordering on the institutional, the rooms had always reminded Paul of his lunchroom cafeteria back in elementary school. The tables were rectangular and covered in the same white linen. Small vases with roses and lavender were set in middle of each. Plates and utensils completed the setting.

Paul was standing behind Katherine's chair, rubbing her shoulders, as friends and fellow parishioners came up to them to offer their congratulations. Jonathan Brown wheeled his wife up and she and Katherine greeted one another warmly. Paul saw Jerry Soule and his girlfriend, Samantha, walk by and he waved. Jerry was a part of Paul's men's fellowship group and a good guy. The couple was scheduled to be married in the spring and Sam had already reportedly been out shopping for her dress and for her chair. Next were Phil and Audrey Knox. Katherine kept complimenting Audrey's dress and how she'd been so smart to get it to match her chair's dyed, leather upholstery.

'Fashionable, and yet so practical,' she'd said.

After that, Paul lost count of all the well wishes, the claps on the back, and the people grabbing his hand to shake it. He looked around the room for Nick and finally found him surrounded by a group of young people. Most were his age or younger, and all were smiling and being so supportive. Some were even handing him envelopes that Paul knew contained money. He felt yet another wave of love and gratitude wash over him as he looked around the room at all the friendly faces.

Thank God for family, he thought.

His musings were abruptly interrupted by Fred Winters who came up beside him, whispering in a low voice.

"The Bride is nearly ready to come out and take her place with the family."

Paul nodded and shook Fred's hand, holding it for a moment.

"Is everything okay?" he asked concernedly, and they both knew what he really meant: were there any complications?

Fred nodded. "She's awake and doin' great; looking absolutely beautiful and has that bridal glow. We've given her something for the pain, but… she should be right as rain within a month or two."

Paul patted him on the arm. "Praise, God."

Suddenly, one of the banquet room's back doors opened with a bit of a clatter. All eyes turned in that direction to see what they all knew would be The Bride's imminent arrival. Some excited guests jostled one another for a better vantage point, but were conscious to leave plenty of room for the wives in their chairs. With the gathering being so small, everyone was soon able to find their place.

Paul walked over and gently pulled Nick from the crowd of young people around him. "Son, I believe your bride awaits."

Nick looked up at him and appeared grateful for the respite from all the socializing. He had a look on his face like he was riding the crest of a gigantic wave and was unsure of whether or not he was going to make it safely to shore.

Both Heather and Alice wheeled Lana into the room and the congregation all burst into a round of applause. Nick walked over and knelt down in order to get close to her. He bent over the handrail of her chair and kissed her lovingly on the cheek. Lana looked up at him happily, although her eyes still looked glassy from the medication.

"I love you so much," Nick said, and Paul thought even he might cry.

The couple was abruptly swarmed by so many loving hands and more wishes of congratulations. Everyone was smiling and hugging. Jeff Gordon had been right; it was a beautiful thing.

Paul broke away and walked over to where he saw Katherine sitting by herself to one side of the group. As he approached, she reached out her hand for him to take. Paul grabbed a nearby chair from one of the tables and pulled it over. Sitting down, he scooted it as close as he could to her.

"You doin' okay, babe?"

Katherine nodded and her blonde hair bounced coquettishly on her shoulders.

"Yeah," she replied as she smiled warmly and leaned into him. "They seem happy, don't they?" she finally said wistfully.

Paul nodded and patted her hand. "Well, as someone very wise once said, 'we always knew this day would come.'"

Katherine smiled warmly, still looking over at Nick and Lana. "She really was beautiful, wasn't she? She's going to remember that Walk for the rest of her life." Still smiling, she looked up at Paul. "I know I still do."

Paul smiled back at her. "Yes, she was." Then, after a moment of watching the crowd move about the room, loving and supporting one another, he looked back at Katherine, and said, "You know, it'll take them a bit to adapt to married life. They'll still need us to be there for them, y'know?"

Katherine turned her upper body and looked at him lovingly. Reaching up, she gently brushed a lock of his hair behind his ear with her finger. Paul grinned at her as he mischievously let his gaze fall onto the sensuous curve of Katherine's knee which was poking out from beneath the hem of her dress. His gaze drifted down her thin legs until he focused on the two Braille-like scars that also slashed across the back of her legs.

"I know they'll make it,' Katherine said, maternally, interrupting his train of thought at the station. "They have us. They have the support of all of these beautiful people. They have God. And they have the traditions that have held us all in such good stead for generations."

Paul smiled at his wife tenderly and his eyes finally let go of their tears of joy.

Then, from across the room, someone abruptly called

out, "Cake! The Cake! They're getting ready to cut the cake, everybody!"

Paul got up and, reaching out, unlocked the brake on Katherine's wheelchair. He stepped behind it and started pushing her forward. Katherine readjusted herself in her seat, feeling content and happy and, ultimately, cared for.

"I think I'm gonna have myself two slices of that cake," Katherine said, and she giggled like she was about to do something naughty.

"Two?" Paul asked, feigning incredulity.

"Yup," Katherine replied, and she rested her head lovingly on his left hand holding her chair's handle. "As the mother of the groom, I think I deserve it."

Paul grinned at her warmly. "Well, hey… if you put it that way, I think I just might join you," and he bent over to kiss the top of her head as he pushed her chair toward the others.

SOVEREIGNTY

For this one, I decided to try and come up with some sort of twisted perspective on the problem of when our courts of law fail to protect us from the real monsters out there, and how some might try to find a solution for that. And, as usual, my brain took it from there. People have mentioned the 1973 film, The Star Chamber (directed by Peter Hyams and starring Michael Douglas, Hal Holbrook, and Yaphet Kotto), and asked if it was in any way an inspiration for story. I can only say, "sorta." I agree that both tales plumb the same rich philosophical ground, but their overall arcs are quite different. I like this tale and think it hides its motive/intentions well.

Santiago Hernandez found himself being dragged to consciousness by the sudden battering of the metal frame of his bunk. In his dreaming, he'd been on a boat, floating off the coast of Santa Cruz with a couple of his good pals fishing, when the planks beneath their feet started bouncing in time with the now incessant kicking. Upon coming fully awake, he found himself in the last place he wanted to be: back in his prison cell.

He slowly opened his eyes and saw, looming over him like balloons in the Macy's Thanksgiving Day Parade, the faces of Johannsson and Miller. The two guards towered over him in their clean, gray prison uniforms with their usual wide, sadistic grins on their faces. All the while, their fucking light was shining in his eyes.

"Wake up, Esse," Johannsson barked in his low baritone. And then, he kicked the bedframe again.

From far off in his dawning awareness, Hernandez heard the other guard, Miller, say something to Hernandez's cellmate in the upper bunk, a guy named Fotius who was doing a dime for Armed Robbery. The guard whispered to him about how 'none of this was any of his concerned' and 'if he knew what was good for him, he'd go back to fuckin' sleep and forget all about it.'

Johannsson chuckled coldly, "Yeah, like… this was all a dream."

Fotius wisely responded only with the sound of his heavy, rhythmic breathing. If he *was* awake, he was doing a good job not showing it.

"Get up, *pendayoh*," Johannsson growled again, having gotten himself back on task.

Hernandez blinked his eyes to see, while still trying to block the flashlight's painful beam with his hand. "What the fuck, man?"

Johannsson leaned in under the upper bunk and put his face to within inches of Hernandez's. His breath smelled of bologna, onions, and an aftershave that had to have had a ship on the bottle. "Get up, you fuckin' mutt. Warden wants to see you."

Hernandez looked confused as he shook the last of the cobwebs from his brain. "In the middle of the goddam night? C'mon, man…"

Johannsson yanked the thin blanket from the bed.

"We promise… we won't keep you from your beauty sleep for *too* fuckin' long," Miller said, tossing the three-pointer in from the cell door.

Realizing the futility of him arguing, and knowing he had little other choice, he swung his feet off the bed and onto the cement floor of the cell. The concrete was like ice on the soles of his bare feet. As he continued to try and get his bearings, he looked up at the two, stone-faced guards.

Johannsson was a big, white guy whose muscles looked like they had their own muscles. He stood well over six and a half feet, and rumor was that he once played for the Dallas Cowboys. As big as he was, though, he wasn't a particularly smart man, and he was about as racist as the day was long. He had this annoying habit of calling people by their wrong names, and those names were usually loaded with racial stereotypes.

Looking up at the man now, Hernandez was surprised he hadn't been called a spic yet.

Miller, while not as beefy as Johannsson, was still as broad as the side of a barn. Word was that the Samoan had been to college, and even had a degree… in philosophy, or some shit. As a result, he was one of those guys who only showed up to work for the paycheck. This wasn't a moral or ethical cause for him. It was more of a financial one. 'Pull the lever, get the treat.' And, as long as you didn't fuck with him too hard, he didn't fuck with you.

Not like Johannsson.

The only reason that prick got up and came to work in the morning was so that he could thump on "the animals," as he referred to about eighty per cent of the prison's population (i.e., the non-whites).

Nazi fuck.

"*Andele*, Paco," Johannsson barked as if to put a period on the thought.

Hernandez grinned. *Ah, there it is…*

"Just give me a second, okay? Christ, I only just barely opened my eyes."

Hernandez stood up and slid his feet into the shower slippers everyone wore in here that he kept by the side of the bunk. The Powers That Be liked to keep anything that could be fashioned into a weapon or used in a suicide (like shoelaces and shards of metal) out of the hands of the prisoners. So, since nobody had, as of yet, figured out how to kill somebody with a Flip-Flop, they went with that solution.

Miller stepped out of the cell first and Hernandez followed. Johannsson lagged behind, leaning close to the sleeping Fotius. He said something else to the inert form lying in the bunk in a low, dark tone that sounded more than a little threatening. Once again, Fotius showed great wisdom by staying still, and not saying shit. Johannsson came out of the cell, and, once he was clear of the door, he touched an earpiece in his right ear with his middle finger.

"Secure Cell 4-7D."

Invisible hands pushed the heavy, metal door into motion,

the metal shrieking like a lost lamb in protest as it slowly closed itself. When it latched, the harsh, metallic sound echoed through the otherwise silent row of cells.

Saying nothing, the guards motioned for Hernandez to start walking down the row. The three of them passed one darkened cell after another with only the snoring and audible breathing of the convicts inside to be heard. They passed through several nondescript corridors, stopping at checkpoints when necessary along the way. And, through it all, Johannsson and Miller kept their thoughts—if they had any—to themselves.

Finally, Hernandez could take it no longer and he spoke up.

"So, hey, man," he asked hesitantly, and his voice fell like a stone in the silent corridor. He cleared his throat and tried again. "What's this about? We're really going to see Warden Conrad, right? This ain't..." he paused and looked at Miller, "This ain't something *else*, is it?"

Johannsson looked over at him, menacingly. He chuckled darkly, giving Hernandez the once-over, but continued to stay silent.

"We don't know shit," Miller finally said quietly. "We're only delivery men. Warden says jump, we put on our jumpin' shoes and ask how high."

Johannsson shot daggers with his eyes at Miller. But it was pretty clear that this little field trip was 'off book.' Prisoners weren't just called for in the middle of the night. Maybe on Death Row, but... He figured that, from here on out, he'd need to be on guard and to be ready for just about anything.

Hernandez never had much trouble Inside and he'd done his best to stay out of the petty squabbles and gang-related activity that fueled this place. Just like on the Outside, he only got involved in bullshit when he had to, when it affected him directly. This... somehow felt like he'd been dragged right into the middle of *something*. He just didn't know what.

Finally, the three of them came to a nondescript door at the end of a long, dark hallway. Truthfully, with all of the walking and the turning of corners and being half-asleep, Hernandez had gotten a little confused as to exactly where they were in the layout of the prison. All he could tell from the looks of things was that they were someplace deep and unused in the building, someplace as far away as possible from any and all prying eyes and ears.

They went into the room and found only a small, undistinguished office space inside. The room looked like someplace where you'd put a desk for a Temp or someone you didn't want to deal with: single metal chair, small metal desk, and a single-bulbed lamp. Johannsson pointed at the chair and motioned for his prisoner to sit.

"Park your ass right there," he grumbled.

Hernandez started to ask another question, but, looking around at the stoic change in the guard's demeanor; he decided against it and sat down. This time of night, these two were usually relaxing in their offices, it was no wonder they were pissed.

They chilled in the waiting area for some time. It could have been five minutes, but also it could very well have been five hours. It was hard to tell. All too soon, though, Hernandez found himself growing bored and felt like he was dozing in and out of consciousness. Fuck it, he thought. If someone was going to shank him, they'd have to do him the courtesy of waking him up first. Then again, maybe it would be better for him if they didn't.

Finally, Johannsson snapped alert at some unseen and unheard prompt. If he'd been a dog, he would have started running around and barking at it. He touched his earpiece and listened intently.

"Yes," he finally said quietly. "We'll bring him in now."

Hernandez opened his eyes and inquisitively cocked an eyebrow at them.

"Up, Cisco" Johannsson ordered as he strode across the room toward his prisoner.

They entered the room on the other side of the door and discovered what could only be described as a classroom; empty of chairs and accoutrements except for a long table that had been set at the far end of the room. The space looked like it was designed for people to utilize, but not spend a lot of time in. Hernandez guessed that it was used mostly for continuing education classes for the guards or as overflow for parole hearings.

Any way you looked at it though, everything he saw told him that he wasn't going to be here for very long.

Behind the table sat three men and one woman. From his left to right, Hernandez noted a white guy who had the bearing of a judge; undoubtedly retired given his advanced age. Next to him was a black woman in her fifties with a close-cropped haircut and broad, round glasses. The other two… were a young guy in an expensive suit—an attorney, Hernandez silently guessed—and a tired-looking, middle-aged white man with a short ponytail who had a stack of file folders in front of him on the table. The Activist. As Hernandez stood taking it all in, he heard Johannsson and Miller take up sentry positions behind him near the door.

Hernandez remembered being in a room similar to this one when he'd had his first assessment hearing back in March. He felt himself relax a little once he'd put it together that he was here for some kind of bureaucratic tribunal, *maybe* a disciplinary action, but not anything more than that.

But that begged the question, what *did* he do?

And why was he being brought here in the middle of the goddam night?

"Mr. Hernandez," the woman said in a voice ground rough by Marlboros. "We're grateful that you could join us here on such short notice."

Hernandez looked back, first toward Johannsson, and then, at Miller, and chuckled. "Well, Ma'am, it's not like I had much of a choice. My escorts were rather insistent."

"Yes, well," she continued, not really listening, and brushing his statement aside. "Be that as it may." She took a minute to look at each of her compatriots; getting a consensus that they were all okay to begin.

"Ma'am, May I ask what this is all about? I mean, it *is* the middle of the night." Hernandez said hesitantly. May as well cut to the chase, he thought. If he *was* here for something bad, they could either get it over with now or let him go the fuck back to bed was the way he looked at it. He made a quick mental note to keep an eye on Johannsson and Miller though… just in case. "I mean," he looked around the empty room, "this whole set-up doesn't exactly look 'standard procedure,' if you don't mind me saying so."

The woman smiled and Hernandez felt cold hands suddenly grip his shoulders. A shiver traced a finger down his spine, and the sensation felt like electricity. As Hernandez and the black woman silently stared at one another, Hernandez wondered how many other people had stood where he now stood. And what their outcomes had been?

"This is a special review board, Mr. Hernandez," she began, talking slowly, choosing her words carefully. "We review cases—*special* cases, like yours—that we feel were improperly adjudicated, and may be deserving of a second examination."

Hernandez smiled. "Oh, am I now special?"

The old guy blanched. He pointed a stubby finger at him and snarled, "Look, son… you'll cut the smart-ass backtalk if you know what's good for you. You play this thing smart, and you can turn it all into a nice little advantage for yourself… and, trust me, that's not a bad thing Inside, as you may have noticed by now."

Hernandez held up his hands, mimicking surrender.

"As I said," the woman continued without acknowledging the interruption. "We are a review board that looks at cases that may have been improperly tried or have… extenuating circumstances. We take a look at the facts of the case, dig deep, and decide if there's anything that can be done… and if we are in a position to do anything about it."

Hernandez's eyebrows leapt onto his forehead. He couldn't help it. The part that was inside of him that still secretly prayed he'd be let out of here sat up and took immediate—and rabid—notice. He was careful to never let the thought of his freedom run too freely in his mind, though. He'd been disappointed too many times in the past in that regard.

"Okay," he finally responded, lowering his hands to his sides. "You have my attention. I'm listening."

The tired-looking guy with the ponytail shut the folder he'd been looking at and set it down on a pile of paper nearby. He looked up and took his glasses off, gently tossing them onto the scatter in front of him.

"Look, Mr...." and he rechecked the name with a glance from a form in front of him. "Hernandez, we've reviewed your case and found that, yeah… there might have been some things that…"

The woman interrupted him suddenly. "Mr. Hernandez, look… I understand. I mean, *we* understand. What that animal did to your little Sophia. Hell, any one of us might have done the same thing had we been in your shoes."

Hernandez went cold at the abrupt mention of his daughter. She was the one subject he couldn't—one that he wouldn't—allow himself to think too much about. It was all just too painful. As for what happened after she'd been attacked, well… Hernandez remembered only bits and pieces of it, but, mostly, he remembered how good the sticky wetness of that *puto's* blood felt on his hands.

Still… the mention of Sophia changed everything for him. Gone were any thoughts of late-night parole hearings or organized disciplinary actions in some far-off closed room. By mentioning his daughter, it had put him on the highest of alerts and it made every nerve in his body come alive. He knew, this… was something *else*.

"I'd appreciate you not bringing her up, Ma'am" he said coldly. He shook his head sadly. "No offence, but you have no idea."

"Can we cut to the chase here, please?" interrupted the young guy in the expensive suit. "Look, it's late. Here's the deal… you're here because we want to offer you something of a *proposition*."

Hernandez chuckled darkly. "A proposition?"

"Mr. Hernandez," the woman said firmly, taking back control of whatever kind of explanation this was. "What we're proposing, as my colleague has intimated, is an exchange of services…"

Hernandez grinned, but shook his head to suggest that he didn't know what she was talking about. In reality, he had a pretty good idea of what she wanted. He just wanted to make her say out loud for all of them to hear. Y'know, so there was no misunderstanding.

"Like meets like," she continued.

"I said I was listening..." Hernandez replied, genuinely curious now that his pulse had started returning to normal.

The woman looked to her fellows for another quiet consensus. When she got what she was looking for, she stared at the uncomfortable man sitting before her. "Mr. Hernandez," she explained. "We exist in a society that has rules. And those rules must be followed and followed implicitly. Do you agree?"

The judge interrupted before Hernandez had time to answer. "But sometimes, son, those rules, by the shear act of them being followed to their letter, creates a mistake."

The guy with the ponytail took over. "And those mistakes need to be reconciled, so that the society can reestablish its balance."

"Do you understand?" the expensive suit asked.

Hernandez looked around blankly as he struggled to follow their logic. "So, you uh... You made a mistake, and you want me to help you fix it?"

The woman nodded, surprised he'd gotten it so quickly. "Yes."

Hernandez thought about it for a minute. Being owed a favor by these people, well... it certainly didn't seem like a bad thing. And besides, what could they possibly need from him, to kill somebody? Not likely. Surely, there was no harm in hearing more, right?

"Like I said," he said carefully, "I'm still listening."

The woman smiled and continued talking, "What we're proposing is... that you will be taken from the prison—much like when you were transferred here from court—and delivered to a drop-off of our choosing. There, it will be your job to 'secure' an asset of our designation."

"Secure, how?" Hernandez interrupted.

The woman ignored him again, as if all of his questions would be explained in their own due time.

"Once that's done, you will return to the rendezvous and you will then be brought back here. You will not deviate from this plan or try anything as banal as escape. We will be watching you at all times and would be only too happy to bring your corpse back here for later discovery."

Hernandez blinked. He'd wanted it straight and she did not disappoint.

"Why me?"

The old judge smiled. "We need someone who can improvise… in order to get what we need done, done." He leaned back in his chair. "And a man who's already in prison is the perfect person to do that for us. You follow me?"

Hernandez thought about it. Sure enough, if you needed something done that necessitated going to *these* lengths, that meant it probably wasn't going to be exactly legal. And who better than someone who was already incarcerated to do your dirty work? He had to admit it, it was the perfect alibi.

He looked back up and waited to hear the rest.

"And, for your trouble," the woman offered, determined to get it all out and onto the table, "and for your subsequent silence in the matter, we would remove ten years from your sentence." She paused to let him feel the full effect of her words. "It means you'd be Out and back home with your family in a matter of a couple of months."

The old guy forward in his chair, his belly testing the tensile strength of his shirt buttons. "That's a sweet deal, kid. I'd think about it if I were you; think about it long and hard. I mean, what could you do with ten years?" He smiled a predator's smile. "But, uh… we're gonna need your answer on this right now."

Not ten minutes later, Johannsson and Miller were leading Hernandez back through the labyrinthine hallways of the prison, back to his cell. The entire way, nothing further was said, and no one ever acknowledged what had been discussed back in that small, cramped room.

When they finally got back to Hernandez's crib, Johannsson called for the cell door to be opened. He motioned for the prisoner to step on through once it had slid itself open. When Hernandez was safely back inside his cell, Johannsson radioed for the door to be re-secured. It closed with more finality than usual.

Then, the two guards just left. They each turned on

their heels and walked off down the corridor, but not before Johannsson leaned his face close to the bars and whispered to him in a low voice. "Smart thing you did back there, Vato. It's about time one of your kind started acting smart."

Hernandez stared back at him and, for a split second, almost felt pity for the big oaf. What it must have been like to grow up with all them privileges (being white, probably raised not rich, but not hurting, and a good-sized guy), but being too oblivious to ever have taken full advantage of them. Let alone be self-aware enough to know just how stupid you were in the first place. It had to make life so much harder. It's no wonder he reacted so violently to, well… everything.

"Hey, man, any idea of when this is all supposed to go down?" Hernandez decided to ask him at the last second before they got out of earshot.

Johannsson smiled and Hernandez got a peek at the real animal that lay behind the man's eyes. "Oooo, a lust for adventure," he said. "I like it. We're gonna have to start calling you, Bond… Juan Bond." He laughed darkly at his own joke. "Don't worry, Esse… Your turn will come soon enough," he chided. He pointed down with his finger at the folder clutched in Hernandez's hand. "You just do your assigned reading, and uh… keep that shit away from prying eyes." He nodded toward Fotius in his bunk. "You get me?"

Before Hernandez could say much of anything in reply, Johannsson walked away from the cell, leaving him standing impotently at the cell door. Hernandez went to his bunk, carefully sliding the folder between his pillow and the mattress. He kicked off his shower shoes and carefully climbed between the now-cold sheets, doing everything he could to minimize the noise coming from the ancient bedsprings. Once he'd gotten himself settled, silence hesitantly returned to settle over the small cell.

"I really didn't expect to ever see *you* again," Fotius finally whispered from the top bunk, his voice barely audible in the cell's quiet. "Not alive anyway."

"Yeah, well…" Hernandez replied, pitching his voice low, but offering up little in the way of information.

"Care to share?" Fotius asked after a minute.

Hernandez knew the place where the question came from. It was the same place every con knew, the place where self-preservation kept its watchful eye.

"Go to sleep, man. It was nothing, and whatever it was, it doesn't concern you."

When Hernandez failed to offer anything else, he heard Fotius finally roll over and go back to sleep. Once there was again only the sound of his heavy breathing in the cell, Hernandez sat up, leaning on one elbow. He grabbed his small reading light from its hiding place between the mattress and the bedframe and pulled the folder he'd been given out from beneath his pillow.

He held the light under the blanket and carefully switched it on. Looking out into the hallway in front of the cell and seeing nothing, he pulled the blanket up over his head. Far off in his recollection, he remembered reading comic books like this when he was a kid. When he'd finally gotten himself situated in his makeshift fort, he opened the folder to find out exactly what he'd gotten himself into.

The first thing he saw was a photograph of a well-dressed, but heavy-set, older man standing at a podium talking in front of a large group of people. His suit looked well-manicured and every one of his salt-n-pepper hairs lay perfectly in place. From the way he carried himself, you could tell that he was a man who was used to talking, and to being listened to. Hernandez turned the photo over and noticed a small, white sticker affixed to the upper right corner that read: 'Dr. Michael Patrick Huesker. Photo taken at a lecture before the Critical Care Unit of the hospital at U.C.S.D. in San Diego, CA.'

Hernandez flipped the photo back over, and stared at the man in the photo again, feeling compelled to already start committing some of the subtle particulars of his appearance to memory. Finally, he set the photograph aside.

The next few pages were a police report regarding Dr. Huesker; something about him being detained in Atlantic City. It seems that was where the good doctor had given a certain sex worker a bit of Rohypnol while in attendance at a medical convention. Normally, something like that wouldn't be particularly noteworthy, however... this time, the aforementioned sex worker died of respiratory arrest in his hotel room, in his bed.

Messy.

The next dozen or so pages were official-looking documents that had been paper clipped together and detailed Huesker's processing and subsequent trial. Not being someone who ever liked to wait, Hernandez turned to the back of the packet. According to the Summary he found there, somehow, in all of the confusion of his arrest and the ensuing press barrage, Dr. Huesker had never been Mirandized. And so, as a result, the entire case against him had been thrown out of court and the good Dr. Huesker was set free. There were some written objections by the Prosecution, but... they never came to much.

Hernandez set these papers aside and picked up the next bundle.

And that's how it went for the rest of the night. He sat and read report after report—about the Atlantic City event as well as *several* others that happened over the years—until nearly dawn. All of them were eerily similar.

There were also included a variety of arresting officer's notes from a dozen or so cases up and down the coast that detailed pretty much everything Dr. Huesker did to those girls. There was a copy of Huesker's bail slip as well, and finally, and most damning of all, a full psychiatric evaluation from one of The State's stable of head-shrinkers.

A psychiatrist by the name of Dr. Eugene Fischer wrote that Huesker was a 'class one narcissist' and was, what *he* called, 'a sexual deviant, sociopath, and potential serial rapist; possibly escalating to killer.' Fischer went on to quite correctly propose that the case at hand wasn't the first time that Huesker had employed his drugs to get his rocks off... and, in his opinion, it wasn't going to be his last. Checking the date on the review he saw that it was stamped a full five years prior to Atlantic City.

Hernandez was suddenly rocked by the memory of the photographs he'd seen like this of this daughter's injuries at the inquest. Those images had been seared as if by a red-hot brand into the meat of his brain ever since that day. The wound may have scabbed over since then, time will do that, but he knew it would never completely heal.

Feeling overwhelmed by everything he'd been reading, he quietly decided that he'd seen enough, and was about to close the folder, when a smaller photograph fell from the bundle of papers he held in his hand.

In the photo, Huesker stood staring—leering was more like it—directly at the camera. Standing in front of him stood a girl, maybe eight or nine years of age—Sophia's age—who was sort of nervously grinning and looking toward something off-camera. Hernandez moved the light and looked closer at the kid's face. Leaning in and squinting his eyes in order to focus, he saw deep lines of fear visible just at the corners of her sea-blue eyes. It didn't take Hernandez much to imagine the good doctor deciding to use his needles on her.

He closed the folder and returned it to its hiding place under the pillow. Switching off his light, he rolled onto his back, clutching the thin, metal tube to his chest like a totem. For longer than he'd like to admit, Hernandez lay there staring up at the underside of Fotius' bunk and chewing over everything he'd experienced in the last few hours. And, by the time sleep finally claimed him, he felt a little better about the decision he'd made.

Hernandez was sitting in his cell, reading a Spillane, and waiting to be rousted by the call to dinner when Johannsson and Miller showed up again outside his cell. They both had on their 'business faces' today, and Hernandez knew in an instant that whatever it was that had been planned for him and Dr. Huesker was about to go down.

"No chow for you, Hernandez." Miller said as the cell door popped open. He crooked a finger at the prisoner. "C'mon..."

As usual, Fotius, who was on his bunk and had his nose buried in a Louis L'Amour novel, stayed wise and kept any thoughts he might have had to himself.

"Where are we going?" Hernandez asked as he got to his feet, even though he felt like he already knew.

"Never you mind, Pancho," Johannsson barked. "You got

told before… We get an order for you to be brought someplace, we bring you there. It's just that simple."

Hernandez raised his hands in an effort to calm the big guard down. "Okay… okay. Jeez, I was just curious." He looked over at Miller. "Man… is he always like this?"

Under his breath, Miller mumbled, "You have no idea."

"Shut up!" Johannsson growled at the both of them as he pulled Hernandez out of the cell by his arm.

The three of them headed down the familiar, gray hallways in silence, and it felt a little like déjà vu to Hernandez; only the lighting was better. They walked for a while, moving through blocks of cells and security stations. All too soon, they rounded a corner and found themselves at a small staging area, just off what appeared to be the prison's loading docks.

Two men stood waiting next to a black sedan that had been pulled up to one of the ramps leading to the outside parking lot, and on to the road that led to The World. Hernandez had never seen the two men before, but he immediately made them for cops. Maybe it was the demeanor, or maybe it was the off-the-rack Foster Grants… but it was probably because they were both were wearing the same slacks and these identical, gray windbreakers.

The two of them popped to attention when they saw the trio approach.

"Over here," Johannsson directed, and they walked to the car.

"This our guy?" the man on the driver's side of the car asked.

Miller nodded. Then, he addressed his prisoner. "Hernandez… Call him, Agent One." He nodded toward the other guy looking at them over the bonnet of the car. "That… is Agent Two."

Hernandez shook his head.

These fuckin' guys…

"In the back" Agent Two ordered. "Over here, on my side."

Hernandez looked with surprise at the guards. "*In*? Are you kidding me?" He looked at Miller incredulously. "Where are… where the fuck am *I* going?"

Johannsson gave Hernandez's back a push, propelling him

toward the car. "Cut the shit. You know why you're here, you fuck. Anything else you need to know will be explained to your dumb ass on the way."

And so, unbelievably, he did as he was told. He got into the sedan. Soon, he found himself sitting in the back of the car and driving out of the prison gate, right passed the guards at the gate. The car accelerated off the prison property, and within a few minutes, they were pulling onto the freeway and heading into the city.

Agent One banked the car around the harbor on the expressway heading into downtown nearly an hour later. So far, the ride had been more or less silent with the only sound in the car coming from the radio. The station was playing one Oldies song after the other at a low volume.

Neither of his two companions had yet to give him any indication as to what the plan was for Dr. Huesker and how it might involve him. All he knew was what he'd been told: that they were going to fill him in at *some* point. Since he'd had patience bred into him by the prison system, he decided that it'd probably be best if he just sat here, looking out the window at the passing world, while he waited to see how it all shook out. For now, he was as happy as a clam just to look at anything going on around him, just as long as it wasn't those same four concrete walls.

"Hey, man, can you lower this window?" Hernandez asked. "I'd love to get a breeze, y'know?"

Agent One didn't respond, but he lowered the window a few inches. Hernandez took in as much of the cool air as he could into his lungs as it flooded into the cabin. Even with the exhaust coming off the highway, it smelled fantastic.

The sedan roared up the expressway, banking to the left, and the array of buildings rose like The Emerald City in the west. Spires stuck up like corn stalks from the underbrush of storefronts, apartment buildings, and tenement flats, while off in the distance, dark clouds amassed on the horizon.

To Hernandez's eyes, he'd never seen anything look quite so beautiful.

Agent Two turned in his seat and looked at Hernandez over the rim of his shades. His manner had become very matter-of-fact and it was clear that this was when Hernandez was going to hear all about the particulars of what he'd signed on for.

"Okay, time to listen up, Leatherneck," Agent Two said and it sounded like something said out of habit. "Here's your deal. There's a package of clothes under my seat. Pull them out and change into them right quick. Do it now. I'll keep talking."

Hernandez reached under the seat and found the package. Wrapped in brown paper, there was a pair of jeans, a black tee, and a pair of Chucks inside. He moved as quickly as he could to comply given the cramped space around him. He stripped without thinking. Being in prison for as long as he had, there wasn't much to be shy about any longer. When he was done, he stacked his prison uniform neatly on the seat next to him.

"Your target," Agent Two continued, "is scheduled to have dinner at a specific restaurant at seven o'clock. We know, from the last time he was here, that he parked a block away at a pay-by-the-hour garage and walked to the restaurant."

"Wait… 'target'?" Hernandez interrupted.

Agent Two stared at him blankly, almost as if he were expecting the pushback. "Is there a problem, convict?"

Hernandez thought about it for a second. He guessed he knew all along what this whole thing was about. Given the extent they'd gone to in order to get him involved, it wasn't like it was all set up just so he could walk up and blow Dr. Huesker a kiss, now was it?

He remembered the look the old judge had given him, back at the prison, 'what could you do with ten years?' and he knew what he'd need to do. Murder was murder and, Christ… he'd already committed one of those. This time, at least, it had to do with more than just his own personal vengeance.

"No," he finally replied. "No problem."

"You got a question, then?"

"Which restaurant?" Hernandez asked.

"The fuck you care?" Agent One shot back. "What, are you going to order something To fuckin' Go?" He looked at his partner and shook his head. "This fuckin' guy," he said with a sneer as he steered the car down an off ramp, heading away from the freeway and on toward the glimmering metropolis ahead.

Two shook his head and looked intently at Hernandez like he was an asshole. "Ricardo's… on 45th."

"45th and what?" Hernandez asked hesitantly. He knew he was pressing his luck here, but he felt like 'where the hell am I on a map' was an important bit of information to have, given the situation.

Y'know, just in case it all unwound somehow.

He wouldn't allow himself to think too long or too hard about *that*. The way he had it figured, if this thing did go bad, he'd either end up shot to ribbons by some cops or left on his own on The Outside… to be shot to ribbons by some cops. He knew there would be no way of explaining his presence out here in The World—or the lack thereof back at the prison—should he get picked up. Either way, he was pretty convinced that, if things did go sideways, he'd be well and truly fucked.

"We'll drop you at the corner of 45th and Jackson. Then, while you see to Dr. Huesker, we'll continue on down the street, like we're looking for an address or something." He looked over at his partner for corroboration, but One just continued looking straight ahead as he drove the car. "So, yeah…we drop you at Jackson, you see to the doctor, and, once that's done, you make a bee-line to the car. *Don't* fuckin run, though, okay? You don't want to draw that kind of attention to yourself. We'll pick you up at the next corner, at Kingston."

Hernandez grinned as he finished getting changed, his dark humor getting the better of him. "So, it's to be, what, a 'stroll-by' shooting?" He chuckled more to himself than anybody else, surprised at how quickly he'd adapted to his role in all of this. The two guys in the front seat, of course, failed to see the humor in any of it.

Agent Two appeared nonplussed as he extended his hand over the seat to Hernandez. He had something small clutched there, wrapped in an oily-smelling, light blue cloth. Hernandez knew what it was immediately, and he felt his heartbeat increase in response. Their eyes met as Agent Two looked over the rim of his glasses. His gaze was straightforward and brokered no bullshit.

"There are two bullets in this and it's untraceable. Double tap this guy, drop the gun to the sidewalk, and walk away. It doesn't get much simpler than that."

Hernandez nodded and took the gun. Removing the cloth, he set the rag onto the seat next to him, next to his prison uniform. Slowly he turned the heavy thing over in his hand, the dim light in the car twinkling with menace off of the polished black metal.

"And before you start getting' any bright ideas about clippin' us both and making for the road," Agent One reprimanded harshly as he wove the car through traffic, "we'll have eyes on you the whole time. We have since we left the prison." He looked out of his side window at the flowing traffic. "You wouldn't make it; not very far anyway."

Hernandez followed his gaze and noticed Johannsson and Miller in the lane to their left. They were wearing street clothes and both were staring dumbly out the front window. They had to have followed them directly from the prison, Hernandez concluded. Miller looked over at them suddenly. He grinned and offered them a salute.

"I sorta figured… and it's not a problem," Hernandez said to Two as he continued to stare back at Miller. He looked over at the back of the agent in the front seat's head, smiling congenially. "I'm not a stupid man. I just want to get this over with so's I can get back to my life as quickly as possible."

"Good boy," Agent One said quietly so as not to be heard, even though Hernandez still did.

A short time later, their car pulled onto 34th Street, heading toward 7th. The streets were sparsely populated at this time of day with most of the people gathered outside the restaurant in the middle of the block as they waited for tables. The crowd was mostly made up of older, well-dressed men with women half their ages on their arms like expensive wristwatches.

Hernandez climbed out of the car and immediately felt submerged in the bloodstream of the city. The noise and bustle of folk moving along the sidewalk and the cars zooming by on the streets, honking and screeching their tires, was almost too much for him after having spent so long in the oppressive quiet of the prison.

It had been a long time.

He heard the car door slam shut behind him and looked back to see Agent Two's all too serious face leaning out the side window.

"You'll see him coming," he said and looked back at the driver grinning. "Lord knows he'll be pretty hard to fuckin' miss." He turned back toward the prisoner and stared at him intently. "You good?"

Hernandez nodded and he touched the front of his belt-line, where he'd stowed the pistol, "I'm good." He took a gulp to swallow the last of his nervousness, and checked the weight of the gun on his belt once more, as he slowly started walking down the street.

"Try not to fuck this up, okay?" he heard Agent One's muffled voice call out behind him.

Hernandez scratched the back of his head with his middle finger; a silent 'fuck you' to his overseers. Making his way down the street, he walked along unhurriedly, enjoying the sights, moving like he had nowhere to go and wasn't in any rush to get there. People brushed passed him, bumping into him, but no one ever paid him much never-mind.

If he were ever being honest, he thought for the briefest second about running. He did. Of just putting one foot in front of the other and getting as far away from there as his feet would carry him. Then, the car with Miller and Johannsson slowly drove by and those thoughts evaporated from his mind like mist. He saw the bigger guard's face glaring at him through the grimy windshield and knew that prick would probably like nothing better than for him to do just that. And so, it was for that reason alone—spite—that he decided the best thing for him to do was to stick to the plan.

Ricardo's was located in the middle of the block and Hernandez marked it in his line of sight. As he got closer, he noticed a woman bending over a baby carriage on the opposite side of the street. The shine from her jacket sparkled in the day's waning light. He stopped to silently remind himself that there were innocent people here on the street. Where he placed his two shots would need to be carefully picked in order to avoid any unwanted casualties.

He focused his attention back to the task at hand. Staring through the crowd in the hope of spotting Huesker early, he scanned the oncoming sea of faces. Regrettably, he failed to catch any sight of him in the constantly moving crowd. He 'bumper-carred' his way through the press of bodies in front of Ricardo's, jostling others and being jostled by them himself.

His stomach growled suddenly at the rich smell of tomatoes, herbs, and spicy meat pouring like honey from the restaurant. What he wouldn't have given to just turn and go inside and eat and drink himself into oblivion. He hadn't had a decent meal since he'd gone Inside.

Suddenly, through the crowd, he noticed a man's wide face striding toward him like he owned the world, and he knew it had to be Huesker. Getting closer only confirmed it. The fat man waddled down the street like a hippo, a cell phone pressed like a Lego to the side of his head. His suit looked expensive, like it cost more than three month's rent at Hernandez's old apartment.

The girl on his arm appeared to have stepped out of a TV car commercial: blonde, pretty, and an undoubted thoroughbred when it came to sex. She looked like one of those Barbie dolls brought to fuckable life.

As he got even closer, Hernandez slid his hand up to the gun on his beltline. Once he felt the knurling of the grip in the palm of his hand, he left his fist fall, concealing the weapon against his jeans at the side of his leg. In the diminishing light, this late in the day, he was pretty confident that no one could see anything.

"I'll tell you what, Larry," he heard Huesker bark into the cell. "I don't much care what you think. I don't exactly pay you to think, Larry. Now, do I?"

The woman walking next to Huesker stared at her manicure, ignoring the bloated gas bag walking beside her. Instead, she played a game with herself of trying to spot her own reflection, like seeing a sprite or fairy, in the panes of the storefront glass. Evidently, this was just the way her boorish date acted on the reg.

Hernandez came walking along in the flow of foot traffic, keeping in his proper lane. A man in front of him suddenly stopped and he was forced to swerve, nearly bumping himself straight into Huesker. But the fat man ignored him, brushing passed, and barely took notice of the interruption in the tide of faces.

POP

The first of Hernandez's bullets struck its target at the base of Huesker's wide skull. The slug pulverized the man's spine at the point where it connected to his skull, severing it like scissors. The bullet arced up and played pinball within the confines of his cranium, whipping his brain into mash.

Huesker pitched forward, driven by the kinetic force of the bullet entering his skull, and fell to his face like lumber. Due to his prodigious weight, his body hit the concrete and bounced a few times like a sack of dropped flour.

Hernandez fired the second round mostly because he'd been told to; his desire not to fuck this all up overriding any sense of overkill. The bullet struck Huesker in the chest, just to the right of the sternum. A red carnation blossomed on his chest in the spot where it landed.

Hernandez continued to walk as if nothing had happened, releasing the gun from his grip; just like he'd been told. He didn't hear it hit the ground, so he looked back. He saw it lying on the sidewalk, people walking heedlessly over it like it was a child's abandoned toy. Content that all was still going according to plan, he continued walking leisurely, heading toward the corner.

Behind him, he heard a woman suddenly scream and there was the sound of some men shouting. His curiosity got the better of him and he glanced back over his shoulder, trying to do so and still appear natural. He figured… give the impression that he wasn't responding to the sound of the shots, so much as reacting to the unexpected shouting. He noticed that a crowd had gathered around Huesker's fallen body and a man was bending down to check on him.

The blonde arm candy stood to the side of the walkway, a dark, maroon liquid splashed like paint across her face and upper body. Tears were streaming from her eyes making streaks of mascara black and blood red run down her powdered cheeks.

"Yo!" someone shouted from the street behind him.

For a second, Hernandez nearly shit his pants thinking something had gone wrong and he'd been caught. He turned and saw the sedan idling a few yards up the street. Agent Two was leaning out the window, holding the back door open and glaring at him. Reining in his rising sense of immediacy so that he didn't break into a run, he purposefully made himself casually walk over to the curb. Without looking back, he got into the car. When he was inside, he reached back and pulled the door closed behind him.

The people on the street barely noticed as the car slowly sped away.

The drive back to the prison was a quiet one. Hernandez changed back into his prison uniform without being told right after they'd gotten a few blocks away. When everything was back to as it had been, Hernandez sat back and did what he could to let the adrenaline coursing through his bloodstream dissipate.

Agent Two abruptly moved in his seat, reaching under it to pull three beer bottles into view. He held them up for everyone in the car to see. They were Heinekens and they still looked cold and absolutely delicious.

"Back in the Corps," Two said fraternally, "we always finished a mission by everyone having a nice, cold beer. Care to join me, gentlemen? These aren't exactly *ice* cold, but… they're wet."

Hernandez squinted at him suspiciously. "Isn't drinking and driving illegal? I mean, aren't you guys on duty?"

Agent One laughed as he veered the car onto the freeway and accelerated. "I think we can handle things if we get pulled over."

The two men in the front seat chuckled and slapped one another on their arms.

Psssssht!
Psssssht!
Psssssht!

The sound of Agent Two opening the beers made Hernandez's mouth abruptly flood with water. It had been a while… Two handed one of the bottles to his partner, and after a second, he handed one back to Hernandez.

"We'll keep this between us when we get you back to the prison, okay?" Agent Two said conspiratorially. "I don't think your warden would exactly understand, much less approve."

Hernandez accepted the beer gratefully, taking the cold bottle into his hands and feeling its chill on his palms. He couldn't remember when the last time was that he'd had one. It had been a long time ago though.

Raising it to his lips, the rich smell of hops and yeast rose to caress his nose and, just for a second, he was reminded of home. He smiled in anticipation of the draught's taste, and then, took a long pull from the mouth of the bottle. His mouth was flooded by the bubbly froth, and it still was cold enough to chill his fillings. Leaning into the seat, he closed his eyes and let the cold beer flow down his throat.

Maaan, that was good!

The whole thing, he silently mused as he took another sip, from the drop off on the corner to the pick-up had taken what, only a minute or two. In the span of a couple of television commercials, he'd transformed a living, breathing man—admittedly a sociopath and a rapist—into a corpse.

And all at the behest of the Federal Prison System.

Jesus…

Hernandez almost didn't believe it had happened at all. He kept half-expecting to wake up back in his cell to the sound of Johannsson kicking his bedframe. Shaking his head in disbelief, he took another long pull on his beer.

At least he was going to be going home soon.

"Don't let it get to ya, man," Agent Two said conversationally from the front seat. "That guy was a piece of shit and everyone knew it. Him getting off on a fuckin' technicality like that was, and remains, complete bullshit. Consider what you just did there… as balancing the scales of justice," and he chuckled darkly, raising his beer in a mock salute.

Hernandez ignored him as he drained the last of the beer from his bottle and stared out the window at the passing landscape, watching sadly as it turned from urban back to rural. Soon, he became lost in his own thoughts and, for once, he let them come.

He'd killed a man twice now: once to satisfy his need for revenge, and once more to regain his freedom. The first time, it had been out of rage and vengeance. This time… this time, it was different. This time, it was a cold, premeditated thing done for purely selfish reasons. Somehow, he knew that he'd turned a corner, and there was no coming back from it.

The drive wore on and Hernandez felt himself—and his nerves—slowly unwinding and returning to normal. His sense of agitation was settling and the ensuing adrenaline crash and lack of conversation in the car was making him feel sluggish and a little dopey. He set his head back onto the headrest and let his eyes fall like drapes.

His mind settled in and he began to feel more and more of the tensions in his muscles unspool. He knew he'd just done a terrible thing, but… ten years of his life back with his family was not exactly trivial. And besides, like the cop said, Huesker *was* a piece of garbage who deserved to die for what he'd no doubt done to those kids over the years… and that was just the ones they knew anything about.

"Hey," Two said abruptly, "I gotta piss. You guys okay with pulling off the road so I can take a leak?"

Hernandez said nothing and he couldn't have cared less. From somewhere far off, he felt the car slow and veer slightly toward the side of the road, tires crunching on the gravel. Once they had stopped, Hernandez faintly heard one of the front doors open, and then shut. The sound of Agent Two walking toward the back of the car seemed to come to him from down some long, cavernous hallway.

"Wait…" Hernandez mumbled, but no one heard him nor cared. "I… I don't…" and his chin slowly slumped to his chest.

Field Agent Jack Corvin shook his dick off and let the last few drops of his urine fall like raindrops to the ground. It struck him suddenly that the wet spot he'd left in the dirt looked like a surprised word balloon you'd see in a kid's comic book. Chuckling quietly, he put himself away, zipping up his pants and smoothing the material straight.

"Speaking of surprises," he said to no one.

Slowly, he walked around the car and approached the driver's side window. Agent Fitzgerald—Bill—had his arm hanging leisurely out the side, drumming his fingers against the metal door. An Everly Brothers' song about dreaming was playing quietly on the radio.

In the back, the prisoner was in his seat, breathing regularly. His head hung from his neck and it looked, for a second, like he was sitting in silent prayer. The beer bottle he'd been given had fallen from his grasp, and now lay abandoned on the back seat floorboard.

"Well," Corvin said to Fitzgerald.

Fitzgerald reached over and turned down the radio. As he did, he looked appraisingly into the rearview mirror and nodded. "Yeah, he's out."

Corvin unceremoniously yanked the back door open.

The prisoner sagged out of the door like The Blob coming out of a theater; the only thing keeping him in his seat was his seatbelt. Corvin reached over him and unbuckled the belt at the buckle. The man's dead weight pressed against him and made it hard to pull the restraint from around him.

"Hey, man," Corvin said sounding annoyed. "You wanna help me with this or just sit there and be a cock?"

Fitzgerald nodded and, with a heavy sigh, got out of the car.

After a bit of wrangling, they managed to pull the prisoner out of the car, and soon, had him suspended like a marionette between them. From a distance, it might have looked like they were carrying someone who'd had too much to drink. Once they had his weight even distributed between them, they walked off the roadway and started across a field toward the grove of trees on the side of the road.

"We'll need to call this in once we get it done," Corvin said and his voice sounded a little winded. "Escaped Prisoner found." He chuckled darkly under his breath. "Fuckin' asshole… is heavy."

Fitzgerald nodded, but said nothing, and trudged on. Then, "So, hey, man… how many would you say this is, huh?"

Corvin shrugged and shifted his grip on the prisoner's belt. "Well, you and I have done… six; another dozen or so in the rest of the state, maybe? You times that by fifty, plus a few in Puerto Rico, another couple in Guam, and you get your number, right?"

Fitzgerald shook his head. "I just can't believe how these guys could think this was ever going to go down any differently than this."

"How so?"

"Well, I mean," and he paused to adjust the weight on his shoulders, "in what fuckin' world do they let this guy just walk free? Knowing what he knows… Knowing who was involved… and how. Nope, never gonna happen."

"Well," Corvin said casually as he reached back with his free hand to pull the 'drop .45' he'd had with him from the small of his back. He clicked the Safety to 'off.' "It's like they say, 'hope springs eternal, right?" He hefted the weight on his arm again. "C'mon, man… Let's get this done. He's getting heavy and Miriam's waiting on me for dinner."

"Yeah, I hear ya," Fitzgerald finally said with a resigned sigh. "I promised Jimmy we'd toss the ball around a bit before it got too late. Did I tell you that he made Varsity?"

"No shit?"

"No shit."

And bearing their burden, the two of agents disappeared into the deepening shadows of the grove of trees.

TOMB OF THE LIVING DEAD

(for Amando de Ossorio)

This one wears its inspiration pretty openly on its sleeve. I love the films of Spanish director, Amando de Ossorrio; most notably for his blissfully depraved Blind Dead films. During The Quarantine, we watched a lot of movies and these films kept repeatedly coming up in our discussion. So, we watched them; all four of them. And they were, well… they were pretty terrible. But, by the end of the marathon, their goofy charm ended up winning me over. And, of course, loving the esthetic, you know I just had to take the idea out for a drive.

Lots of other influences come bound up with this one. In addition to the Ossorrio films, there's the filmography of Mario Bava, a few Italian and Spanish giallo directors (particularly the work of people like Sergio Martino, Aldo Lado, Luciano Ercoli, Umberto Lenzi, Carlos Aured, and Javier Aguirre), some American slasher tropes, and, of course, my signature 'taking a goofy idea and approaching it way too seriously' way of doing things and voila! I wanted to somehow include the great film scores of Anton Garcia Abril, but, for the life of me, I couldn't figure out how to make it work. Please consult your streaming services for his music. It's totally awesome. Anyway, I hope you enjoy this little excursion into mood and monsters set amidst the beautiful Spanish countryside as much as I did.

"Oh, c'mon, man! Shit!" Chris Sandler shouted as he reluctantly stumbled to a stop.

He'd been running to catch the last bus into town and they'd just missed it. He watched benignly as the small, renovated school bus disappeared into the distance in a puff of dust.

They… were he and his girlfriend, Jill Scott. The two of them were midway through a two-week hiking tour through the Spanish countryside, and, well… things hadn't exactly been going according to plan. In fact, things couldn't have been going worse. Nothing so far had gone according to schedule.

Back home, Chris was a mid-level marketing manager for an electronics company in Palo Alto, California. Jill worked as a Civil Engineer for the city. They'd been together for almost a year now and this trip was their first extended one together, and the first *real* testing of their relationship.

Jill came running up to him from behind, bumping into his shoulder, and breathing heavy. "Are you fucking kidding me right now?" she whined. She turned and glared at Chris, her brown eyes flaring. "What are we going to fuckin' do now, Chris?"

Chris hugged her and tried to calm her down, wrapping his arms around her shoulders and holding her tight. He knew how she could get when things went sideways in her life… and things had definitely been going sideways as of late, so he didn't exactly blame her.

They'd already missed one flight. Then, they had their hotel say that they had no idea who they were and wouldn't be able to put them up, even for the night. This in spite of them having confirmed their reservations with Trivago months ago. He remembered the clerk, shrugging and mumbling something like, 'Hay una convencion en la ciudad.' before finally walking away from the front desk.

And now, this… a missed bus.

And, not by minutes. No, fuck that, seconds.

"Shit, baby," Jill moaned, pressing her face to his chest. "Seriously, what do we do now?"

Chris stared down the long, empty Spanish road, first to his left, then to his right, and held her a little tighter. For a second, he thought about going back to the gas station they'd just been at but… It's not like anyone there could—or would—want to help them. They hadn't exactly been welcoming when they were there, and why should they be? They were foreigners.

"We walk, I guess. Maybe hitchhike, if we can."

She looked at him blankly and he thought she was going to cry. He pulled her close and, despite everything, the scent of her hair made parts of him stir slightly.

"It'll be fine," he said, trying once more to reassure her. "If it gets too late, maybe we can find a place to camp."

Jill sighed and stamped her feet impotently. Crossing her arms, she walked away from him, leaving the bags for him to carry.

"I love you," he called after her.

"Love you, too," she replied, but the sentiment somehow got lost on the wind.

Two and a half hours later, the sun was slowly slipping behind the rolling hills just outside Castelo Branco in Spain. If their situation hadn't seemed so dire, Chris thought to himself, the scenery around them might have been considered to be beautiful. It was like a postcard come to life everywhere he looked. Now, though, with the sun going down and their options quickly running out, there was more of an immediate sense of menace in the air. Chris knew that they needed to figure something out for themselves as quickly as possible.

"Hey," Jill suddenly said from where she was walking on his right. "What's that?" She pointed toward a grove of dying trees off to the side of the roadway.

Chris looked over and saw the upper eaves of a building poking its head up beyond an acre or two of what looked like apple trees.

"I think it's a house," Chris guessed. "Hard to tell from here."

Jill stopped walking and took Chris by the arm, turning him around.

"Ooh, Chris," she implored, "We should maybe go there, huh?"

Chris eyed her suspiciously. The last thing he wanted to be doing was bothering more of the locals. Somebody might call the cops. "Do you really think that's a good idea?"

"I mean, look… there's either someone there," she said, pleading her case, "or there's not. If there is, we can ask them for a ride or for a place to sleep until that fucking bus comes back in the morning. And, if there's not, then I'm sure they wouldn't mind if we camped on their land for the night. Maybe on the porch… or, y'know, inside the house where it's warm."

Chris smiled and put an arm around her. She looked so cute standing that way, looking defiant, that he almost asked her to marry him right then and there. He'd been thinking about popping the question for a while now. This trip was supposed to help him decide one way or the other. They'd been dating for longer than either of them had ever dated someone before. And even with the hiccups on this trip, he was still crazy about her.

One thing that had been impeding him though was finding the perfect ring. She had been so specific whenever they talked about it: red stone with smaller white gems surrounding it; 'supporting it,' she'd said. Everywhere he'd looked for anything even close to it, never seemed to yield the right one.

"Okay, look," he conceded without much heart. "We'll go there and check it out, but we're *not* going inside unless we're invited. You hear me?"

Jill leapt into his arms, pressing her full brown lips to his. They enjoyed the moment for a moment before reluctantly separating and heading toward the old, dark house that was set back beyond the apple trees.

Approaching the house, Chris was struck by the simplicity of the building's design. It looked like a rectangular box set on its side in a field near the foothills of a low mountain. Low shrubs of hibiscus, lavender, and passiflora surrounded the house and gave it a lived in, almost homey appearance.

The long plane of the box—upstairs and down—had a total of twelve windows. The upstairs rooms each featured small balconies that were surrounded by a wrought iron railing. Tubs of dead and dying flowers hung from the sides of the metal barrier by hooks. The short plane of the house was the same but had only six windows.

The roadway descended onto the property, creating a natural entryway onto the estate. A short, dirt road divided the apple orchard directly in the middle. They both commented that the lot had seen better days. The apple trees themselves were bare of leaf and fruit, now nothing more than bony hands protruding up from the depleted soil.

Behind the building, rows of withered grapevines were hung on splintering stakes. Their leaves were long gone and more branchy skeletons remained. Not too far beyond them rose some sizeable hills that continued upwards to join the larger mountains beyond. Pretty much all the landscape was carpeted by beautiful, tall Aleppo pines.

The couple walked up to roadway and, as they got closer to the house, they instinctively reached out to hold one another's hands. No birds sang in the trees above them, but the wind ran its fingers through the branches, and it made the boughs sway hypnotically.

At the top of the porch, the entrance to the house was large and divided by a central post. Oval windows split the middle of each of the panels with stained glass latticework. When the waning light struck the panes, it created a kaleidoscope of rainbows that slowly moved across the porch with the setting of the sun.

Chris approached the door and knocked firmly. They heard the booming from it echo throughout the house. They waited for someone to answer the door, both smiling and doing their best to appear friendly, but no one ever came.

Jill got up on her tiptoes so that she could peer into the house through one of the windows. She moved her head back and forth, in order to get a clearer picture of what was inside.

"It's empty," she finally said as she dropped back down and set her backpack onto the porch.

Chris scrunched up his eyebrows and knocked again, even harder this time.

"No, really," she repeated. "There's nothing inside, Chris. No furniture. Nothing on the walls. It's empty."

Chris stepped off the porch and went over to one of the building's side windows. He hoisted himself up, pressing his face against the cold glass, and stared inside. Sure enough… the place was completely deserted.

The room inside was large, like a sitting room or family

living area. The wood flooring was bare and it stretched across the entire visible space, snaking down a hallway. There were some nails left sporadically around the four walls, but whatever art had once been there was now long gone.

"You're right," he said, jumping down to the ground and walking back to her.

He came back up onto the porch and approached Jill. He hated to admit it, but she might be onto something here. The way he had it figured, the sun was going down, the temperature was dropping, and it was getting late. They really only had one of two options. They could set up a base camp where they were—either under some trees or even here on the porch—or they could keep moving in the hopes of finding someplace else to crash a little further down the road. Either way, they were chasing the clock.

Jill presented a third option by checking the door. She gripped the doorknob and looked over at Chris inquisitively. Then, raising an eyebrow, she turned it, and the door popped open and swung inward.

"Jill!" Chris exclaimed, looking around as if someone might hear.

"Calm down, Honey," she said smiling indulgently. "The place is clearly empty. There's no one here."

Chris shook his head. "But… what if someone comes home?"

Jill laughed and reached down for her pack. "Chris," she said earnestly, "There's no *home* here for anyone to come to." Then, assuming that the matter was settled, she walked inside.

They ate trail mix and Power Bars from their packs for dinner that night. Chris surprised her with four little airplane bottles of Jack Daniels he'd pocketed from the flight over. They toasted the night, their trip (despite its setbacks), and spoke of their love for one another before finally settling down in front of the fire that Chris made in the fireplace. The night wore on and they settled into their makeshift camp. The hours passed, and they talked some more, and ended up making love before falling asleep in front of the fire.

Outside, the crickets fiddled, and some far-off frogs croaked, and the Spanish night passed without either of them ever really noticing.

The next morning, the couple discovered, much to their delight, that the house still had its power and that the water was still running. They hadn't checked either of them when they'd come in last night. 'Broken in,' was more like it, he thought. Anyway, they'd just assumed it was off. They ate more Power Bars for their breakfast and decided to take some time for a much-needed shower and to recharge their electronics.

In the shower, they had sex again, and held each other close as the water cascaded down the length of their bodies. Once they'd dried themselves off and gotten into a change of clothes they'd pulled from their packs, they went outside onto the porch to sip some instant coffee and map out what they were going to do next.

"Y'know," Jill said into her steaming cup as she leaned against the open frame of the front door. "I was thinking..." She turned her back to him and stared out over the grove of wilted apple trees.

"Uh-oh," Chris replied smiling. "Here we go."

She turned back toward him with a conspiratory smile on her face. "Just hear me out, okay?"

"Okay, okay," he said, raising his hands in surrender. "What were you thinking?"

She turned to look back out over the property. "Well... it sure is nice here, and, by all appearances, no one seems to be using the house."

"And?" Chris asked, nervously waiting for the other, presumably illegal, shoe to drop.

"Well, I thought... we could stay for another day." She turned to once again face him. "Just one more day. We can leave in the morning."

He looked at her and was about to say no, when...

"We can lay by the fire again," she said, looking up at him seductively.

He knew she did that sort of thing—trying to look cute and acting coquettishly— whenever she desired something. He'd come to understand over the course of their relationship that, the more she played the role, the more she wanted it. He figured it was a hold-over from what he knew was a complicated relationship with her dad. He thought about it for a bit, though, and could only think of one reason to argue against it.

"What if someone does come?"

She stared at him blankly and cocked one of her eyebrows; as if to say, 'we've been through this already, Chris.' Despite his misgivings, he found himself slowly nodding his head. Maybe she was right. They had enough to eat in their packs for another couple of days if they were careful, and the house had running water and warmth. They'd looked the place over after their shower and there wasn't a stick of furniture anywhere. It's like whoever had once lived here left and had no plans of coming back. No reason not to take a day for themselves, to rest and recharge. He looked out over the scraggly apple trees and idly wondered why they'd been left to die.

"Okay, we'll stay one more day," he finally said. "I know we could both use the rest and we can use the time to figure out what we want to do next. Decide where we want to go."

Jill hopped up and down, clapping her hands excitedly. She bounded over the Chris and hugged him. "Thank you! Thank you! Thank you!" she said happily, and she kissed him.

He smiled at her and ran his hand up her back.

"I want to go out on a hike, don't you?" she continued. "Y'know, explore this place a little bit. It'll be fun. We won't go far. We can go check out the grape fields I saw out back to start."

"Uh, okay," he replied reluctantly. "I guess we can leave the packs here; hide them in a closet just in case someone *does* come by. We can bring a something to munch on in case we need it. Maybe find some apples that haven't rotted. And we have our water bottles…"

She smiled broadly and kissed him again, more passionately this time. "This is gonna be so cool," she said excitedly as she let go of him and ran into the house to get ready.

The sun was just reaching its highest point in the sky when Jill and Chris arrived at the far side of what turned out to be an anemic vineyard. The plants had all gone to rot; dried leaves withered and lying dead on the ground. The soil itself was a barren clumpy powder that offered only a prolonged death to the emaciated plants that were still struggling to hold out.

They'd reached a wood rail fence that separated whose ever land they were on from their neighbors and stopped to drink from their water bottles.

"What do you think?" he asked her.

Jill squinted against the light and looked around. Her face had a dissatisfied, almost annoyed look, like she'd been expecting something else, something fun, to happen. Now that it looked like the chances of that were rapidly fading, she clearly felt cheated and disappointed.

"I don't know," she finally replied. "This place is kind of a dump, right? It looked way better when we saw it yesterday." She giggled a little. "In the dark."

Chris chuckled and nodded. It had looked better last night; like some romantic chateau that had been put here just for them. Now, it looked like Tara gone to seed.

"Hey," Jill yelped suddenly. "What is *that*?"

Chris turned his head in the direction of where she was looking. He could just make out the roof of another small building poking up over the next hill. The gables and frieze boards were painted white and they plainly stood out against the clear, blue sky.

"What do you think *that* is?" she asked curiously. "Is it another house?"

Chris shook his head. "I… I don't know."

Without waiting for any further discussion, Jill suddenly bent under the top wooden railing and dipped through the fence. She immediately started walking into the grove of trees that lay beyond. She strode away without waiting for him even as Chris was reaching out to stop her.

"Hey, c'mon, Jill… Wait!"

She turned to look at him but kept walking backward. "Hola! Soy Dora! Let's go explore!" She laughed and doing so caused her to stumble.

"Jill, please…"

She stopped walking. "Look, let's go check this place out, and, if there's nothing to see, we'll go back to the house, I promise." She flashed him one of her cutest grins. "Deal?"

He considered the proposition for a second, and then, finally agreed. They did pretty much have the rest of the day to kill, and there were more reasons to go satisfy her (and his, let's be honest) burgeoning curiosity than to not. He shook his head.

"If we end up in a Spanish jail on this vacation, I'm gonna be so pissed."

She laughed and extended her hand to him, smiling widely. "C'mon, Clyde… let's go do crimes."

Chris grinned and followed along after her. "Okay, Bonnie."

Then, once he'd gotten through the fence, the two of them walked off through the trees.

The house, as it turned out, wasn't a house, at all, but rather a small, stone and wood structure that looked like it was built as a chapel. Whoever constructed the structure had, for reasons known only to themselves, hid it away here in a cleft between two mountains.

Jill immediately ran ahead and started searching around the building's perimeter for a way in. Chris walked up to the door and used some spit on his fingers to try and clean the small glass window that was set in the middle of it. He was unable to remove much of the mud, just smear it around a little, but he got enough off that he was able to make out the empty, open space of the gallery inside. Almost without thinking, he put his hand on the door and leaned his weight against it. Unexpectedly, the door swung open.

"Jesus, doesn't anybody lock *anything* around here?" he mumbled under his breath. Then, leaning out from the doorway, he shouted for Jill, "Babe… I'm in."

She came around the corner of the building in a hurry, grinning like a kid who'd been sent on a secret mission. "Man… you think you know a guy, then you go on vacation with him, and you learn, not only is he good in bed, but he's a wiz at Breaking and Entering, too." She chuckled warmly as she stepped up onto the porch.

Chris peered into the building from the doorway suspiciously. Jill leaned against him, and her breasts poking him in his back were making it hard for him to concentrate. If she kept it up, he had a pretty good idea of what might happen; especially now that they'd found someplace secluded. As she pressed against him, though, her additional weight pushed them both deeper into the door. They both stumbled bit but quickly regained their footing.

"Do you want to take a look around?" she asked. "It looks pretty creepy in there, doesn't it? But it also doesn't look like anyone's been in here for months; years, maybe."

Chris still wasn't convinced. The place was a duplicate and every bit as empty as the house where they'd stayed last night. He didn't see much of a reason to go snoopin' around.

"I don't know… it's just as empty as the house. I mean, I don't see shit in here of interest," he finally said. "Maybe we should just go back, huh?"

Jill's expression soured and she waved his concern away as if she were annoyed. They'd been on this trip for, what, over a week now? And, the entire time, they'd been walking; trudging their way across the admittedly beautiful Spanish countryside, but still… If they weren't doing that, they were getting ripped off by the locals. Now, just as they'd started having some adventures, they could tell their friends about back home, he was wussin' out.

"C'mon, Chris," she said matter-of-factly. "It's a dilapidated, old church in the middle of nowhere. But, just like the house last night, nobody gives a shit."

Chris laughed and shook his head. She was right. Maybe he was being a stick in the mud. After all, who was around to care whether they had a look inside this empty church or not? With the way the trip was going, so far, well… it was safe to say that it hadn't been panning out in the way either of them had hoped. They were finally just beginning to have fun. He smiled at her and invited her inside with a gesture of his hand.

"After you, Ma'am…" he finally said with a flourish.

Jill bowed royally, and without hesitation, stepped into the room.

"Man, it smells funky in here," she called from inside.

"Well, for god's sake, don't touch anything," he advised as he reluctantly followed along after her.

They found themselves in an extended foyer with white marble sides and a gray slate floor. Two thin windows in the shape of a cross were embedded in the stone of the far wall, allowing the late afternoon sunlight to fall like a golden mist across the floor.

He followed her into the main chamber and was surprised by how big it was. The room was long and had a multitude of ornate carvings made into the old wood paneling like some kind of vestry. There were no pews, but he could tell by the scuff marks on the floor that there had been some once. He could see discolorations in the wood from where they had been through the layer of dust that had accumulated there.

At the furthest end of the room from them, at the back of a slightly raised dais that seemed to dominate the room, Chris noticed that was a recessed altar. He was able to make out some low containers sitting at the far end of the platform. From here, they looked like shipping crates. Shadows lay over them like a shawl, obscuring a clear view, and making it so that he could only see their vague shape.

"What do you think?" Jill asked and her voice sounded like an intrusion in the quiet of the place.

"I don't know," Chris replied. "I mean, it's doesn't exactly look Catholic, but it does feel like something pretty similar."

Jill walked over to the far wall and touched the cracking surface with her fingertips. The dried paint came away in small, brittle chips. She turned around and caught Chris' attention when her black hair caught a thin beam of light coming into the room though a window and flashed like polished onyx.

"Well, the place is old, that's for sure," she said. She took abrupt notice of the altar and began walking toward it. "I can't believe someone would just leave it open like this, though."

Chris looked up and saw that the ceiling was open and its wooden beams spread out over them like the ribcage of a giant bird. A lone, metal candelabrum hung from the center of the ceiling, nearly all of its candles now gone, its sockets now empty and gone fuzzy with dust.

By now, Jill had walked up onto the altar, and was peering into the darkness at the very back of the room. She noticed the oblong boxes tucked into an alcove against the back wall of the church and went over to them.

"What are *these*?" she asked, mostly talking to herself.

Chris looked over at her, and then, toward where she was looking. He could now see the long boxes and immediately knew them for what they were. His uncle used to work at Saint Francis Memorial Park and he'd shown him pictures.

"Those look like burial vaults," he said, proud of himself for remembering the correct term.

"Burial vaults? Like, there are *bodies* in those things?"

Chris smiled indulgently. "Sort of. I mean, there may have been at one time. But, by the look of the place, it wasn't exactly recently, so..." He followed her up onto the dais. "Now, there's probably nothing more than dust and some spiders inside."

Jill wrinkled up her nose but didn't stop approaching the crypt.

Chris walked over to the furthest vault, putting his hand on top and brushing the thick layer of dust from its surface. Once it had been cleared of grit, he noticed that these containers were not like anything his uncle had ever shown him. Ornately carved and very, very old, Chris noticed that the lid had a large cross as big as a man etched onto the lid. Some words had been cut into the hard stone, but he couldn't make much sense of them. The only ones he could recognize were 'Caballero,' which he thought meant 'cowboy,' and 'Templarios."

"Hey," Jill exclaimed. "Is that one broken?"

Chris looked where she was pointing, and, sure enough, the lid on the vault in front of him had been split open. He dug a Maglite out from a pocket of his pack and, after clicking it on, he shined the light inside. As expected, the vault's interior was dark and dusty but, by angling the light's beam around, he was able to get a pretty good idea of what was going on inside.

His light first fell upon a long length of muddy, white fabric. He could see that there was deep red piping that had been sewn around the length of its border. He also caught a glimpse of something that looked like a red cross embroidered over the chest of the garment. It was identical to the one carved into the vault's lid. A skeletal hand rested alongside the figure's body. The hand still had small bits of flesh clinging to it, its bony digits reflected back white in the Mag light's beam.

"Christ, there *is* a body in here!" he cried out.

Chris pulled the light out of the hole and a few of the smaller, loose stones fell away. With his line of sight now clear, he was able to get a better look inside. He bent down over the lid, and was shocked when a large piece of stone, about the size of a dinner plate, came away in his hand. Removing it caused a thick cloud of dirt to leap into the air. The fog it created sent Jill stumbling away, coughing.

"Shit!" he exclaimed.

"Chri-is!"

"Sorry," he said apologetically. "The damn thing just came apart."

He set the chunk of stone aside and returned his attention to the inside the vault. The beam of light fell next onto the body's stick-like arm. Chris was surprised. The corpse didn't look nearly as disgusting as he thought it would. It looked almost fake, like it was made of model airplane wood and papier-mâché.

"Is there really?" Jill said, now back over by the chapel entrance. "Okay, this is getting a little too creepy now. I don't mind a little B & E, but I draw the line at desecrating a grave. I thought we'd find something cool in here, but... this is just sad."

Chris grinned, but kept searching the rest of the vault. "Okay, but it was an accident, just so's we're clear." He chuckled, finally giving up on finding anything of worth inside.

"Yeah, yeah," Jill called from over by the front door. "Very funny, smart guy. Let's go, okay?"

Chris braced one of his hands on the side of the vault and the other on his thigh and pressed himself to his feet. His back barked and cursed at him for all the nights he'd spent sleeping on the floor this trip. Not for the first time since leaving, he momentarily longed for his bed back home.

Then, just as he was turning away from the vault, something shiny caught his attention. It happened just was he was pulling the light away, a glint of metal from within the blackness.

Bending back down, he directed the light toward where he thought he'd seen the reflected light. He swept the Maglite's beam back and forth across the interior like a searchlight. Then, just as he was about to give up, he saw it, on the corpse's right hand: an ornate-looking ring with a large stone at its center. The illumination of the flashlight lit the metal up like it was Christmas, the stones glittering in the gloom.

Angling the light up to where the body's face was, he saw the extent of the occupant's mummification. And although the corpse was now nothing more than a withered husk, he could still see where a beard had once grown. Shafts of hair stood out from its skin like burned trees across a parched landscape. The broad, white teeth shone through a rigid smile like ivory tombstones. Tufts of his fallen hair lay about the pillow on which his head lay like candy floss.

Returning his attention to the ring, Chris reached in with his free hand and tried to pry it from the bony fingers. He wasn't even sure why, but he told himself it was to get a better look at it. He worked the metal circle round and round on the dead man's finger, but it kept getting caught on a knuckle. The brittle digit finally broke off in his hand from all the wrenching he was doing, and the freed ring fell off into his palm. When he withdrew his hand, he got his first real look at his prize.

The jewelry was old, 'antique' didn't even come close to its vintage, and beautiful. The central stone was large, but it wasn't ostentatious. And the smaller, surrounding white stones framed the ring's simple beauty.

In a flash, Chris knew Jill would love it.

It was perfect.

He looked around the room and the idea that he was about to break another law in a foreign country suddenly struck him. The absurdity of the idea that he was about to pocket a ring he'd just taken off a corpse that was lying in a casket in some forgotten church in the middle of Spain was not lost on him. It probably meant that, somewhere, he was probably in some kind of trouble, sin-wise, but… he'd been meaning to propose to Jill for a long time. He'd just not had the ring with which to do it. And now, here was this one, literally falling into his lap…

And with their trip had been going to poorly…

It was like it was all meant to be.

"Hey," Jill called him again from the door. "Are you comin', or what?"

Chris took a guilty last glance back at the hole in the vault lid. Then, he dropped the ring into his pocket, and ran to catch up with his soon-to-be fiancé.

Later that night, just as Chris and Jill started packing their gear into their backpacks, a storm blew in and rain began pelting the outside of the house. As much as they'd enjoyed the last few days alone together, they both knew it was time for them to start thinking about how they were going to get back home.

All good things must come to their end, and all of that.

They'd snacked on the last of their trail mix and dried fruit for dinner, and neither of them talked much about this afternoon, much less about the trip to the chapel. Chris kept looking for an opportunity to show the ring to Jill, and to ask her to be his bride. He'd pretty much decided on the walk back that he was going to ask her to marry him but somehow things never seemed to come together. She always ended up changing the subject or he would get distracted by something or the other.

It was just never seemed *right*.

They finally settled themselves back in the house's living room. The front windows faced the dying apple orchard and the road that led off the property and back to the road. Chris built another fire that was now roaring in the hearth.

Outside, darkness crept up on them like a thief.

"This is nice," Jill finally said with a deep sigh, sitting down on the floor in the little nest they'd made of their sleeping bags.

Chris smiled and nodded but said nothing. He looked over at her face in the flickering firelight, feeling so much love for her in that particular moment. And, the whole time, he felt the weight of the ring sitting in his pocket. Like a millstone, it was a constant reminder of how he'd been unable to gather the nerve to ask her his one important question. He took a deep breath, and, making up his mind that now was the time, he turned to face her.

"It *is* nice. It'll be hard to go back home after all of this."

"Well," she said with a grin, "It won't be *that* hard..."

They laughed together and the world seemed perfect for the both of them. Chris reached into his pocket to grab the ring, and once he had it in his grip, he looked back over to her and smiled.

It was now or never.

"Hey, Jilly... since this is, uh... pretty much our last night here. I wanted to, um..."

Jill grinned at him. He always got like this when he had something on his mind; like a little boy trying to ask for a new toy. She wasn't exactly sure what he was up to but seeing him act like this amused her to no end.

"What?" she asked, seeing no reason to make whatever it was easy on him.

"Well, I uh..."

Just then, a loud crash shattered the silence and the mood. At first, Chris thought it was only branch breaking in the apple trees outside, but it was pretty clear by its proximity that it was much closer than that. It *almost* sounded like it came from inside the house.

Chris got up from where they were sitting to go check the overhead lights. He found the switch and flipped it. The room around them exploded in a sudden, blinding flash, and then, everything went dark again. Once again, the only light in the room came from the fireplace. Shadows from the flames danced like sprites across the flat, bare walls.

Jill gasped in surprise and immediately drew her feet up under her. Her head whipped back and forth as she scanned the room, her eyes brightly flashing from behind her knees.

"What the hell happened, Chris?" she hissed.

He went back over to her and took hold of her hand. "It's okay. We probably just popped a fuse or lost electricity from the storm."

"Really? Do you think that's what it is?" she asked, and her voice shook with distress. "Fuck! That scared the shit out of me."

Chris got up and retrieved his Maglite from his pack. He smiled reassuringly at Jill in the hope that it would help her calm down. "I'll go check it out. You stay here. I'll be right back."

"No!" she replied emphatically. "Don't you dare leave me here, goddammit! I swear to God, Chris! I've had this weird feeling around here ever since we got back from our hike. I can't really put my finger on it, but… something just feels off."

Chris knelt down again to hug her.

"Look, it's gonna be fine, I promise. Just stay here and I'll go check it out. It'll only take a second, okay?"

Jill glared at him and crossed her arms, staring at the floor. "Don't leave me here alone, Chris." She looked back up at him. "Please."

Chris smiled indulgently. "Honey, it'll just be quicker if I go alone. I mean, I may have to go outside. There's no need for both of us getting wet, right?"

Before she could rally any kind of defense, he got up and walked away. As he disappeared down the hallway heading toward the kitchen, he heard her call him an asshole under her breath.

Which he figured was fair.

When he got to the kitchen, he began looking for the fuse box. But after checking every cabinet and behind every door, he couldn't find it. He finally decided it must be someplace else and went to go check the rest of the house.

Jill sat on the floor by the fire, her arms still angrily crossed over her chest. She was pissed. Shit, yeah, she was pissed. Who knew what the hell happened to the lights to make them go out? Maybe it *was* the storm, but then again, what if it wasn't? What if it was something else? What if it was the owners of the place coming home? Would they think them burglars? Were they both now in some kind of danger? It just made sense that they *both* go to try and find out what was wrong. Splitting up like this was the stupidest idea ever.

"What is this, a bad horror movie?" she asked the fire, annoyed. "Fuckin' *men*."

The fire fanned its flames, but it didn't feel much of a need to reply.

Behind her, the quiet sound of something slowly creeping across the floorboards broke the crystalline silence in the room. It might have been the house settling into its foundation the way old houses do or it might have been just the battering the building was taking from the storm outside. Even if it was only just a mouse, it all made her skin crawl.

"Chris?" she called out hopefully into the gloom. She held her breath and she waited for him to respond. Nothing. Then, under her breath, she softly hissed, "Fuck!"

The house kept its silence and the only sound in the room was the whipping wind and sporadic thunder outside. The fire crackled and popped and the air of expectation that came after made the room seem all the more heavy and electric.

"Chris? C'mon, man… Stop foolin' around."

Quiet; like no sound dared to interrupt the stillness of the moment.

Jill hugged her legs tighter with her arms, her knees now coming up under her chin. Her eyes moved around the room distrustfully, pupils now gone wide from her growing fright.

What was it about men, she thought to herself. They always seemed so fucking determined to make everything they did into some weird, boy adventure. She once caught Chris trying to duel the neighbor's dog using a garbage can lid and a broomstick when he was out cleaning the garage. Who does that? Despite herself, she grinned at the memory.

"You dick," she whispered under her breath.

Suddenly, something fell in front of her eyes, covering her entire field of vision like a curtain. She felt hands roughly clasp themselves over the lower part of her face and hold on tight, pulling her back. Whatever it was that had grabbed her, it was weirdly strong and felt slimy and gross against her skin. She tasted something old and dusty on her lips where the surface of the thing pressed itself against her mouth.

She reached up and tried to pry whatever it was away but felt only wet sticks pressed firmly over her face instead. The rods felt weird, like they were made of bone and mud, and her hand came away wet with what she hoped was rain.

Bracing herself against the ground, she used her arms to

break free, whirling them about and leaping to her feet, she turned to face the intruder.

"What the hell, man?" she coughed as she glared at her attacker.

Standing before her was a man, but it most definitely was *not* Chris. This guy was stick-thin and stood in front of her rocking unsteadily on his feet. He wore some kind of muddy, hooded monk's robe or something that bore a large cross over the front.

The man's face looked impossibly ancient and was dried to old leather. A wiry goatee stuck out from his withered flesh like brush bristles. But it was his eyes that demanded all her attention. Where normally there would have been eyeballs within their sockets, now only charred and ruined pits remained. She gasped when she realized that his eyes had been burned out and he was blind.

The figure stood silently in front of her, its arms outstretched. He slowly tilted his head, first to one side, then to the other, as if he were searching for something and could only use sound to find it. Jill took an involuntary step away from him and heard the floorboard beneath her feet creak like a ship's mast, betraying her position.

The man in the robe's head turned as if he had somehow zeroed in on exactly where she was standing. He took a hesitant step forward and sniffed the air as he tried to catch any scent of her. Then, he took another step, again reaching out for her. His fingers were splayed and searched the air in front of him like antennae. And all the while, his mouth continued working at something, like a cow with its cud, forever chewing.

Involuntarily, Jill gasped, and even as she did it, she knew what a mistake she'd made. The man began moving closer to her, coming at her much quicker than she'd expected. He came relentlessly forward, moving like a shark with a fiendish intent.

She took another step backward, and was about to run—*run to where?*—when she felt another pair of hands suddenly grip her shoulders from behind. The bony fingertips dug into her flesh and dug deep. As she flinched and tried to move away, the first hooded man was on her, pulling both her and whoever accompanied him to the ground, where they both held her.

Jill felt a final blind panic course over her body before everything went black. Her last thought was of Chris and where he might have gone.

And why he'd left her all alone.

Chris climbed the staircase that led to the kitchen from the basement. When he'd been unable to find the fuse box in the kitchen, he went to check elsewhere, starting with the cellar. All he'd found down there though was an old, long unused boiler, and a couple more empty rooms. He closed the basement door behind him and decided to go and check on Jill before continuing on.

Walking down the hall toward the living room, he hoped that she wasn't freaking out too badly being alone. He knew she was a little mad at him because he'd left to go look for the fuse box, but… who knew what might have happened to the lights? And who might have done it? If it had been something that was dangerous, he figured it was better if she stayed someplace safe.

Coming around the corner into the living room area, he immediately noticed the change in the room's temperature from the fire. A deep orange glow tinted the walls as the fire's light enveloped the room in its warmth. Outside the windows, the storm raged on, continuing to dump a torrent of water on the house.

Chris searched the room looking for Jill, but he was unable to find her. Where could she have gone, he asked himself. His heart dropped when he thought of a few possibilities. The best of which was that she went off to look around for herself, pissed off that he'd left.

Stepping deeper into the room, he approached the fireplace, slowly moving across the empty floor to get to the hearth. As he came closer, he was surprised to find Jill lying face down on the floor. Her dark hair hung in front of her face like a curtain, but he could tell it was her by her clothing.

"Jilly, honey?" he asked, and his voice sounded like an unwanted intrusion in the quiet room. "I couldn't find the damn fuse box. I think it might be upstairs, but… I wanted to come back to check on you before I went to look. You okay?"

Jill still didn't move, and she didn't answer. She just lay

there on the floor silently pouting.

"Look," he stammered, "I know you're probably pretty pissed at me, but I just thought that it would be better—safer—if only one of us went to look. Don't be mad, okay?"

Remained still, she just lay there without moving.

Man, he thought, she must really be pissed.

"C'mon, honey," he said, and he went over to her.

Bending down, he put his hand on her arm as a way to show his contrition. When he did though, her skin felt cold and clammy and his fingers came away with something on them; something that was wet and black in the firelight. He put his hands on her back, rolling her gently over, and her body felt hard; almost like it was made of marble.

"Jill?" he asked, his voice starting to crack with worry.

He reluctantly pushed her onto her back, and it was like moving a plank of wood. Easing himself back in order to see more clearly in the firelight, he noticed that the black fluid he'd seen was all over her chest, soaking her shirt to the skin. There was so much of it, he thought. It was everywhere.

But it was her face that truly horrified him. The skin of her cheeks had been pulled tightly back, exposing a torn and ravaged musculature beneath. Her eyes were empty orbs, rolled up and put away behind their heavy lids. The pearls of her teeth shone through the rendered flesh of her mouth like shiny coins stuck in mud.

Chris' legs abruptly gave out and he fell back onto the floor. Feeling the rough embrace of panic, he started scrambling, kicking his legs violently, as he tried to get away from her. To his horror, he slipped and ended up kicking Jill in the side of her head, but she didn't even flinch from the blow. It was at that point that he thought he heard himself scream. And, as his mind reeled, he felt his sense of logic and reason start to fold in on itself.

All the while, he couldn't help but continue to stare at Jill's ravaged face.

What was left of his mind quickly began sorting through its available options, trying to come up with a reason, no matter how implausible, that this might all be happening. Could she have run into the house's owners? Could they have come home and mistaken *them* for intruders? Maybe it was the owners who cut the lights and they were now lying in wait for him somewhere else in the house?

But why would anyone do something like *this* to another person?

Whatever the reason, he forced himself to admit one thing: Jill was gone; murdered apparently. And that did not exactly bode well for him. He knew he would have to grieve later, after he got out of here and called somebody, the cops maybe. Right now, he needed to get out of here, and to find the nearest farmhouse up the road to get some help.

He crouched before getting to his feet since it took him a minute to himself sorted. His breath came in short gasps, and his limbs suddenly felt sluggish, like he was swimming in a thick soup.

"Must be shock," he mumbled softly to himself.

Suddenly, from the shadows at the far corner of the room, he heard something move. At first, it seemed like it was nothing, like something from his imagination. But then, there was an ominous shuffling, like someone had hesitantly moved their feet across the bare flooring. He turned and looked behind him, but saw nothing, only the black of the shadows.

Then, from deep within the blackness, something stirred.

A cloaked form drew itself from the inky black, becoming more and more distinct with every one of its steps. Its width and bearing showed that it was a person—a man, from the size of him—moving inexorably toward him. The figure had on a muddy, white robe and it bore a large cross on his breast. A hood covered his emaciated head, casting his features in perpetual shadow. And, as it stepped fully into the firelight, it took a moment before Chris recognized why his manner of dress looked so familiar.

Chris couldn't help but notice how the intruder took every step as if he was unsure as to the stability of the ground in front of him. He moved tentatively and hesitated for a moment before each step. But then, the man turned his face more toward the firelight, and Chris saw the heavy scarring around his eyes.

The man was blind. His eyes had been burned out.

The hooded figure slowly raised his arms as he continued moving like a viper across the room toward him. His hands searched his vicinity for somewhere to grab, something to hold on to, in order to gain access to his prey. And as the hands reached for him, Chris noticed how one of the thing's fingers was missing, broken off at the knuckle of the third finger.

The sudden realization of who this was hit Chris like a hammer to the back of the head. But how? How could that mummified corpse get up and walk? It was crazy!

Chris retreated a step back and, in doing so, tripped over one of Jill's splayed legs. Teetering for a second, he saved himself by stumbling away in two loping steps. He felt himself caught suddenly in another person's arms. Even not knowing who it was, he clung to them as he fought to keep himself upright and on his feet. And just as he was about to speak, to warn the person that had caught him of the impending danger, he looked up to see another of the same hooded figures. His withered facial features were different than the other, but both were still very much the same: desiccated, blinded, and unfathomably old.

Then, Chris noticed another of them.

Then, another.

He struggled to get to his feet, but the dark figures soon surrounded him, and roughly dragged him back to the ground. And, as they all fell on him, Chris noticed the ring, having fallen from his pocket, lying on the floor near the fireplace.

THE DAGGER OF GOLGOTHA

This story came about as a result of me doing what I do: staring out of the window and thinking about the world (something I've been doing a lot as of late). I wasn't raised in what anyone would call a religious household, but I did end up looking into different religions as I got into my pre-teens. I also worked with clergy extensively while I was in Funeral Service. What I found was that it wasn't for me. That said, I do continue to have an appreciation for its iconography (something we'll get to in the story itself) and its sense of pageantry. But back to the window gazing… This story features the inimitable Father Thorpe who people (and I) seem to quite enjoy. This story gives a little more background on the guy and helps detail the early days in the relationship between him and Dr. Flemish (reference "The Sword of Saint Michael" from Moonlight Serenades). It also gives me a chance to flesh out the world in which he operates a little more… which is always fun! I'm hoping to one day pull all of the Father Thorpe stories I have together into a single narrative, but… we'll have to see if it's something that time will allow.

Sunlight glinted off the whirling blades of the twin-engine Bell 230 as the helicopter dropped out of a cloud-filled sky. The aircraft was sleek-looking with long elegant lines and a futuristic tone to its overall hardware. The helicopter spiraled down, spinning on its axis, using its mass to slow its rotation. It finally settled onto its three wheels, the tires sinking like pylons into the soft, sandy ground.

The pilot cut power to the engines and the rotors wound down like an unattended child's toy. The weight of the craft settled onto its landing gear and the hydraulics grunted as they accepted their heavy load. Father Thorpe stepped out of the wide, side door once it had been opened by the lone ground crewman standing by waiting on the tarmac.

The man was a local; rail-thin, Hispanic, and dressed in worn dungarees and a beige, button-up shirt. He looked tired and acted like he couldn't have cared less about anything going on around him.

Thorpe waited, stretching out the kinks, and composing himself after the long flight from Rio Gallegos. He let his gaze wander around the Aeropuerto de Ishuala, a small airfield in the Tierra del Fuego province of southern Argentina, and saw little to impress him. Essentially a waystation/jumping-off point for those looking to either get to the Antarctic to the south, Australia to the west, or the African continent across the Atlantic to the east.

The air was warm and still around him; not hot enough to make him sweat, but still not so cold as to make him want a jacket. He looked up and took in the darkening sky dotted with stratocumulus clouds that stretched out over the airport like a loosely crocheted blanket.

The grounds man came up to him hesitantly and set Thorpe's single, black travel bag down at his feet without saying anything. The priest handed him a fistful of Argentinian pesos. The silent man thanked him with a bow and hustled off to finish seeing to the Bell.

Once the helicopter had been refueled and tended to, the pilot gave Thorpe a thumbs-up through the front windscreen and lifted off, the aircraft disappearing into the rapidly darkening sky.

Not too long after the helicopter left, a car came driving into view, stopping first at a large gate in a far-off cyclone fence. Thorpe recognized the vehicle as a Russian-made GAZ Tiger, an all-terrain infantry vehicle he'd seen a lot while doing work in Eastern Europe. He idly wondered about the car and the trip it had to have made to get here. Russia to Argentina... It was a long way from home. He also stopped to consider its Russian connections and the possibility of *that* particular involvement here. Knowing that he lacked the necessary information to make a proper decision, he set the topic aside for later examination.

The car pulled up alongside the landing pad where Thorpe was standing, tires crunching on the loose soil. Up close, the GAZ looked like a big SUV that was painted a flat brown with small windows on the sides up near the top. Even as the car was coming to a full stop, the back door swung open to reveal a shadowed interior.

"Father Thorpe?" a man's reedy voice called out of the car's gloom.

Thorpe raised his hand in greeting, squinting in order to better see. "Dr. Flemish?" he asked, remembering the name from his itinerary. He pitched his voice so as to sound friendly, but its tone still displayed an edge that he'd not intended. The priest reminded himself that he was tired from the flight, and that he should be more mindful of that. There was no use in the two of them getting started off on a wrong foot.

He'd read in the report he'd been given by his superiors that his point of contact here was to be this Doctor Joaquin Flemish. The man's dossier said that he'd been educated in Europe at any one of a number of prestigious schools, and that he'd specialized in the treatment of 'disturbed and in crisis' individuals. As a result, his reputation as an academic was beyond reproach; not that that Thorpe was here to impeach the man's character.

But as this was the first time Thorpe was meeting the man, he was cautious. He'd heard good things after having done some of his own due diligence (and having had a few of his friends run their own dossiers on him). He'd learned that Flemish was unorthodox, but fearless, and had a lot of experience with high profile discoveries having been kept quiet. In the end, Thorpe had only verified what he'd already been told: that the scientist was educated, accomplished, and possessed just enough brashness as to make him useful.

"Hello!" the voice responded from the dark. "Please, Father, get in. It looks like a storm is coming in, and we can't have you standing out in the rain."

Thorpe smiled as he picked up his bag and got into the car. No sooner had he gotten himself seated than Dr. Flemish turned toward him and began to talk excitedly. Now that Thorpe was closer to him, he saw that Fleming was a bookish man in his mid-thirties with dark hair that looked perpetually windblown. His manner was one of intense, albeit slightly scattered, focus.

"We're very happy that The Vatican has seen fit to send you to us, Father. We're convinced that we're on the brink of something that I feel is an incredibly important find here," the doctor explained.

Thorpe cast a glance at their driver in the front seat: a man in his twenties with short-cropped hair who appeared to be Israeli. He was looking straight ahead and was clearly not paying attention to them or anything happening in the back seat. His eyes remained fixed only on the road ahead.

"I read a bit of the report that you sent to my offices," Thorpe replied. "It was fascinating, even to a layman. And I agree, the dig you described does sound promising. But, to be honest here, Doctor, The Vatican feels that there were some details that were left out of your account that my superiors had a couple of questions about. Like what exactly it is that you're out here looking for, Doctor?"

Flemish nodded sheepishly. "Yes, I know. I know. Look, Father," he said, appearing a little flustered. "I'm going to need you, and by extension of that, The Vatican, to extend to me just a little trust."

"I think we have, Doctor."

"Yes… and I agree. But, if my calculations are correct, this artifact we think we may have found is something *very* special. My worry, and the reason for my having been a bit vague with you all thus far, is the disappointment should we be wrong."

Thorpe stared at Flemish and considered the variety of his options. His bosses were curious about what he was doing with their money, but they'd also had been pretty specific when they'd ordered him to give the doctor more latitude than he was normally comfortable with—*if* it produced results. And, since they were signing the checks, he figured he'd go with that. For now. Orders were, after all, orders. But he also knew, if circumstances changed, how prone to improvisation he could be.

And besides, from the sound of things, and the look of hope in his eyes, Flemish could well be onto something. And it's not like he was going to run off anywhere anytime soon. Thorpe would be patient until he had a better idea of what this was all about before he decided what he was going to do.

"Well, this had better be good then, Doctor," said the priest as he settled into his seat for the drive to Flemish's dig site.

After nearly an hour on the road, the GAZ Tiger clawed its way over a final hill and a wide valley opened up before them. Looking out of the front windscreen, Thorpe noticed how the land dropped off at a precipitous rate, the terrain dipping into a valley that was shaped like a bowl. At the far end of the basin, he could see an assemblage of bivouacs all centered against the canyon wall.

They took a dirt road down through the foothills and across the valley floor, and soon found themselves entering the camp. A dozen canvas tents had been erected around a large cleft in the rock wall. Like a crack in the mountain itself, the fissure dove deep into the rock, violently marring the otherwise pristine cliff face.

The car wound its way slowly through the encampment. Thorpe was able to see that each of the tents was occupied by tables laden with bits of pottery and shards of shattered stone. In a few of the enclosures, young men and women toiled to catalog everything in the waning heat of the day. Keeping it all straight and adequately documented, Thorpe knew from first-hand experience, was a task of Herculean proportions.

He looked over at his traveling companion, Dr. Flemish, and saw that the man had unbelievably fallen asleep. His head was back and to the side, resting against the closed car window. His mouth hung at half-mast as if he were a Pitcher Plant trying to catch flies.

Almost as if by some internal alarm that sounded solely in his head, Dr. Flemish's eyes suddenly opened, and he sat up to get himself together. He wiped at the corners of his mouth with the back of his hand, looking embarrassed.

"Eitan," Flemish called to the front seat. "I've gone and done it again."

"Fallen asleep, Sir?"

"Aye, the very thing." He looked over at Thorpe. "Forgive me, Father. We've been working such long hours lately and, well, any time I sit still for even a few minutes…"

Thorpe grinned and waved the comment away. "Doctor, I assure you, of all people, I understand, and can even empathize. People in our business, well, we catch our sleep where we can, *when* we can."

The car suddenly began to slow, and they were both pitched slightly forward as Eitan applied the brakes. He angled the car off the dirt road and parked it by some shipping crates that had been set to one side of the road. Without waiting for assistance, Flemish threw the car door open and hopped out of the still-moving vehicle.

Grinning, Thorpe followed along after him.

Flemish stepped out of the car and onto ground that, while not sandy, was definitely loosely packed. His shoes sank into the dirt easily, leaving clear, visible tracks. The scientist stretched his back and grunted every time he turned to his right. He hadn't wanted to spend the last several hours penned up in the car's cramped confines, but escorting this priest from the airport to the site, meeting him personally and getting an initial take on him, was of paramount importance to the project.

The Vatican had put up a sizable portion of their funding and Flemish was well aware of that. He also had known that, sooner or later, they'd want to come and have a look at their investment. He'd expected it, even planned for it. But now that the time was here, he was filled with apprehension.

But then again…

Flemish smiled slyly when he thought about the look on their faces when he finally showed *it* to them. Provided, of course, that they could ever find the damn thing. They were close. He just *knew* it. He'd studied every document, travelled the world over, and looked everywhere the science had directed him. If the damn thing wasn't here in this desolate valley at the ass end of South America, well… it could well have never existed in the first place.

Dr. Flemish looked over the bonnet of the car at Thorpe and

watched as the priest got his first real look at the place. The scientist shook his head. The man looked like no kind of priest Flemish had ever encountered. Sure, he looked the part… sort of. He looked at the expensive-looking vested, black suit the priest wore appreciatively, his eye lingering on the white square of his clerical collar at the base of his throat.

But it was the way in which the man looked at things—at people, at situations, at his environment. It was unlike anything Flemish had ever seen. His gaze was more like that of a predatory hawk or wolf rather than a shepherd of men. Flemish knew that men could oftentimes lead full lives before they ever entered the priesthood. From the look of this Father Thorpe, his must have been one wild ride.

"Doctor!" a woman's voice suddenly called from behind them.

Flemish glanced over and saw that it was his assistant, a graduate student of his named Janet DuBois, coming toward them through a crowd of workmen. Janet had been with Flemish for so many years now that he'd lost track. He'd helped her get into Stanford back when she'd first applied, and he'd given her a job on his team the moment she graduated and felt she was ready. These days, Flemish didn't know what he'd do without her.

"Janet!" Flemish said cordially once they'd gotten a little closer to one another.

Janet was a short, stocky woman in her twenties with short, brown hair and stern, green eyes. She had on her de rigueur attire: a worn, decades-old Nirvana shirt that she was very proud of, some dusty, brown cargo pants, and a pair of Docs that looked like they may have been original prototypes. Their greeting was warm, but tempered, both knowing from experience that it was always too hot here to be bothered with much more.

She leaned into him and spoke to him in a voice that was barely above a whisper. "Is this the priest?"

Flemish smiled indulgently. "Yes."

She scrunched her nose up, her green eyes flaring. "He doesn't look like much of a priest, does he? He looks more like… muscle."

"That's what I said."

They both glanced over at Thorpe who was busy appraising his surroundings: the tents, the cargo shipping containers, and all the research assistants, grad students, and local laborers that made up the busy dig site. They both noticed how his eyes drank in every detail of what was happening around him, never missing a thing. It was like he was loading everything he was seeing into some kind of short-term memory for future retrieval.

Thorpe strolled around the front of the car, coming in their direction. As he walked, he adjusted his suit, paying additional, albeit brief, attention to the jacket under his left arm. As he approached, he once again smiled, doing his best to appear affable, if not downright friendly.

Flemish pulled the girl gently closer and softly said, "I'll be honest, Janet… I'm starting to suspect that there is more to our theocratic friend than we might have originally suspected."

Fleming then turned, directing her toward the priest.

"Father, this is Janet DuBois," he said, "one of my most-trusted assistants."

The young woman gazed at the ground, looking almost embarrassed by the flattery.

"Everything I know, she knows. And if she doesn't know it, then she knows where to find the person that does." He chuckled. "Feel free to ask her anything you wish about the project. We have nothing to hide here." He turned back to the young woman. "Janet, this is Father Thorpe."

DuBois reached out hesitantly to shake the priest's hand. He took it, his grip enveloping hers like a hungry octopus, and shook it gently. For a brief moment their eyes met, and the connection left DuBois feeling a little shaken.

"It's a p-pleasure to meet you, Sir," she managed to squeak out as she took an involuntary step back the instant he released her from his grip.

She was used to being around intimidating people, professionals, and those who were gifted. Her parents had been college professors at Rutgers and they'd, as was said back in those days, 'entertained.' Additionally, the family did a lot of moving around the world, meeting important people, as a result of her parent's work… it all meant little to her. But no one had ever left her feeling the way meeting this Father Thorpe had. Intense, she thought, didn't even come close to covering what it was like to be in the focus of his gaze.

"Miss DuBois," Thorpe responded cordially, as he retracted his hand. His eyes scanned her, and once again, it left her feeling invaded somehow. He smiled to try and alleviate any lingering anxiety and saw her cheeks bloom crimson in response.

"Um," she stumbled, "We, uh…" She cleared her throat. "We are nearly, um…" She turned to face Flemish. For some reason, she was finding it hard to think while talking to the priest. Seeing Flemish's face in that moment felt like being in the desert, and suddenly seeing an oasis "We're nearly through, Doctor. Matteo says that he thinks he's figured a way around the vault's final locking mechanism. He said it was 'old school,' and then, he laughed."

She smiled at her friend and mentor, grateful to no longer be in the crosshairs of their unnerving guest's gaze. She felt exposed by the man, like he knew things about Life, about the world, about *her*… that he shouldn't. She shook her head slightly in an attempt to clear it. Admittedly, it was a lot to get from an initial handshake, she mentally chastised herself, but something deep within her could just tell: this was a man whose life was fundamentally different from other peoples.

Flemish reached out and took her hand protectively. He knew the young woman to be highly organized and a skilled colleague, but he'd noticed that she could get flustered being around other high-functioning individuals. It wasn't about competition for her; it was more about her never feeling like she belonged—or deserved to be—in the room. Flemish blamed what he knew was a complicated relationship with her parents for that.

"Are there any other updates?" Flemish asked her. "Is Matteo in the burial chamber now?"

"Yes," she replied nodding, but she still couldn't keep herself from shooting a glance over her shoulder once more at the priest. "He's in the inner chamber, and, as you can imagine, he's pretty anxious to see you. He's got most of the vault excavated and the grave site is pretty much cleared. He says he'll be able to get through that final seal on the vault, but it's still gonna take a little time."

"Excuse me," Thorpe finally interrupted, smiling at DuBois. "May I speak with you for a moment, Doctor?"

Flemish nodded and came closer to him, a few feet away and out of earshot of the young woman. Thinking better of it, Flemish turned back briefly to tell the girl to go on ahead and they'd see her inside. She nodded and walked off, returning to her work elsewhere at the dig.

Flemish invited the priest to walk with him, taking his guest by the arm, and guiding him deeper into the camp, back toward the fissure in the rock. As they made their way along a path that ran through the middle of the camp, Thorpe waited until he had the scientist's complete attention before continuing to speak.

"I appreciate how accommodating you've been so far on this trip, Doctor but…" he said carefully. His voice, while still remaining friendly, definitely reflected a more serious tone. "I am forced to exert a more forceful position here, and once again ask…" His eyes flashed with intensity. "Putting all pretense and vaguery aside, what are we doin' here, Doctor Flemish? What are *you* doing here? What are you looking for? What do you think is there inside this mountain?"

Dr. Flemish's face sagged a bit at the priest's directness. He'd expected this conversation to reoccur at some point, just not quite this soon. At least not until after he'd been able to show some results. His face changed, becoming more determined, as he appeared to make a quick, mental decision.

He looked up at the priest and simply said, "This way, please."

Thorpe followed the scientist down another dirt pathway that led him between some tents, moving them deeper into the camp. They finally arrived at a small, nondescript bivouac that was pretty much just like all the others. The doctor pulled the door flap open and gestured for Thorpe to step inside.

Within the canopy, Thorpe found living quarters for one.

There was an old Army cot tucked into one corner and a small table on wheels that looked like it doubled for a desk sitting nearby. The tabletop was covered by stacks of books and papers set in a chaotic jumble. Flemish followed the priest into the tent and invited him to sit down. However, the priest declined, preferring to stand in the center of the room.

"So?" Thorpe asked pointedly. He knew he was tired from the flight when the words came out sounding annoyed and a little angry. He silently chastised himself and, again, vowed to be more patient.

The doctor picked up a cup that was sitting near the edge of the desk. Inside, a very cold cup of black coffee stared back at him and dared him to drink. Flemish accepted the challenge, taking the remaining liquid down in a single, bitter gulp before setting the cup aside. He took a minute to compose his thoughts. Then, he turned and looked directly into Thorpe's eyes.

"Tell me, Father Thorpe, how much do you know about The Crucifixion?"

Despite himself, Thorpe chuckled out loud and shook his head. "Need I remind you of what I do for a living, Doctor?" He shook his head, genuinely amused, and pointed to the small, white square at the base of his throat. "Trust me, Doctor; I think it's safe to say that I know a thing or two about one of the most important tenets of my faith." He looked at him inquisitively. "Care to elaborate?"

Flemish grinned. "Touché, Father. But, I mean, *beyond* that, beyond what you were taught in seminary school."

Thorpe cocked his head like a dog hearing a strange sound, and squinted, not understanding where he was going with this. "You're kidding, right?"

Flemish looked back at him intensely. "I assure you, Father, I'm being quite serious here."

Once again, he offered his guest a seat on the cot. This time, Thorpe took him up on it. He had a feeling that he'd better sitting down for this.

"Father, the story of The Passion is one that we all *think* we know; especially if we were raised Catholic. And for the most part, we do. It's one of the great tales in all of Man's history:

the suffering, the injustice, the brutal death and torture, and, of course, the Resurrection… You won't find a better tale in all of Theology anywhere in the world.

"And so, we know—as best as is humanly possible—that Jesus died on the ninth hour of the day, after having been forced to carry his cross along what's known as the Via Dolorosa, or The Way of Grief… The, uh, The Way of Suffering.

"We are told as children of the story of Saint Veronica, the woman who wiped Jesus' brow with her fabled handkerchief. We know of the Crucifixion itself… the hammering of the nails into His flesh. Some say there were three, some say four," he looked down and began staring into his hands. After a minute, he said under his breath, "I've heard it was as many as fourteen.

"Scholars will tell you," he continued, "how the nails were placed in Destot's space in the wrist, between the capitate and lunate bones." He paused to point to the center of his palm. "Others will say that they were put between the radial and ulna bones in the forearm. Either way," he shook his head and shivered, "quite painful. And then, there was what they did to his feet."

Thorpe held up his hand to interrupt him. "Yes. Yes, Doctor, I'm well aware of all of this, but…"

Flemish was undeterred. "Some say, though, that He never even died that day. They say that it was Simon of Cyrene, the man who bore the cross for Jesus when He could no longer carry it. Others say it was his betrayer, that it was Judas himself, attempting to show contrition and seeking forgiveness from the Father."

He looked at Thorpe intently.

"In the Quran, verse 4:157, it says, 'and [for] their saying, 'Indeed, we have killed the Messiah, Jesus, the son of Mary, the messenger of Allah.' And they did not kill him, nor did they crucify him; but [another] was made to resemble him to them. And indeed, those who differ over it are in doubt about it. They have no knowledge of it except the following of assumption. And they did not kill him, for certain.'

"Anyway, we know that they took Him after He died and entombed him. We know of The Resurrection and of the sighting of Him by the women. We know all of that..." He paused for dramatic effect.

Thorpe leaned forward to listen, getting frustrated, and thinking, this had all better be good.

"But," Flemish continued, "There is no record anywhere of what was done with the cross after He had been taken down." The last few words came out in an excited rush, syllables stumbling like drunks over syllables.

Thorpe looked openly confused. "I don't follow..."

Flemish's excitement began to slowly rise the more he talked about the project that had consumed his live for the last few years. "The cross, Father, the blood-drenched gibbet of wood that they hung Him on to die." He gave the priest a second to put it all together. "And the nails, Father. The nails that were driven through His flesh; His *actual* flesh," he added sardonically. "Not His transubstantiated flesh."

The spark of Thorpe's curiosity suddenly caught, and the flame quickly grew in its intensity. The scientist was right. Once Christ had been taken from Golgotha, there was no mention of anything else regarding the Crucifixion site, much less the physical Cross itself.

"Okay, Doctor," Thorpe said. "You have my attention. Please continue."

The scientist smiled knowing that the worst of this was over; he had the theologian's interest piqued. The rest was just the explaining of it all to him. "Now..." he said slowly, "imagine that, Father. His *actual* flesh. If we could find and verify something as tangible as, for example, the actual nails that crucified Jesus..." He leaned back in his stance and looked damn pleased with himself.

"Okay," Thorpe asked, still not getting his point. He shrugged. "So, where are these nails?"

"Well," Flemish said as he reached over and pulled a small, foldable canvas and wood chair closer to the bed. He sat down on it and leaned close to the priest. "According to my research..."

"Wait," Thorpe interrupted, already trying to vet the story. "Please define research, doctor."

Flemish looked momentarily irritated by the question, but

the expression on his face came and went like a cloud passing by on a windy day. Clearly, he'd had to explain himself like this before to somebody… even if only the girl and whoever this Matteo was.

"Over the years, this has all been a sort of pet project of mine: finding these items lost to history, or at least attempting to figure out if they ever existed in the first place. It's why I took—and didn't take—different assignments at hospitals and research facilities over the years. There were certain places I needed to be in the world, and at specific times, and I'd arrange to go there for some reason or the other. And, little by little, I started to piece it all together."

"Piece *what* together?" Thorpe insisted.

Flemish stared at Thorpe like he'd been struck dumb. "Why, what happened to the nails on the cross, man?"

The doctor got up from his seat and grabbed a large, leather-bound book from one of the makeshift shelves against the tent wall. The book had to be three or four inches thick and was loosely wrapped in worn leather. He laid it across the portable table like it was a venerated prize. Opened up, the manuscript more than covered the piles of paper that were already there.

Inside, there was a kaleidoscope of maps, charts, and handwritten notes, and they all came spilling out in a papery flood. Most of the material looked familiar to Thorpe, the maps and geographical documents, but there were some pages written in a script that he had no experience with. Of course, that just served to heighten his curiosity.

"So, again, according to our research," Flemish continued to explain, his voice having switched over to his 'professorial mode' in tone. "Once it had been established that He was indeed dead, the cross was lowered and His body was freed from its pitons.

"Family and worshippers came and claimed Him, taking His body to be prepared for burial. Meanwhile, according to a letter I purchased from a dealer in Iran - a Bedouin who'd found it in a demolished home in the Gaza Strip - soldiers were instructed to take the gibbet away to be cleaned and prepped to be used again. A Syrian who was blacksmithing in the area for traveling money reportedly took the nails in a game of Senet, claiming them for his own."

Thorpe shook his head in disbelief. "Why have I never heard a whisper of this?" He ran his fingertips over his forehead as he tried to put it all together. "No offence, but how is this even possible? And no mention of it anywhere…"

Flemish shrugged. "I know… it's the damnedest thing." He paused. "Sorry, no… poor choice of words there, Father."

Thorpe shook his head, ignoring the faux pas. "So, what happened once this Syrian had them?"

Fleming once again shook his head. "Well, according to *several* of my sources, he took the nails and hid them amidst his clothing, reportedly leaving Jerusalem, and traveling through Egypt, and on into Africa. It's said that somewhere along the line, somewhere in the Sudan I believe, he reportedly found a place safe enough to forge them."

"Forge them?" he said inquisitively. "Into what?"

"Into a blade, Father."

"A blade?" Thorpe asked, shaking his head in disbelief. "What kind of blade?"

Flemish shook his head and shrugged. "We're not sure, but what we know is that it's not large, given the amount of material they had to work with; maybe about the size of a large chef's knife near as I can figure. I mean, there was only so much iron, right? It couldn't be *that* big."

He paused to catch his breath and to make sure that the priest was still following along. "From what I can piece together from descriptions I've found, it was forged into something called a 'Shibriya,' or 'Shabria.' It's also known as a 'Janbiya.' It's a traditional blade of the nomads of the time, which, when you think about it, makes perfect sense."

Thorpe shook his head. "Do we know what it looks like?"

"Well, that's the thing, no one knows exactly. I mean, I've seen a Shibriya before, of course, but we just can't know for sure what this thing really looks like until we actually find it. We should be able to verify it from whatever it's hidden in… or alongside."

Thorpe reluctantly nodded his agreement.

"But normally," Flemish continued, "they are thin, plain-looking knives with a short handle and a blade that tapers radically at its point. The overall shape looks more like a metal shard than something crafted by any determined hands."

Thorpe silently considered what he was hearing. The idea that any of this was possible staggered the mind. He could only begin to imagine the religious significance of such an object. Let alone its potential. There was nothing in any text he'd ever read that even hinted at such a thing. He had to work to keep himself calm.

"And you think this blade is here in Tierra del Fuego? How do you figure it's in this particular spot? I mean, why here?"

Flemish shrugged. "We've tracked it for years and everything we've found points to this place. Now, I'm compelled to add that it *has* been two thousand years. Things may have been moved."

"I'm sorry. I hate to keep repeating myself here, but ... why hasn't this *ever* been mentioned, well... *anywhere*? I mean, my god, man."

The doctor ran his hands through his dark hair. "I don't know, but I can guess..."

Thorpe raised his eyebrows as an invitation for him to go on.

"Given just the political potential that an artifact like this could have had at the time, the smartest thing to do was to get it the hell out of Jerusalem, get it out of the Middle East, get it to someplace as far away from there as possible, to a place where no one knew or cared what it was *or* where it had come from."

Thorpe considered it, finally agreeing that he was right. The smart money—whether they knew the knife's history or its potential or not—was to get it someplace safe, some place far away from those who might be looking for it.

"Okay, so," Thorpe continued, "You spend some time looking..."

"Decades," Flemish said, sounding a little sad.

"Fair enough," the priest conceded. "Decades looking into it."

"There..." Flemish nodded toward an open shipping

container set at the back of the tent, small filing boxes filled it in a Tetris-like configuration. "That is my research; every bit of it. You may look at any of it, if you like."

Thorpe declined, but reminded himself of the importance of going slow with this scientist. Now that they were getting close to his find, the thing he'd been trying to locate for so long, his fear of having it all taken away from him would undoubtedly be growing. It would be up to the priest to convince him otherwise. Thorpe had already made up his mind that this scientist was smart, naturally inquisitive, and therefore, an asset that needed to be protected and brought into the fold.

Not just for this job, but for the future as well.

"How'd you make the leap to Argentina?"

Flemish rubbed his hands together excitedly. "That's the interesting part. See, we were in Namibia on an unrelated study, when a villager approached Janet…" He looked up. "You remember Janet, right?"

Thorpe nodded.

"Well, they told her that there was something that a relative had possession of in a nearby village that was, and I quote, a 'very, *very* old book.' When she checked into it, it turned out to be a ship's log from a Captain John Vincent Rogers, who I guess made regular shipping runs between Africa and South America." He thought for a minute. "Slave trader as well, as I recall.

"Anyway, the log spoke of a man 'dressed in a manner of a far-off land' who booked passage with him across the Atlantic Ocean. Along the way, he reportedly showed the Captain a unique 'desert knife' one night at dinner.

"This Captain Rogers, by the way, ultimately ended up spending the last years of his life here in Tierra del Fuego. Locals—the really elderly ones—say he spent his final days, quote: 'looking for something,' end quote."

Thorpe shook his head, incredulous. "It's unbelievable."

"And yet, is it not the unbelievable something with which we both find ourselves routinely involved?"

Thorpe smiled and gave him that. "But why here?"

Flemish smiled again. "Captain Rogers named this place

specifically in his writing as where this traveler disembarked. He mentioned it several times, in fact. I'm guessing he became obsessed, returning here year after year, looking for either the traveler… or the knife."

"Why?"

"Who knows? Maybe, over the years, the area grew to be special to him. Maybe he picked it as the place he wanted to grow old in and die. Or just maybe… he was looking for the knife all along. We spread some pesos around to the locals and it didn't take long before someone remembered hearing a story from an uncle or something about a 'knife from across the water.'" He shrugged. "We began following other such stories like bread crumbs."

"Pardon me, but… I still don't get why he chose here, in this particular place?"

"Well, I can tell you that finding out all of this wasn't as easy as I'm making out. I mean, this is the twelfth or thirteenth site up and down the coast we've looked at, Father. But I can assure you, in all cases, we've spent The Vatican's money *very* judiciously. Discoveries *were* made. Artifacts have been found and are being documented and sent to be dispersed amidst The Vatican, museums, and private collectors. These findings will reside in museums all over the world."

Thorpe chuckled at the scientist's base-covering. "I never doubted your frugality for a moment, Doctor."

At this point, Thorpe figured he had a pretty good idea of what he was up against with this case. The artifact was either here or it wasn't. If it wasn't, then no big deal. He'd write his report and he'd move on to his next case. But, if it *was*… then, that would change everything. He'd be forced to take possession of the piece and go offline until he could get it to a Vatican safe house. One thing, though, was gnawing at the back of his brain though, like a squirrel trapped inside a tin can.

"Does your research say anything about the artifact's, uh… capabilities?"

Flemish waved the question away like he was shooing a fly. "Father, if you're asking me if this is something akin to, say, the legend of The Grail, we simply don't know. But, like I say, what we do know for sure is that it's of great archeological significance. Beyond that..." he shrugged. "Only God can say."

Thorpe sat up in his chair and was about to elaborate on what he'd meant regarding the artifact's potential, when a thin, Hispanic man in his late thirties with salt-and-pepper hair suddenly poked his head through the tent's front flap. His face was powdered in a patina of dust and clay, but a wide, bright smile gleamed from within the muck.

"Excuse me, Mister Doctor," the man said sheepishly.

"Ah, Matteo," Flemish said, his mood noticeably lightening, "just the man I was about to come and see. What is it, son? I hear you found us something."

Matteo looked over at Thorpe, and he reflexively crossed himself. His gaze returned to the doctor and he somehow grinned wider. "Si! We've found something."

Matteo led them into something that Dr. Flemish called The Anteroom through a long, slim corridor that had been chiseled through the rock. The way was tight, and they were sometimes forced to squeeze themselves between the sheer, rock walls. Dust fell like sprites about their heads. The doctor and Matteo didn't seem to notice and acted as if being covered in dirt was a regular part of their day. Thorpe remembered having been on hundreds of these sites even as he looked down at his Corneliani suit and sighed. The apparel had cost him a pretty penny and he knew it was about to get ruined. He sighed again, and then, he stepped on through.

They sidestepped their way along the passage, stepping over loose rocks and basketball-sized stones lying on the ground. When they reached a natural pinch-point in the rock, Matteo went through first, followed by the doctor, and then, Thorpe.

Once they were through the crack, a vast cavern opened up in front of them like a storybook. A high ceiling stretched like the sky itself over them, creating an immense all-encompassing stone dome. The priest guessed the entire space at roughly fifty or sixty feet across, at the least.

Off to the left, off toward the back of the cavern, was a semicircle of small, electrical generators that seemed to be supplying the energy to all manner of jackhammers and hydraulic transports. The majority of them were being used to widen another fissure in the rock face. How in God's name they got all this stuff in here was anybody's guess. Maybe there was another way into the cavern, Thorpe mused. Any way you looked at it, it had to have been a logistical nightmare.

To the right, he noticed more tents like the ones outside which were surrounded by piles of canvas duffels that were all stacked on their sides. The priest understood it immediately for what it was: the site's secondary headquarters. Thorpe noticed Matteo immediately walk off to the left, toward where the hub of work activity was. Flemish followed along after him like a kid being led to a birthday party.

As they progressed across the gallery, Thorpe sped up his gait to catch and keep abreast of the scientist. "Are we going to the burial site now?"

Flemish pointed over toward where the generators were. "Matteo just filled me in on his progress. He's excavated the area around something in what we've been calling The Crypt. He said he was going to try and open it but stopped to come fetch me because he knew how important it was that I'm there."

Thorpe caught Flemish's arm and gently turned him to get him to look directly at him. "Wait. You forget, Doctor, I only just arrived here, I don't know anything about what you're talking about."

Flemish stopped walking and stared apologetically at Thorpe. "Sorry, Father. It's just that, in all this excitement..." He took a step and, when Thorpe did the same, they continued walking, albeit slower than before, so it would be easier for them to talk.

"After we read through everything in Captain Rogers' log," the scientist said, continuing his story, "we became even more convinced that the dagger was indeed somewhere here in Tierra del Fuego. And so, we began a systematic exploration of the area using thermal and deep, magnetic resonance imaging. But, sadly, we found nothing.

"Then, about a month ago, we caught sight of what we thought at first was a shadow on one of the photographs our surveyors took. We did some more testing, but still nothing. Finally, a few of our grad students who spelunk as a hobby volunteered to try and find out what was in the rock."

"Spelunkers?" Thorpe asked shaking his head. He was beginning to like this doctor and the way he thought outside of the box. That could prove helpful.

Flemish nodded. "Geoff Taylor told us that he'd done it for years. Anyway, he and his team discovered this Anteroom and recorded video. They found enough here to warrant us cracking into the mountain and doing some further looking around inside. That," he said with a smile, "was a little over a year ago."

"Mister Doctor!" Matteo suddenly called from where he was next to phalanx of humming generators. "Andale, please!"

Flemish grinned at Thorpe and he looked like a boy going to his first circus.

"Come on, let's go!" he said excitedly to Thorpe. "This is gonna be so cool!"

Then, he ran off without waiting.

As he got closer, Thorpe saw the extent of the excavation going on beyond where the generators were parked. Another deep gash had been cut into the stone wall, and smaller boulders and loose stones lay around the makeshift entrance like spilled pocket change.

As the priest moved closer to where all the work was being done, he saw that there was what could only be described as a hallway beyond the breach in the rock. Ornately decorated with meticulously-laid tiles, the passageway led even deeper into the heart of the mountain.

"This way," Dr. Flemish instructed just as he disappeared into the gloom beyond.

Thorpe followed along behind as quickly as he could, picking his way through the rubble. Once he was inside the passageway, he could hear the hollow sound of his shoes as they came into contact with the tiled bricks that made up the floor, walls, and ceiling, their clicking echoed into the dark.

At about twenty feet in, he bumped blindly into a wall in the gloom. Looking around him, he quickly figured out that the walkway made an abrupt turn to the right and followed it. Turning his head, he saw the warm glow coming from the digger's lanterns in the next chamber not too far off

Following the shadows ahead of him like he would a specter in the moonlight, he soon found himself at the entryway of yet another sizable chamber. This one was a lot smaller than the other, and the ceiling was considerably lower, but it bore the same starkness. Several portable light arrays were hung on poles that had been positioned around where a lot of new activity was centered.

Flemish waved him over, and Thorpe stepped up on his right-hand side. In front of them lay a grave measuring roughly seven feet long by four feet wide. The workers had pulled away most of the dirt and rock from around something that looked like a long, stone box half-buried in the dirt.

Matteo hopped down into the hole, shouting at the other workers to move aside in Spanish. Thorpe was only able to translate a bit of what he was saying, but he could tell that the man knew how to motivate people and could get things done. Flemish got flat onto the ground, lying on his belly, near him. He leaned into the grave and examined where Matteo was directing his attention.

Thorpe peered over their shoulders and was able to see that they were focusing on an odd-looking contraption made of wooden dowels set into a stone case. Whatever it was, it had been attached to the side of the larger case in some unseen fashion.

Flemish looked back at the priest, indulging his innate desire to instruct and educate. "The locking mechanism is deceptively complex. I mean, it looks like it's made only of a bit of wood and carved stone, but we'd tried everything we could to get into it over the last few days, and nothing's worked. In the end, the material—whatever it was - was just too strong."

"That's not wood?" Thorpe asked. "I mean, it *looks* like wood."

Flemish shook his head. "No. We tested it every which way from Sunday. But, while it may look like wood, it certainly is not. We subjected it to an immense amount of stress and the material wouldn't even crack.

"Finally," he reached over and clapped Matteo on the back, "I let Matteo here take a look at it. He now says he's found a slot we'd not noticed before." He paused a second, and then, "Hopefully, it'll work."

Matteo barely noticed the conversation going on around him due to being so fixated on the job at hand. Inserting a screwdriver he'd retrieved from one of his pockets into a small hole in the lid, he made himself busy by doing something with it to the mechanism inside. His face contorted from his effort, twisting his expression into a frustrated mask.

Finally, something deep within the casket made an unexpected 'ping' noise that reminded Thorpe of the sound a grenade makes as it's being sprung. He angled himself to get a better look in time to see the entire mechanism suddenly came apart in Matteo's hands; like a puzzle set free from its locking pin.

Everyone in the room took a step back when they heard it, many half-expecting some kind of adventure novel snare to be suddenly sprung. They all held their breaths: some in anticipation of what might happen next, some because of the stories they'd heard during boyhood of the traps of Qin Shi Huang, The Red Queen of Palengue, and the perils of Baphuon, and if there was to be some kind of noxious gas expelled, they didn't want to breathe it in.

But, to everyone's surprise, absolutely nothing out of the ordinary happened. And so, at some unspoken command, the workmen all abruptly picked up where they left off and returned to what they'd been doing. It was as if everyone instinctively knew that the potential for danger had shown itself, passed, and was now being all but immediately forgotten.

Several of the work men gathered around the vault and tried to move the heavy lid by lifting it using a system of rope and pulleys. Once they finally got things secured, everyone began pulling. A loud scraping sound, like fingernails being rubbed raw across a blackboard, erupted from the coarse stone. From the amount of exertion it took to move it, Thorpe could tell how heavy it was. Soon though, the lid was off and suspended precariously over the vault, the hoist bowing alarmingly under the weight. After their lines had been secured, the remaining workers climbed out of the hole to give Dr. Flemish more room in which to investigate.

Thorpe peered over the edge and tried in vain to get a glimpse of what was within the vault. He only saw shadows though inside the long, stone case. Joined at the corners by some bindings of an indiscernible origin, the crypt looked very much like a modern burial vault, only impossibly old. Other than the simple binding methods used to craft it, there didn't appear to be too many differences from what he could see.

Matteo brought a lantern closer and it became easier to see.

Inside the vault, there were a collection of bones laid out in a roughly human configuration. It was easy to identify the two femurs, the ribcage, and the bones of the upper arm out of the jumble of tattered clothing.

Flemish, of course, immediately dove right in.

"Man," his muffled voice said, and it sounded hollow as it echoed back against the ancient stone. "The clothing, the craftsmanship, the way the body seems to have been posed for burial… It certainly fits the time period. The heavy, woolen material, the wide ankle-length pants, the hip-length blouse. I…" He paused. "Wait, hellooo… what's this?"

Thorpe angled himself so that he could get a better look at what the scientist was talking about. He could see Flemish fussing with something inside the vault on the far side, just to the left of the remains. Whatever the object was, he was pulling at it from deep within the crypt, along its inside base. Thorpe could see the muscles in his shoulders flex through his shirt from the effort.

"What? What'd you find?" the priest asked.

"If I…" Flemish grunted. "Can just… get this… Shit!" Something suddenly cracked beneath him and, whatever the scientist had been tugging on came away in his hands. *"There it is!"*

"What?" Thorpe repeated.

Flemish looked up at him and the excitement in his eyes was infectious enough to light up the room. "Father, I think," he said cautiously, "I think we may just have found what we've been looking for."

Thorpe helped Flemish crawl up out of the hole. He waited as the scientist dusted himself off. Then, the two of them went over to a table that had been made from two sawhorses and a wide piece of thin wood along the wall. A couple of lanterns were set at each end, casting their light over the tabletop and their prize.

Meanwhile, shadows danced across the wall keeping time with their slowly burning muses.

Flemish placed the small box in his hands onto the center of the table and stood back, eyeing it appreciatively. He fumbled in his pocket for a second, and then, pulled out a cell phone that appeared to be from the Pleistocene Era, and flipped it open. He handed it to one of the workmen, instructing him in Spanish to take as many pictures as possible, before turning back to the item on the table. The confused workman did what he could to comply.

Matteo stepped up to the doctor and they had a brief conversation that Thorpe wasn't able to hear. They spoke for a moment, and then, the Hispanic man left the burial chamber, presumably going back to the other cavern to prepare for the artifact's reception.

Now that the thing they'd been searching for was out and in the open, Thorpe saw that it looked like, well… a stone shoebox, covered in mud and dark clay. The sides might have been carved or decorated, but there was so much dirt on it that he couldn't really tell. Flemish bent over the object, returning his attentions to the artifact once again, his body obscuring Thorpe's view.

The priest moved closer, leaning in over the scientist's shoulder, and was able to hear the doctor mumbling to himself as he worked. "The construction, the size… it's all about right. Ooooo, wait. What's this?" An empty-sounding pop, like a metal soda can being dropped, echoed in the room. "Whup, that's got it. Well, it's got something."

Thorpe leaned in, edging his way in between Flemish and a curious workman. The Hispanic man took a long look at the priest, and then, moved away from the table, crossing himself.

Thorpe circled the table and got himself situated directly across from Flemish. He saw that the doctor was in the process of tearing away as much of the dirt and mud from the box as he could with his hands and setting it aside in a wet heap.

Flemish finally gave up and walked over to a side table to grab a brush that was soaking in a rusted coffee can. He filled it halfway full with water from a canteen sitting nearby. Back at the table, he returned to his labors, scrubbing at the surface of the artifact to get it as clean as he could.

When he'd made some progress, Thorpe was able to see that the box had indeed been inscribed with carvings of small peony flowers and grapevines. There was also something etched into its lid, but Thorpe couldn't see what it was due to the scientist's rapidly moving hands obscuring his view.

Then…

"Jesus," Flemish gasped.

Thorpe leaned even closer and, as Flemish dumped the water from the coffee over the box, he was able to make out a few letters: 'B a a u g.' Flemish used his fingers to clear the last of the debris away and Thorpe was finally able to fully make out the rest of what was written there: *Batu ya Mungu.*

"What is that?" Thorpe asked pointing at the lid. "Portuguese? Spanish?"

Flemish staggered back a few steps from the table. His legs suddenly abandoned him, and he dropped into a cross-legged sitting position on the floor. His complexion had gone pale and he was breathing sort of heavy.

Thorpe knelt beside him and supported his weight against his leg. "Are you okay?"

Flemish nodded his head. "Y…yeah."

"What language is that?"

Flemish put his face into his hands and shook his head back and forth for a second. He looked up at Thorpe and his eyes were wide and excited. "After all these years…

Thorpe snapped his fingers to get him to focus. "Doc, what does it say?"

"It's Swahili… of all goddam things."

Thorpe retracted a bit in confusion. "Swahili?" He looked

around as if someone else in the room going to explain it all to him. When no one volunteered, he continued on to the next obvious question. "So, what does it *mean*?"

"It means," Flemish said, his mouth slowly breaking into a wider and wider grin: 'Dagger of God.'"

Thorpe almost laughed out loud. It was an involuntary act, like sneezing. He'd come to Tierra del Fuego not more than a few hours ago, having been told that the trip could well end up being a wild goose chase. He'd still been told to come here though, to investigate the case as was usual, but his bosses said not to expect much to come of it. No disrespect to Doctor Flemish, but even now, as he was thinking it through, the idea that they'd found something of this importance seemed so implausible as to border on the ridiculous.

And yet, here we were.

The priest eyed the box on the table warily. "Open it," he demanded.

The doctor looked up and nodded. "Yes, I'm sorry. It's just…" He got back to his feet, staring over at Thorpe. "We've just been looking for this for so long."

Thorpe nodded. He knew what it was to search for something for an extended period of time and not find it. Something suddenly occurred to him, so he asked about it. "But why Swahili?"

Flemish considered the question for a second, and then, he nodded. "As I believe I mentioned to you before, the artifact was taken through Egypt. Then, it was brought through Africa before crossing the South Atlantic Sea to South America. It makes sense that, once they got it someplace safe, they'd try to conceal it."

The scientist re-approached the table. The artifact sat patiently waiting for him, as it had for decades. His hands reached out, moving over the box's surface as if it were a musical instrument and he was trying to gently coax a melody from it. However, nothing he touched or pushed on did him any good.

He set the object back down and thought the mystery over for a minute. Suddenly, he slapped his hands together. "Wait a second," he exclaimed. "It couldn't be, but…"

He rushed back over to the side worktable and reached under it, grabbing a gray, cloth bag. He set the bag down on top of the bench and opened it, rifling through its contents.

"At the risk of repeating myself here, Doctor," Thorpe said. "What are you looking for now?"

The scientist glanced back over his shoulder at him as he continued his search. "When we were still searching in Africa, we were taken to another burial site by some locals near where we suspected the artifact had been buried. We were under the impression that looking there would prove fruitful, but we only found a rather elaborate burial chamber of a local tribal king."

"Okay, so," Thorpe replied, not exactly sure of his point.

"In that burial chamber, we found an object that had inscriptions on it that looked incredibly similar to *those*," he pointed at the box on the table. "In that grave, we found something we first thought was a favored grooming object, but I just realize that it could very well be something else."

"What?" Thorpe asked, shaking his head. He was beginning to sound like a broken record.

The doctor raised a short, slender rod into the air like it was a magic wand. "A key!"

He strode back to the tab excitedly, setting the rod down, and reaching for the box. Once it was back in his hands, he turned the object over and over as if he were looking for something.

Thorpe took the opportunity to get a better look at what he'd found. The rod wasn't long, but it was slender, and looked more like a pointer than anything else. He noted more of the same grapevine and peony inscriptions on it he'd seen carved into the box; they were almost identical.

"Here we go," Flemish said, setting the box down and moving it closer to one of the lights. He picked up the rod and directed one, tapered end into a hole in the flat, bottom panel. Wiggling the wand around inside, fitting it, he began to exert a distinct downward pressure. Suddenly, the key dropped slightly, locking into place and another sharp snapping sound echoed in the room.

"A box without hinges, key, or lid, yet golden treasure inside is hid," Flemish quoted softly.

Thorpe recognized the Tolkien quote which he thought was apt. A number of the workmen who were still gathered around them abruptly crossed themselves for some reason, and Thorpe felt an odd impulse to follow suit.

Flemish removed the rod and gently set the box back onto its base on the table. He rubbed his hands together in nervous anticipation. He'd been waiting for this for a long time, had endured *so many* disappointments. No one could blame him for relishing the present moment for a little bit. He gripped the lid and started manipulating it, trying to figure out how to pry it open. At first, nothing happened. Then, once he got a different grip on it, the lid moved slightly.

"I guess that's to be expected," Flemish said, chuckling slightly, even as he kept working at the puzzle. "I mean, I can't imagine the last time this thing was opened?"

He put the flat of his thumbs on the top and pushed. The lid slid with a sand-on-sand grating sound before finally sliding completely off in his hands.

Thorpe leaned over and peered inside; he couldn't help himself. There was something there, he could see that. Wrapped in some ornately decorated cloth, whatever it was had roughly the same dimensions as the interior of the box, like it had been made specifically to hold it and keep it safe.

Flemish carefully reached inside and pulled the object out into the light. Whatever it was, the thing had weight, and the doctor had to get a better grip on it for fear of dropping it. He finally set the parcel down, gently lifting the covering away.

Light from the lanterns played like sunbeams over the dull, metal surface of what could only be described as a small sword. Not as large as, say, a Japanese *Tanto,* but still plenty big enough to cause someone a lot of trouble. Made of a forged metal, the blade was flat and slightly curved, sloping at a dramatic angle toward a needle-like point. The handle was made of some kind of pale polished wood, and it had an Arabic cross and more braid work carved into it.

"I uh... I think this is it, Father. I'm... I'm pretty sure of it," the doctor said, unable to hide his excitement. "The engraved cross, the braiding, the inscriptions... I have copies of documents that show illustrations that look *exactly* like them." He looked up at Thorpe and his eyes flashed in the dim light. "We'll need to do further testing on it, of course, but I'd be willing to stake my reputation on the fact that this, Father, *is* the Batu ya Mungu; The Dagger of Golgotha."

Thorpe shook his head. It was taking him a minute to get his head around everything that was happening around him. The whole thing still seemed impossible, like someone was playing an elaborate joke on him. A blade made from the nails that crucified Christ? He shook his head again to try and understand it.

His superiors at The Vatican clearly had no idea. How could they?

Flemish covered the dagger back up and returned it to the box. "Let's take this to my lab. It's near my tent. I have some equipment there that will help us get a better look at it; maybe even verify its age. Or come close."

Thorpe nodded. Yes, yes, he thought, all of those things would need to eventually happen. But right now, the most important thing to be done was to secure the area and to protect the artifact. If this thing was what they thought it was, who knew who else was out in the world looking for it every bit as ardently as Flemish had been? Or who might have been following the scientist around, for what, decades?

"Look, Doctor, I think I should be frank with you. I don't really have the luxury of being anything else. We need to lock down this entire site, protect it from anyone who might be out there, watching you, waiting for you to do the impossible by actually finding this thing."

Flemish shook his head. "I don't think you understand the world of science, Father. No one knows we're here. Nor does anyone care. We're not in some movie serial adventure, I assure you."

Thorpe smiled. "Doctor, I'm going to need to remind you once again of the claim my superiors have in this project, and of the agreement to which you agreed attached to it. Remember," he stated matter of factly, "you came to *us* in order to find your money for this expedition. You asked that we come here to verify the find—*if* there was one—and to keep it safe. And now that we're here, and now that we have... Please, with all due respect, follow my instructions, even if you don't understand them, even if you disagree with them. Follow my instructions to the letter. Can you do that for me?"

Flemish slid his prize a little closer to him, and slowly, but resolutely nodded.

"I also don't need to reiterate that, with the finding of this artifact, we could all well be in danger here. Imagine the secrecy and guile by which the blade came to be her in the first place. Then, imagine how many lives were lost over the years in order to make that happen."

Flemish looked genuinely surprised, like the idea—and all of its implications—had only just now occurred to him. But Thorpe knew. He'd seen people slaughtered by 'artifact pirates' over pieces with far less significance than this one. He'd even once seen a house burned to the ground because one of the tenants had a toaster that etched an image of Jesus into bread when they used it.

People, he thought... so unpredictable.

Especially when you added Faith and Fear to the mix.

Flemish nodded sheepishly. "I... I agree, Father. We'll need to tighten our security. I'll inform Janet and Matteo once we get back."

"I'd also feel better, Doctor, if we got out of these tight confines. Strategically, this place is a nightmare. Will you do me the favor of leading the way out?"

Flemish nodded and Thorpe followed him as they walked back through the tiled passageway to the cave's larger room. He took a peek at his cell phone, but of course, this deep beneath the rock, he had no service. He knew he needed to contact his office as quickly as possible, so that they could prepare for what they'd found.

As they wound their way back through the tiled tunnel, Thorpe noticed some water weeping from the walls as they walked by. He momentarily wondered about the stability of the mountain over them.

Thorpe and Flemish heard the soft thrumming of the generators as they turned the final corner, and knew they were getting close. The light increased dramatically, and soon it became a lot easier for the priest to see. He looked over at the package in the doctor's arms, as they strode into the larger, anteroom of the cave. He tried to imagine all of the places it had been, all the hands that it must have passed through. He knew he would be amazed by it—and its mystery—until the day he died.

They'd taken only a few steps into the cavern, when they were both brought up short by the sound of a woman calling out.

"Doctor Flemish!"

The two men both turned and saw Janet DuBois standing in front of one of the tents on the other side of the cave floor. A man was standing a little too close to her, his body pressed close to her side. Thorpe assumed that he was just someone with the dig, another one of the workers, but Flemish showed no immediate sign of recognition in his expression when he saw him.

The man was white, middle-aged, and a little overweight, wearing a desert coat and dark pants. There was nothing unusual or exceptional about him, just another someone that you might see and overlook in a crowd. But then, Thorpe noticed the gun in his hand and the barrel pressed against the young woman's side.

"Doctor Flemish," the man said, and he pushed Janet forward with the barrel of his gun, so that everyone could see her.

Flemish looked up, shielding his eyes from the glare of the portable lights. "What's this? Who…? How did you get in here?" he asked the figure in the dark. He cast a quick glance over to Thorpe, but the priest's attention was focused elsewhere, as his eyes quickly scanned the room, weighing out options.

Thorpe felt the switch in himself the instant he saw the gun, felt the sting as the adrenaline poured into his bloodstream like hot oil and made straight for his heart. His pulse accelerated and his brain reflexively twitched and switched over to High Alert.

Without any thought, he instantly began processing the scene. The space was, for the most part, open; roughly sixty feet across at its widest diameter. He had the generators behind him to the right; beyond which lay the burial chamber. In front of him was the wide, open floor of the cavern.

Scanning from his left to his right, Thorpe marked a man to the right of the tents who was casually holding a shotgun at his waist. Another stood at the mouth of the cave with an old AK-47 in his hands. There were two more just to Thorpe's right. One held an old .38 in his fist, and the other had the AK's twin draped across his arms like it was a baby.

The priest sighed. They were spread out; *too* spread out, he thought. By the time he could get to the first two, the others would have plenty of time to pick him off at their leisure; like shooting a very large fish in a very small barrel. He needed a distraction, and a pretty big one; something that would level the playing field a little.

"I believe you hold something that I would very much like to see, Doctor," the stranger called out. His voice echoed hollowly in the open air.

Flemish took a step forward, cradling the still-wrapped box into the crook of his arm.

Thorpe faded like octopus ink back into the shadows.

"I'm not sure I know what you're talking about, Mister...?"

The stranger raised the pistol and put it to the back of Janet's head. The girl winced, but to her credit, she didn't cry out.

"I won't ask you again, Doctor."

Thorpe kept the configuration of the armed men within his peripheral vision as he edged closer to the junction box that fed power to all but one of the generators. Located less than three feet from him, the power supply was a mass of tentacle-like cords that jutted out from a small metal box.

He had a sudden idea and prayed it would work. He was well aware of the danger he was putting the girl in, but he hoped that she'd know when to duck when the opportunity presented itself, because it was going to be doing just that in about a second.

Flemish took a few additional steps forward, drawing the man with the gun's attention toward him. "I'm not sure I know what you mean, my friend. And, I'm not sure what you think you're doing here, but I'm going to have to ask you to leave. We are only a small archeological dig, nothing more. There's nothing anyone would want here."

Thorpe had sidled over to the power box by now. Standing over it, he kept one vigilant eye on Flemish, and the other on the position of the armed men. He knew he'd gotten lucky. Whoever this guy was, and whoever his hired help were, they didn't appear to be pros. No one seemed to know who Thorpe was or where he'd come from… and they didn't much care. It was pretty clear by their lack of concern that he'd been dismissed as 'just a priest,' which was fine. Others had done that in the past and had been quite unhappy with the outcome.

The big man with the gun laughed in response to Flemish, and took a step forward, lowering the pistol from Janet's head. The girl, frightened but still focused, took several small steps, moving slowly, but inexorably away from him. Once she was sure his attention had focused on Flemish, she ducked into the shadows between two tents.

"I think," the stranger said, "we both know what you've been looking for down here… and whether or not you've found it. I'm sure your priest friend is here to verify the find. So, where is it, Doctor? Show it to me!"

He motioned impatiently to the man standing closest to Flemish, the one with the automatic rifle, to bring the doctor to him. The man walked over and pointed the scientist in the direction of his boss with the barrel of his gun, indicating the way to go. The two of them slowly walked across the wide floor of the cave, moving toward the man with the pistol.

"What about the priest?" the henchman with the rifle asked as they moved across the stone floor.

"Leave him…" the white man ordered.

Thorpe grinned.

He waited until he felt the time was right, and then he moved, dropping to his knees. In one swift action, he drew the Beretta from its holster under his arm with one hand and hit the main power button on the electrical box with the other. Darkness fell like a guillotine over the inside of the cave. A shot went off at the far end of the cave. Then, another, a little closer. The priest silently hoped neither of them had found Janet DuBois or Flemish.

Thorpe couldn't really allow himself to think about that now, though; he was already on the move. He hit the first guy—the one with the pistol—like a rhino, picking him up by the throat, cupping his lower jaw in his free hand. Torquing his body around, Thorpe drove his head over and into the ground in a tight Fibonacci curve.

Snatching up what turned out to be a 9mm. from the now-unconscious man's hand, Thorpe moved on to the next guy. He caught him just in back of the ear with the butt of his friend's pistol, driving his head forward. He then struck him across the nose with the barrel of his own. The scissoring effect rocked the man on his feet, and he fell unconscious before he ever knew what hit him.

Thorpe now had an automatic pistol in each hand. He momentarily wondered how many rounds there were in the other guy's weapon, but he had no time to check and he didn't much care. He didn't want to start any shooting in these closed confines for fear of where the ricochets might go.

There were far too many friendlies around him to start 'Wyatt Earping' it.

Using the pistols like palm loads, he moved on to the guy near the cave's entrance. More shots rang out and every one of them made the priest more and more nervous.

Overhead, red safety lights abruptly came on and it made it a little easier for him to see. Unfortunately, it also made it easier for the bad guys to spot him as well. The knowledge of this motivated the priest to move quicker and hit all that much harder.

A quick jab-cross-hook made quick work of the next guy he came upon. With the additional weight of the pistols in his hands, he was confident that his punches were landing like sacks of wet cement. He looked back at the unconscious man on the ground and the AK lying near him, and grinned.

Fighting instincts now in full bloom, his heart pumped furiously to fuel the machine. He clobbered the next guy (the one with the shotgun) with a quick, Mike Tyson right hook-uppercut combination. He made sure he was out before disappearing into the shadows between the tents. By his count, his only concerns left were the white guy with the pistol and the guy who was ushering Flemish; the one with the machine gun.

Not exactly ideal.

After running around a bit to lose any potential trackers, he popped out from between two of the canvas tents and damn near ran into the guy with the AK. He saw the guy's eyes drop momentarily to his clerical collar a second before Thorpe had his hands on him, silencing him with the sound of cracking knuckles.

"That will be quite enough of that," the white man suddenly shouted out. He was silent for a second, then, he growled to someone unseen. "Speak to him!"

Thorpe winced in his hiding place. He figured it could only be one of three of things. The first was that he had the girl—Flemish's assistant—again. The second was that he'd found Matteo or one of the workers. The third…

"Father Thorpe? I've, uh…"

"Gone and gotten yourself captured?" Thorpe asked as he stepped into the red glow of the security lights.

"Yes, I'm afraid so…" he replied, and his voice dropped to show his contrition.

Thorpe walked toward the doctor and his captor slowly. Things looked bad, Thorpe was forced to admit to himself, but he knew he still had a trick or two up his sleeve. Literally.

"Yes, Father," the man said, "and, if you would, please drop the guns in your hands. I'm surprised. A militant priest is not something I would have expected." He hoisted the heavy, cloth-wrapped box in his one arm. In the other, he still gripped the pistol.

Thorpe complied and dropped the two pistols into the dirt, marking their place in his memory. He liked that gun and meant to come back for it. "And you are…?" he asked as he took a few steps closer, closing the distance. "And what exactly do you plan on doing now?"

"The name is Crocker, Father. Hans Crocker." He grinned and a gold tooth glittered in the dim, red light. "And, to be honest, I had planned on leaving. And, I was thinking about taking this along with me."

Thorpe grinned and he took another step closer. "Well, I'm afraid I can't allow you to do that, Mr. Crocker. And I'm afraid my boss' authority carries a little more weight than whoever yours is."

Hans Crocker smiled, but again, Thorpe didn't much care. Not anymore. His brain was busy rifling through his memory for the name. Crocker... Crocker... Suddenly, it clicked in his head: Hans Crocker... financier, owner of a chain of low-rent hobby stores, and artifact privateer. Thorpe had never met the man, but he'd definitely heard his name.

He closed the mental file, having now done the required: he'd assessed his environment, measured his adversaries' intent, and made an informed decision on a plan. It was time to act.

"Well, Father," Crocker said, "I seem to be the only one left with the gun, so..."

Thorpe took the last few steps, comfortable in the fact that he was now within the distance he needed to be in order for him to do his thing. Now that he was this close, he was just waiting to see the point of no return in Crocker's actions, and in his eyes.

In the meantime, he shook The Array of Five, the five small knives he always carried with him, from their sheath on his forearm. The blades were long and thin, and measured six inches in length. The blades were of a unique design in which each blade fit into the other, making them easier to use. The flicking of a small clasp along the back of the knife unlocked them and the five blades could then be separated with a fanning of a thumb. The slim blades fell reassuringly into his hand, their sharp points digging into the flesh of his palm.

Just then, he noticed the muscles in Crocker's gun hand tense, tightening his grip on the trigger. Thorpe threw his blades at him with a practiced hand. The silver shards sailed like bullets across the short space separating them. The first three blades went regrettably wide. It was dark, so he forgave himself. The fourth struck Crocker's upper deltoid, and the last one sank deep into the soft meat of his bicep. Thorpe heard him cry out and the pistol clatter on the ground at his feet.

Silently, he started chasing after Crocker.

As the priest passed Flemish, he saw that the scientist had been knocked to the ground in the scuffle but was otherwise okay. He didn't have time to check on anybody else. Feet digging into the pliant sand, he followed behind the now-running Crocker, who was still clutching the box. The fat man couldn't run fast, so Thorpe made up the distance quickly, moving diagonally across the room to cut him off from the door leading to the outside. And, all the while, his eyes scanned the ground, looking for a weapon, but finding none.

With no other option left to him, Crocker sprinted toward the back of the cave, ducking into the tiled hallway that led back to the burial chamber.

Thorpe was a freight train coming up right behind him.

Stepping stealthily into the passageway, Thorpe held up a second to let his eyes readjust to the change in light level. The priest knew there was literally nowhere for Crocker to go since the crypt was a dead end, so he didn't feel any pressing need to hurry the confrontation. What he also knew was that Crocker had crossed the line and was bound to be a lot more dangerous—gun or no gun—especially now that he was wounded.

And, he still had possession of two of Thorpe's knives.

Thorpe followed Crocker into the burial chamber and immediately saw him as soon as he entered the room. Realizing he was cornered, Crocker set the box down onto the table with the two lanterns to free his hands for the fight. Thorpe stalked the room like a predator, slowly closing in.

As he got nearer, Crocker turned on him, having picked up a length of wood that had been leaning against the table. He swung it at him with his good arm. The board struck Thorpe across the upper body, even though he'd managed to raise his arms in time to deflect most of the blow's kinetic energy. The priest was nonetheless dropped to his knees by force of the impact, his breath leaving him like a ghost. Crocker made the standard 'tough guy' mistake of grabbing Thorpe by the throat and trying to strangle him. Thorpe hit him repeatedly in the sternum with a Wing Chun straight blast, and felt the hands relent a little. Somehow though, Crocker still managed to keep his grip.

Just then, Flemish came stumbling into the room, distracting Crocker long enough so that Thorpe could crack him on the jaw with a lateral Muay Thai elbow. The blow broke the hold and Crocker stumbled backward. Thorpe struggled for a second to catch his breath, but he managed to crawl back a few feet to create some distance between him and his adversary.

When he once again had more room, he scrambled back to his feet. The ground they were on was uneven though, and it caused him to stumble a bit coming up. Crocker took advantage of the fumble, and slugged Thorpe behind the ear with his fist. The blow knocked the priest away and he hit the table with the two lanterns in a sprawl. The force of his momentum sent the table, and everything on it, flying. The lanterns hit the ground, spilling their oil, and burst into flames.

The wrapped, stone box hit the floor and fell open with a heavy thud.

Thorpe heard the big man coming up remarkably fast behind him, and he scrambled for something to use to defend himself. Crocker tackled him from behind, using his weight to knock him to the ground. Thorpe's hands continued to rapidly prowl the soil in front of him.

Crocker grabbed him again from behind and aggressively yanked him back to his feet by his jacket collar. Thorpe went with the energy of the pull, using the force to increase the torque at his centerline. As he came around, he drove the point of The Bata ya Mungu he'd picked up from the spilled contents of the box into his opponent's abdomen.

Crocker's mouth fell open like he was about to say something, but nothing came out. The blade cut deep into his belly with little resistance, just under the rib cage, angling up. He slowly let out a rasping, lungful of air and took a few faltering steps back. His mouth continued moving, opening and closing, but he said nothing. Then, when his legs went to water and could no longer support him, he dropped to his knees, falling back onto his haunches.

Suddenly, Crocker arched back and his entire body started to convulse. His hands clutched at the hilt of the dagger, as he tried to get a grip on it, so that he could pull it out. But the priest had buried it so deep he was unable to remove it. Blood coated his fingers as he pawed feebly at the pale wood handle.

Then, what only could be described as an eruption of bright, incandescent light burst from the portal of his open mouth. The illumination was blinding in its intensity and seemed to completely engulf the room. Like mercury, the light poured out of him from every orifice, spreading out and oversaturating Thorpe's entire field of vision. The room's temperature abruptly spiked, like a great fire was raging, and then, it was gone.

When the priest's vision finally cleared, he saw what was left of Crocker lying on the floor. Where the man's body had once been, now only a charred husk remained. To Thorpe's eye, it appeared as if he'd been burned up from the inside out like a road flare. A single gold tooth lay amidst the ash. And there, sticking out of the scorched remains like an appendage, was the dagger.

"A purifying fire..." Thorpe heard Flemish whisper to himself from the corner.

The priest looked nodded over at him, concerned. "Is everyone okay out there? Janet? Matteo? The workers?"

Flemish shook his head. "Everybody's fine. I saw Matteo and some of the workmen taking the rest of Crocker's men captive as I ran in here. They'll contact the local authorities once we've put a lid on things."

"And gotten our collective stories straight," interjected the priest, eyeing the scientist darkly.

Thorpe walked over and picked up the box and the dagger's embroidered cover. He handed them to Flemish. "These will get you started in your investigations."

"What about the dagger itself?"

Thorpe stepped over to what was left of Crocker's body, and bent to retrieve the dagger. "I think it best that I take possession of this. First... for *everybody's* general safety. And second, because we need to get it away from here to someplace safe, someplace where our people can really look into it."

He held up his hand in anticipation of Flemish's protest.

"And before you start complaining about anything, I promise you that nothing will be done with the artifact without you being directly involved. I appreciate everything you've done, Doctor… and for what you did by distracting Crocker.

"So," he held out his hand for it to be shaken, "do we have a deal?"

Flemish considered the proposition and ultimately nodded his agreement. Reaching out, he shook the priest's hand. His interest in the dagger was solely for its archeological and historical value. All he wanted was to be involved in the piece's investigation. Now that he'd been guaranteed his spot on the research team, he was good. He could play along, especially… if it got him the data he wanted.

"We won't mention the dagger from here on out," Thorpe said. "I need to check in and let my people know what's coming."

He tucked the dagger into his coat, improvising a spot for it amidst the straps of the shoulder rig he wore for the Beretta. It didn't hide much of anything, but it did set his hands free. Looking down, the priest took a moment and silently mourned the state of his suit. Out of everything that had happened today, that hurt the worst.

The two men turned and started walking toward the exit.

"Now that we've seen a bit of this thing's potential, Father, I'm even more curious as to what *else* it can do?"

Thorpe followed along after him, doing his best to dust himself off. He trusted that Flemish would get Matteo or one of the workmen to tend to Crocker's remains before the local police inevitably got here. He felt the weight of both the weapon under his arm, and of the sin he'd just committed to protect it and hoped he and God might be able to call it square. And besides… it wasn't like this was the first time he'd been forced to compromise his vows to serve The Church. He was sure, given the kind of work he'd been called to do, it wouldn't be his last.

"Well, I want you to know, Doctor Flemish that you are welcome to help us as much, and for as long, as you'd like in that regard. We'd appreciate your expertise," Thorpe suggested.

"Please, Father… Joaquin. My name is Joaquin."

Thorpe smiled and draped his arm around the scientist's shoulders. "Okay, Joaquin it will be, then."

And, as the two men disappeared into the shadows of the

tiled hallway that lead back to the main dig site, Thorpe looked over at the doctor. "See, Doctor," he said, "I'm pulling together something of a team to investigate things very much like your dagger. You interested?"

Flemish's excited laughter echoed back to the burial chamber and the sound reverberated in the cavern until it finally settled back into silence.

HYPOXIA

I wanted to include this piece as another postcard from Cleese and his camp. I also wanted to remind readers of a few things. First off… that Father Handel was still in play. I have a lot planned for him and I wanted to let people know he was still around. Second, that there was, and has always been, activity going on at the Training Facility during the time that No Flesh Shall Be Spared: Don't Look Back was occurring. And finally, that time was passing, and that Kekoa was growing older and becoming more self-reliant. This story also sets up, in a REALLY subtle way, a critical plot element of the soon to be written, No Flesh Shall Be Spared: War, but I can't really tell you much more than that right now. I am compelled to say that I tried really hard not to lean into the 'creepy priest' trope in this tale, but… given who Father Handel is (and, again, what I have planned for him), it was hard not to have it happen a little bit. I hope you dig the story, though… and yeah, No Flesh Shall Be Spared: War is in the works. I can only ask your patience.

The sound of her own feet striking the ground was the only thing Kekoa heard as she jogged along the path that led away from the Training Facility. The League had chosen to build a trail that first circled the broad, flat exercise field leading to the running track, and then, on toward the shooting range at the back of the compound. From there, the trail then wound around the rest of the fenced property, passing an archery range and the ever-present specter of The Holding Pen, before it circled back and returned to the main facility. All in all, the loop was a little over eleven miles.

She'd decided to go out for a run today for a variety of

reasons; the first being that it was such a nice day out. The sun was shining. It was warm. And there wasn't a single cloud floating in the deep, blue sky.

The second was that it had been kind of a rough week for her: physically, mentally, and emotionally. Her anatomy and geometry classes were rough, sparring was becoming more and more intense, and, even though she felt like she'd been here for a while, she was still trying to get used to the place's grim routine.

She doubted if she ever would at this point.

Right now, there was nothing she needed to do more than to unplug her brain and drift away on the pain-numbing adrenaline that was only now beginning to course through her bloodstream like hot fire.

And finally, she simply needed a break from the day-to-day intensity of her trainer and mentor, Cleese. She loved him like a parent, but… she just needed a break.

He'd come out of nowhere to save her at a point when many could—and did—leave her behind to die. They'd both been caught in some twisted game the corporation put together up, and she'd lost everything: her family, her home, her way of life… in what could only be called, a living nightmare. But he'd taken her in, helped her, given her a place to live, healed her, and provided for her a life with a renewed purpose.

But he'd been on a tear as of late though, going on about some obscure thing from the Malay Archipelago he'd called 'Kuntau.' The fighting style involved a lot of squatting incredibly low and using physics and geometry to affect some impressive damage. He'd pushed her for hours going over the same drills and holding poses for impossibly long periods of time. He'd been obsessed with it along with something he called 'Mande Muda,' both Indonesian Silat-based fighting systems; obscure, but extremely effective.

But yeah, the guy could get a little intense. Much like someone else she'd once known. She shook her head to clear it of any further thoughts of Father… and of what had become of him. And of what he had become.

Rising up onto the balls of her feet, she increased her speed.

Blood flooded to her leg muscles and the stiffness of inactivity she'd felt a moment ago unwound in her leg muscles like a clock spring.

Plodding along, her breath settled into its natural rhythm, oxygen feeding her tissues. The sun overhead soon warmed her, and between that, and the blush of her exertion, she felt her mood slowly improving.

It felt good to get away from everything, from being chained to a computer screen at the tape library, from the searing pain of the weight room, and from the fear that often came during their time in the Training Hall. Things could sometimes just get overwhelming for her here. It was difficult for a lot of people, and they were all adults.

She was just a kid.

But she knew that there was a lot at stake. Cleese tried to keep her away from the worst of it, protect her like a fierce lion protects its cubs, but… she *had* eyes. She saw the men when they came to train, and she also saw when they didn't come back from their live events. And no one knew better than she how dangerous the UDs could be when improperly managed.

She breathed in deep and the air tasted clean and fresh on her palate. It reminded her of home, of the beautiful, tropical island that she'd grown up on. At the very least, it smelled a *lot* better than the air in the Training Pit did. That was an odor she prayed she *never* got used to.

Once she'd circled the field and come up on the track, she noticed a group of four men gathered by the bleachers which sat to the side of the oval track. When she'd gotten closer, she saw that they were from a group of fighters who were known around the compound as the Budo Warriors.

They were an intense group of people who looked like they came straight out of a Kabuki play… or an anime, all painted faces and formality. They fought hard and had this whole mythology thing going that bordered on a religion. Cleese told her it was best not to listen too much to the things they had to say. He said it would be better if the only person she listened to was him. So, since she trusted him, that's what she did.

One weird thing she'd noticed, though, was that the group

treated Cleese like he was some kind of royalty. Everyone here did, but *especially* the Budo Warriors. They gave him ample space, and an almost clergy-like respect. She knew it had something to do with their leader, a woman Cleese once had a lot of feelings for. She'd never asked him about it—or her—but she could tell it was a sensitive subject with him.

The men by the bleachers all turned in her direction as she approached. She'd seen them before, training on the practice floor, and at Mess. And, while she'd never spoken with any of them, they had no quarrel. The men all bowed in her direction once she'd gotten closer, affording her a little of the respect they so often showed to Cleese. Truthfully, all that stuff made her feel weird.

On a whim, she decided not to go too near.

Impulsively, she continued on passed the track, deciding that she would do her laps by running the compound's perimeter instead. The slightly longer distance would give her time to think, to clear her head, and to check out the rest of the compound. In all the time she'd been here, there were still parts of the complex that she'd never seen. And she knew how important it was to know one's environment. It's something that Father had always tried to tell her.

Reaching up, she activated her ear buds and thumbed through the music library on her watch until she found her 'running playlist.' Once she had it, she hit 'Random Play,' and music expanded in her ears to fill her reality. She settled into the groove and tried to match it to her body's natural rhythm. When she'd gotten herself into sync, she lowered her head and continued on.

"Such a beautiful day. The Lord's day," Father Handel sighed as he sat beneath one of the big, red maple trees that lined the perimeter of the training complex property.

He'd come out from his office about an hour ago having completed the last counseling session he'd had scheduled for the morning. His congregation here at the complex tended to want to talk to him for either counselling or fellowship at odd hours of the day. It was usually early in the morning (after the fighters had woken up from a night of drinking), or very late at night (when they were drunk and had gotten philosophical). So when windows in his schedule opened up like this, he tried to take advantage of them.

The priest sat with his back against the thick trunk of the tree, his head tilted back and his eyes closed. He felt tired, so he was purposefully taking this time to relax. Life had been more complicated for him than usual, as of late. And his life was usually pretty complicated.

He'd had a video meeting with his Diocese at dawn (due to the time difference) for his weekly check-in, and to give them an update on how things were going in his admittedly unique ministry. They'd ask their questions and he'd dutifully answer them. And he did it knowing that they were assessing him for signs of wear and fatigue, searching for indications that he'd somehow become compromised in his control of the situation, and in his Faith… given his extraordinary surroundings.

Of course, the Diocese knew nothing of his nightly excursions to the Holding Pen for what he considered to be his real mission: bridging the ecclesiastical gap between the Living and the Dead… and, if he were being truthful, he doubted that they ever would. But he'd seen things, instances of the connection he knew was possible, of the Dead doing what they could, in their limited capacity, to communicate with the living.

He'd first read about it happening on one of the Internet sites he so often visited. Most of the things they talked about there were obvious nonsense; ludicrous conspiracy theories that bordered on the fantastical. But every now and again, he'd see stories that could be corroborated by the simplest of searches; stories (and, in some cases, video) of the Dead speaking in short, semi-coherent phrases; acting in ways that were unheard of.

And again, he'd seen it happen himself over the years, mostly during his night visits to the Holding Pen: small instances of recognition… and even understanding.

And they'd all seen it happen a few years ago with Monk.

So he knew there was *something* there.

For now, though, he left it all back in his office. For now, he was content to simply sit and relax under this tree, eat his lunch, and leave all those grave concerns for another time.

Kekoa passed the Archery Range just as she was slipping into her zone. Every runner had their zone, the place where their perspective shifted, where the pain of exertion receded, and true objectivity could be found. Hers was a silent, comforting place of warmth that she usually only got in two places: training and distance running. When she was in that space, reality tended to slow down and become more manageable for her. She was able to zero in, see the subtleties, and to think. When she was there, she always seemed able to figure out just about anything that was bothering her. She counted on that now, counted on it to help her forget, and to help her continue with her healing.

Her feet pounded the dirt flat beneath them, kicking up little clouds of dust at her heels. Her legs no longer existed for her. They were just pistons now that powered her body forward. Driving the machine, her heart beat in her chest like a kick drum.

The music in her ear buds abruptly changed to something slower which broke the spell, causing her to return to the here and now. Abruptly, she noticed a sour/sick/sweet odor that hung in the air and grew stronger with every step. Annoyed, she looked up to see where she was.

Far off in the distance, set off at the furthest corner of the property, she saw the foreboding specter of the Holding Pen. Large and sorta barn-like, the structure gave off a terrifying aspect; like a place you *didn't* want to go. Not if you were smart.

Cleese had taken her there once, right after they'd first gotten here.

"We need to get this over with," he'd said. "If you freak and rabbit when we got inside, we'll at least know that this ain't for you."

The part that she still felt weird about regarding what she'd seen was how little it all bothered her. How fine she was with being around the dead; how little fear she felt. She'd gotten all of that out of the way back on the island, back when her entire world fell apart. To her… they were only opponents now; things to be put down. Like rabid dogs.

Something you just had to do.

Cleese said to think of it as something like 'immersion therapy,' in which a person gets over their fear of something by overwhelming themselves with it.

She'd done that.

She'd done that in spades.

Her plan was to follow the fencing passed the Holding Pen and circle back around to the main facility. She was already planning in her head to shower, and then meet up with Cleese at the Mess Hall for dinner. He had a live event coming up and wanted to meet with her for an hour or so before Lights Out to do more drilling. He had a habit of doing that before Shows. She thought that it came from his sense of perfectionism and a desire to not get caught unawares. It couldn't be that he felt something as human as fear.

No… not him. No Cleese.

Breathing in deep, she continued on her way.

Father Handel saw the girl coming down the trail long before she was able to see him. At first, she was only a small dot bobbing along on the horizon. But, as she came closer, he was better able to make out her features and start to see who she was: the kid Cleese brought back with him from the Paradise Project.

He'd never met her, but he was well aware of everything that happened on the ill-fated Paradise Project, and how it had been such a debacle for the League. They'd lost—and had to pay out quite a bit of capital on that one, to workers, to survivors, and to countless others. Luckily, Handel hadn't been anywhere near that mess. He'd been here at the Training Complex, but he'd seen the fallout. Money had gotten tight there for a while. Budgets were slashed. Belts had been tightened.

But then, as always, The League bounced back in no time.

Then, out of nowhere, Cleese came back, and not a thing (not Monk, not Monroe, not him going AWOL, not the missing money, nothing…) was ever said about it; like all had been forgiven and forgotten.

But now, Cleese had this kid in tow.

Handel had heard all the unsavory innuendo amongst the

fighters, but after the girl carved her way through most of them in sparring, those crass comments got quiet real quick. The priest had seen her in training and it was impressive, even to someone who'd never fought.

The only thing he knew was that being under a man like Cleese's wing certainly seemed to have its advantages. The League gave him the best accommodations and left him pretty much alone to do as he wished, just as long as he performed for them at their live events. In exchange, he was able to raise her in relative luxury. The priest was sure that the girl being able to sue Weber and his investors back to the Stone Age—her being one of the aforementioned Paradise Project survivors—helped immensely. She knew *everything* about what had happened there and had even lost her parents there, reportedly. It was probably best to keep her happy in order to keep her quiet.

The priest smiled when he saw that the girl noticed him and slowed her pace.

Kekoa slowed her steps and paused the music in her ear buds the instant she noticed the man sitting under the tree. At first, she mistook his shape as a fallen tree limb, but when he moved, she knew it for what it was: a man, and she went on high alert.

She slowed to a trot, but continued moving forward, as she approached where he was by the side of the trail. Still unsure as to his identity, she figured, this far away from the main facility, it had to be someone who worked in the operation of the compound; maybe some supportive personnel out catching a smoke.

Whoever it was, Kekoa had already decided to simply jog passed him, and give the appearance of being lost in her own head. Leave well enough alone, she thought to herself. And then, if this person proved to be a threat or, god forbid, something like an escaped UD, she was already on her guard, and therefore, prepared for anything that might happen.

She put her head down and continued jogging on.

"Hello!" Father Handel called out as he walked to the side of the trail, dusting off the seat of his beige cargo pants. He smiled broadly, and said, "Hello! Hello, there!"

The girl slowed to a stop. Jogging in place in order to keep her wind up, she checked her pulse and silently marked it in her head, all the while eyeing the priest suspiciously. "Can I help you with something?"

Father Handel shook his head. "No, no... I'm just out here for a breath of fresh air and saw you there. I thought I recognized you. You're Cleese's ward, aren't you?" He stepped into the middle of the road, blocking her way. "Anyway, I realized we'd never met and I wanted to introduce myself." He extended his hand. "I'm Father Handel."

The girl smiled but found herself moving back involuntarily. She suddenly realized that she knew this man. He was the League's clergyman. She'd seen him at her Orientation right after she and Cleese arrived here. He just didn't remember it. Cleese had less than complimentary things to say about the man and had said that he had some odd ideas about things. Other than Roman Catholicism, he'd said. She wasn't too interested in finding out more.

There was something about him that bothered her. Now that she'd gotten closer to him, she could tell that he smelled a little like the Holding Pen. If she had to put it into a word, he smelled of Death. And his eyes... they had this probing aspect to them, like he was constantly searching for a way to get beyond your defenses, like he'd be the type to come into your house and start searching through the cabinets.

"So, how do you like it here at the compound?" Handel asked.

"It's okay," she responded before she had time to think about it. Her tone though remained stand-offish.

The priest moved closer, his hand still extended for her to shake. "Yes, they've provided us with a good place here." He looked out over the vast, open area. "To train. To learn. And to provide to the world their much-needed outlet, eh?"

Kekoa smiled as she continued to slowly maneuver passed him. She'd decided not to be distracted from her workout by the Budo Warriors at the track, she wasn't going to let this strange priest interrupt her either.

As she padded passed, she felt Handel suddenly take hold of her wrist. Instinctively, she yanked it away, and turned to square off on him. It took her a second to remember… this was a priest in front of her.

You don't go hitting priests, girl.

Kekoa eyed him balefully, still not sure if he was a threat or not. She knew from talking to Cleese that the man was odd. And now, he'd touched her without her permission. Best that she have done with it and go back to her life.

"Whoa! Whoa! I'm sorr'. I didn't me' to alar' you. I jus' wan… duh… taw…" he slurred, and his tone sounded suddenly drunk.

He took a sloppy step back, his head suddenly lolling to the side. His arms fell uselessly to his sides, his fingers spasming like spiders. At first, Kekoa thought he might have 'turned' and had somehow become a UD. But then, she remembered his manner just a moment ago and wondered if it might be something else. This… had to be something medical, right? She tried to catch him as he fell back into a sitting position on the ground, legs splayed openly out in front of him.

"I don'… I don' fee…" the priest mumbled, his head abruptly tipping him back.

He rolled onto his back on the ground and it was like his head was suddenly too heavy for his neck and it needed to be set down. He rolled over, his eyes swimming like guppies, and Kekoa thought that he was going to vomit. She pushed him over onto his side, so he wouldn't aspirate if he did puke.

She'd had impressed on her since birth the need to know how to treat injuries, and she did what she could to settle him down, helping him to ride out the spasms. Taking off her watch, she put it between his teeth to keep him from biting his tongue. She wasn't sure if what he was having was a seizure, but she knew taking a few precautions would help him if he was.

After a minute, the priest settled down, but she still held him on the ground, holding his hand and cradling his head. He looked up at her, but his eyes were still rolling around in his head like marbles.

Looking around at her environment, she knew she had a

decision to make: leave him here, tucked under a tree or something, so that she could go and get help… or she could *carry* him back. The man weighed, what, one-forty? How hard could that be? She gazed off into the distance and estimated there were still a few miles to get back to the compound. Carrying him would be hard on him… and it wasn't exactly going to a picnic for her either. But it seemed to be the most prudent move.

"Hey, uh… Father," she gently said to him. "I'm going to have to get you to the Infirmary, so I can get someone to check on how you're doing, okay?"

The priest's head rolled on the post of his neck, and his eyes remained glassy and unfocused.

"Okay, so… I guess I'm carrying him," she said to herself.

She grabbed the priest under his arm and, using some leverage she'd learned in Judo, she pulled him to his feet. Ducking under his torso, she hoisted him up and across her shoulders like a long sack of flour. Her thighs trembled under the weight at first, but they soon stabilized once she'd gotten moving. Father Handel groaned and, for a minute, she prayed he wouldn't puke down her back. She took the next few steps haltingly, but soon picked up steam, and she was on her way.

"You wanted a workout," she grunted to herself, and she took her next step.

And then, she took another… and another.

Soon, she was on her way.

Cleese came busting into the Compound's Infirmary like a bull entering into a china shop a little more than an hour later. He stopped once he'd cleared the door, scanning the small reception area and triage desk like a predator. Past the lobby and the bustling staff, he saw Kekoa sitting in a small, metal chair in an alcove off to the side. Without waiting for anyone to talk to him, he went over to her.

"Hey," he said as he came up to her.

"Hey."

"You okay?"

She nodded as she stood up. "I'm fine. I'm just tired. It's been kind of a weird day."

"Someone came and told me you were here, but all I heard was your name and 'infirmary,' and I came right over."

She grinned imaging him roaring through the hallways on the way. Cleese was a lot of things, but subtle was not one of them. "Well, thanks for not killin' anybody on the way over."

"De nada," he laughed and shrugged his shoulders.

She liked it when he laughed. He didn't do it often; not around her, and not as of late. She knew he had a lot on his mind, having an inkling of the responsibilities that were on his shoulders. His already grim demeanor had only gotten darker over the last few months as they trained and he got used to doing live events again. His teaching remained excellent, and his televised matches so far had been pretty amazing, but… he'd developed a reputation around the compound for being a bit of an asshole.

"So, what happened?" he asked.

Kekoa shrugged. "I was out… running and getting myself some air. I ran into him on the back part of the trail, back by the Pen. We started talking, and I remembered what you'd said about him, so I kept my distance."

Cleese smiled. "Good, girl."

"Then, he started having trouble talking and just collapsed. I didn't want to leave him out there, so I carried him back so someone could look at him."

Cleese barked out a laugh. "*Carried?* I'm impressed."

She looked over with a strained expression. "I didn't think he'd be so heavy."

Cleese grinned and put his arm around her, leading her back toward the reception area. "I guess we can skip leg day tomorrow," and he chuckled. "C'mon, let's see if we can get an update on the padre."

Kekoa smiled, but her eyes showed her concern. "I just hope he's okay."

By now, they'd gotten to the desk and Cleese waved a nurse over. She was middle-aged, pretty, and seemed pretty excited to be talking to someone as famous as Cleese. She quickly broke away from what she was doing and came over to talk to him.

They spoke for a minute, and Kekoa noticed how the woman

kept touching her hair. The young girl rolled her eyes to no one. After a minute, she saw him shake her hand, sign something for her, and she reluctantly returned to her work. He strolled back over to Kekoa, grinning mischievously.

"Well, it looks like they'll be keeping him for a few days for observation. She said that she wasn't able to legally tell us much more than that for privacy reasons."

Kekoa smirked at him. "But…?"

"But… she said he'd had some kind of Grand Mal seizure and they're checking him to see what caused it, and how much damage it's done."

The girl rolled her eyes again and shook her head. "So much for patient confidentiality…"

He grinned and took her hand. "You sure you're okay?"

She nodded, more than a little grateful for his concern. "I'm just glad it wasn't what I first thought."

"Which was?"

She looked up at him intensely. "That he'd been bitten and had turned."

Cleese shrugged as he led her toward the door. "I wouldn't be too worried about that," he said paternally. "I have no doubt in my mind that you could handle the situation pretty easily if so. You're as solid a fighter as I have ever seen."

He opened the door for her and let her go out into the hallway first. He'd meant what he'd said. At this point in her development, especially given her history, there was nothing that a UD—or a Man, for that matter—could throw at her that she couldn't handle.

Kekoa proceeded down the hallway following along behind him. She didn't remember much of the walk back to her Crib. She was physically tired, and now, her head was spinning. Cleese didn't give out compliments often, so him saying that she could handle herself was a big deal.

At least it was for her.

Since their meeting on the island, he'd become like a father to her. He'd become her teacher, her confident, and her friend in that time, and his opinion meant the world to her. And as they walked along the hallway that led back to the main part of the compound, Kekoa looked back over her shoulder, silently hoping the odd, little priest would be okay.

Father Handel lay on his back in his hospital bed, looking out of his window. He had no idea what happened earlier, with the girl. But one second, he was feeling fine, and the next, the world just sort of slid out of his grasp, like molasses. It felt odd, and it frightened him a little. Luckily, the girl had been there to help him. He made a mental note to thank her.

There was a part of him, though, that had been able to stand back from the experience; to be an objective observer of his own intellect short-circuiting and shutting itself down. He'd have been scared when it happened, had it not been for how amazing it was.

Like being in the presence of God.

His room door suddenly opened and a young, athletic-looking man came in. Handel knew him; he knew who everybody was here at the compound. Jefferson was his last name, and he was the main doctor at the Infirmary.

"Things must be bad," Handel said with a smirk. "I get the Big Guy here right out of the gate."

Jefferson smiled. "Hello, Father."

The physician was a white man in his mid-30s with dark brown hair cut short, and light grey eyes. He had a look of someone who'd once been Prom King back in high school and he'd somehow managed to parlay that into a medical career. The priest chastised himself for his sarcasm, reminding himself of the need to be more compassionate—even in difficult situations such as this.

"Father Handel, I wanted to come see you in person to give you the results of the tests we ran on you. I just thought it important that we talk..."

The priest stared at him for a long time, already knowing where he was going with this. He should. He'd delivered the same speech a time or two; to people who'd also just had something happen and were about to learn that they were going to die. It didn't make it any better.

He opened his mouth a few times as if to speak, but nothing

came out. Tears glassed his eyes, and no matter how hard he tried, he couldn't blink them away.

"Oh?" he finally gulped out as he labored to keep the smile on his face.

Doctor Jefferson nodded solemnly, and the priest braced for the punch.

"Yes. You see, Father… we found a mass."

Father Handel chuckled darkly. "A mass?"

The doctor nodded, but Handel's perception was already slipping away into a womb of introspection. Of course, he'd always been aware of Death in the abstract. As a priest, it was an important part of his job. He'd especially seen so much of it since the Dead rose; at St Joseph's, while he was on the run, and now, here with The League. But somehow, he'd never connected it happening to himself.

That he, too, would one day die.

Slowly, he raised his gaze to look at the doctor. He focused on his lips as they moved, but his words though, kept phasing in and out.

"Tests… positive… Craniopharyngioma… affecting pituitary and frontal lobe function… metastasizing…"

The priest raised his hand in an effort to stop the doctor from continuing. He'd heard enough. He knew how this song ended. The physician slowly stuttered to a stop, looking at his patient with visible concern.

"Doctor, I am a man God, and I believe that He has a plan, for me… and for you… and for all of us. Apparently, he has a plan for us even after we die; for our spirits and for the bodies left behind. But, right now, you've given me a lot to think about, and I think I might need a minute to process all of this. I hope you understand?"

Jefferson nodded, almost as if he'd been expecting the response, like he knew he'd been pouring some difficult information into his patient and he shouldn't be surprised now that he was showing signs of being full.

"I understand, Father. We'll talk again in the morning. Rest now. I've given the nurse's orders to give you something to help you sleep. I wish… I wish I had better news for you, Father, but... You of all people should understand."

Handel smiled a perfunctory smile, like the ones he'd pasted on for parishioners for years. He tried once again to speak, but his throat felt tight, and it made it hard to breathe. He settled on waving the man away, silently watching him as he exited the room.

Later, after the sun had gone down and the hospital building had grown dark and quiet, Father Handel lay in bed, awake. He stared out the window, idly watching the moon as it inched its way across the onyx sky.

The Infirmary was quiet at this time of night, the majority of staff having retired to their respective homes elsewhere on the property. The skeleton crew left behind was busy making rounds, seeing to the few patients (fighters injured in training, mostly), and tending to the responsibilities of their shift.

And down the dimly-lit corridors of the hospital, silence kept its lonely vigil.

Handel had dozed in and out of consciousness for several hours, until he finally awoke just after three in the morning, not being able to go back to sleep. This late, the early morning quiet pressed down on the building; almost oppressively so.

The priest swung his legs out of bed, and, after testing his stability, he slowly hobbled over to the window. He reached up with one hand to unlatch the clasp on the lock, and the noise it made sounded like a gunshot in the silence.

He gently pushed the windowpane open and felt a rush of cool, night air flood in. Handel breathed in deeply and felt better than he had all day. He leaned against the windowsill, and quietly spent a few minutes drinking in the liquor of the night. He listened to the sound of the early morning calling out to him, the birds as they began their day, and the crickets just ending theirs, and he smiled at the world's simple beauty.

God be praised.

Then, another sound crept in.

It was the same sound that he'd heard so many times before, during his excursions to the Holding Pen to give to the Dead their Last Rites. It was a low, forlorn moaning that sang of lost lives and missing loved ones, and of being given a glimpse of Heaven, only to have it cruelly snatched away.

He looked out over the property, listening to the chorale of the Dead, until his gaze finally fell upon the shadow of the Holding Pen. The building was an imposing obelisk presiding over the compound like an angry parent at Sunday dinner.

"Soon," he whispered with a wry smile. "They'll see... They'll all see I was right."

Leaving the window open to let the night air into the room, he turned and slowly made his way back to his bed.

ANAMNESIS

This one was pretty easy for me to come up with, since it actually happened to me; sort of. I was cleaning out a closet and discovered an old box of my mom's (who passed in 2010) under a bunch of photo albums. When I opened it, I had much the same initial reaction as the hero in this story does. Anyway, the whole thing really got me thinking… and, as usual, a story—this story—was the result.

The last of the day's sun trickled in through the dining room window of Bill and Nadine Potter's Georgetown home. The day had been a lazy one for the both of them. They'd taken a late breakfast, did The Times' crossword puzzle together, and even had some early afternoon Mimosas. They'd worked hard this past week at the store they owned, and, quite frankly, they both could have used a day off.

Nadine Potter was in the kitchen, preparing their dinner. They'd invited some friends, Bob and Nancy Slater, over for dinner last week, and she'd been busy getting things ready since they'd cobbled together their lunch.

Bill was in the Living Room, reading the last of a Joe Lansdale Hap & Leonard book. He was lounging on the couch, intently focusing on the folded-over paperback he held in his hand. He turned to the past page, which was only a couple of paragraphs, and quickly scanned it. Feeling a small level of accomplishment, he clapped the book's covers closed triumphantly.

Suddenly, the front doorbell rang.

He got to his feet, tossing the book onto a side table, and went to get the door. Before he opened it, he looked down to check how he was dressed. He had on the same pair of running shorts and Steely Dan tee he'd woken up in. For a second, he thought about waiting for Nadine to come and get it. He peered through the peephole and saw that there was a UPS driver, dressed in brown shirt, cap, and shorts, waiting on the porch, holding a box in his hands.

"I'll get it," Bill called to the kitchen as he opened the door. "Yeah?"

"Potter?"

"You got him."

"I got a delivery for ya, so I'm gonna need your signature on this, okay?"

Bill nodded. "They got you working on a Saturday, eh?"

The UPS driver nodded and smirked as he gave him his package. "I have a good agent."

Bill accepted the box and set it down inside the door at his feet. The driver handed him a small electronic pad on which he scribbled something that loosely resemble his signature.

"Who's it from?" Bill asked conversationally as he handed the device back.

"No idea, pal," the driver replied, taking the pad back and stepping off the porch. "I just bring 'em and drop 'em, y'know?"

Bill laughed and gave him the perfunctory, 'well, have a good day' response, as he stepped back into the house. He wasn't sure where the guy got his attitude, but... his whole demeanor had rubbed him the wrong way. It wasn't Bill's concern if he wasn't happy about having to work on Saturday.

Shaking his head, he picked up the box and closed the door with his foot.

The box was square, maybe a foot high, and heavy—solid—like it had something heavy, like a lot of paper, inside. Maybe it's just packed really well, he thought.

"Who was that?" Nadine called from the kitchen.

She came out into the hallway, wiping her hands off onto a dish towel. Not too tall and dressed in loose gray sweatpants and a white button-up blouse, Nadine Potter was the light of Bill's world, and, together, they'd built a good life together. They ran a small convenience store in town; nothing big or fancy, just a place for people to get essentials when they needed them.

And, for them, it was enough.

They'd been married for a while now—thirty plus years—and their kids were all grown up, moved out, and gotten themselves married. Now, unless the grandchildren were visiting, the two of them had the luxury of spending a Saturday like this every once in a while: lazily, and without much direction.

"UPS," he replied. "Somebody sent us a box. It's kinda heavy, too. The delivery guy was a bit of a jerk, too… thought he was funny, I guess. He wasn't."

She approached him, putting her arm around his waist. "Oh, stop… we're 'chillaxing,' remember? Who sent it?"

Bill flipped the box over in his hands until he finally found the shipping label. He searched for his own address, and then, he looked above it.

"Shit," he said with a resigned finality, his shoulders sagging involuntarily.

"What?"

"It's from Penny."

Nadine narrowed her eyes in distrust. "Your sister?"

Bill walked to the dining room and his wife followed him. He set the box down onto the table, stepping away without opening it.

"Yeah. Goddamn it. What could she possibly be up to? I bet it's a human head… like in that movie."

Bill and his sister had never been what anyone would call 'close.' Especially not since their mom died a number of years ago. It was a long story, but the nuts-and-bolts of it were that he and Nadine were at a weekend sales conference when they'd gotten The Call that his mom had passed. She'd been sick with dementia and they'd been told by hospice that it was only a matter of time. He talked to the funeral home and they said that she'd paid to be immediately cremated and placed at some property at the cemetery she'd selected. There really wasn't any pressing need for him to hurry there. They could meet on Monday when he got into town. Even with this reassurance, Bill and Nadine had gotten there as quickly as they could.

By the time they'd arrived in town, though, Penny had gone ahead and had her own funeral service, scattering their mom's ashes at the beach. Of all places. Mom *hated* the beach. Anyway, they'd not spoken to one another since.

"I said, stop," she said sternly, even though she thought his reference funny. "What's inside?"

He looked over at her blankly. "I have no goddam idea. As you can plainly see, I haven't opened it yet."

She took a second to let the snappy response float passed her. She looked him in the eye and calmly suggested, "Well, why don't you?"

He nodded his head, looking sadly resolute. "I'm sorry. I will. I just need a minute."

Nadine patted him on the arm and kissed his cheek. She knew all about the conflicting emotions he had when it came to his family. They'd not treated him the best while he was growing up, and they'd done a lot worse to him as of late. She knew that if he really needed someone to talk to, he'd come to her. That was just his way. Thirty years had taught her at least that. Any prodding on her part would only make him mad, and she didn't like it when he got moody and sulky.

"I'm gonna go back, then. I have some potatoes that need mashing. So, if you need me, or want to take out your aggressions…" She jerked her thumb toward the kitchen.

He smiled and kissed her again.

"Thanks. If I can't figure out how to open it, I'll call ya."

He could hear her chuckling as she disappeared back into the kitchen to presumably go rough up some tubers. When she was gone, he reluctantly turned his attention back to the mystery of the box. God only knew what his sister had sent. She'd always had a vindictive streak and had been really mad when he'd cut off communication with her after the funeral.

The package sat waiting though, waiting patiently for him, on the tabletop.

"To hell with it."

He pulled his car keys out of his front pants pocket, singling out his house key, and dragged its teeth across the cellophane tape holding the package closed. Whatever it was that Penny had sent him, he knew it wasn't going to be good.

May as well get this over with.

Tiny strips of plastic spiraled up from around the key as the metal tore through the packing tape. When it was all cut, one flap of the package popped open like the lid of a Jack in the Box, inviting him to look inside.

Just as Bill saw a quick flash of some yellowed paper and a manila folder, a smell from inside reached out to slap him across the face and fifty years into the past. The odor, and the memories it inspired, rocked him to his core. It was the smell of old cigarette smoke and of a perfume he didn't know if they even made anymore called Emeraude. The odor was old and musty, and smelled of only one thing: his mother.

His reaction was immediate and physical, reflexively pushing the box away, and sending it skidding across the surface of the polished wood. It came to a stop just before sliding off the table and onto the floor.

The next thing he knew, he was bent over the table, sobbing uncontrollably. There was a part of him that was surprised he hadn't felt the usual welling up that he usually did just before crying. This… was more immediate and out of his control. He smelled his mom and it all just hit him all at once: the weight of her loss, how much he missed her, his regret over the soured relationship with the rest of his family… the raw open wound of it all, and the dam just broke. His knees suddenly felt weak and he feared that his legs might abandon him, so he sat down in the nearest chair. All the while, his body was wracked by an irrepressible weeping.

He sat for a few more minutes and quietly cried, doing everything he could to not make any noise doing it. There was no use in unduly worrying Nadine and having her get upset, he thought. He knew what this was. He and his therapist had talked about it. This was merely another expression of his grief. He knew that, while the wound of his mother's passing may have been still healing, it was pretty obvious that it wasn't completely healed. This… was just him further processing his loss and being triggered by an unexpected memory. He was confident it would pass in time.

But still…

"Please, Buddy," a woman's familiar voice suddenly said in

the room. "It's important that you go through what's there."

He looked up. "What'd you say, Naddy?"

But Nadine wasn't there.

Instead, he saw a young woman in her late twenties with bright red hair styled in a retro-fashion which crowned her head like a halo, and deep green eyes. Her lips were painted a Woolworth red and she was sitting in the chair opposite him, hands clasped in her lap, and smiling. He knew he knew her from *someplace*, but he couldn't quite…

Then, "Mom?"

"Hi, Honey."

Bill looked around the room and silently wondered if the stress of it all—the store, his sister sending this strange box, his long-held and undealt with grief—had finally gotten to him, and he was now starting to hear and see things. "You're here?"

She smiled and he recognized the gap between her two front teeth. "Yes."

"Are you a…?"

"A what, honey?"

"A ghost?"

"No…" She smiled indulgently. "I'm more of a memory."

"A memory?"

"Yes."

He sat for a minute, not really sure of what was happening, much less what to say. But then again, his mother—whether real or imagined—was here, in front of him and his heart was supremely grateful for it. His mind quickly rifled through all for the things he thought he might want to say to her, to ask her.

He finally decided to start with the basics.

"I miss you."

"I miss you, too, Dear…"

"I love you."

"And I love you, you know that. You've always known that."

And he did, as surely as he knew anything in the world. She *had* always loved him. If he ever had to be honest on the topic, there had been times in their long marriage when he'd doubted Nadine's love for him. But his mother… not ever.

"Are you… okay?"

She smiled, but only said, "I am. I am… atoning, as we all must."

He wasn't exactly sure what she meant by that, but his brain was on fire with how surreal the situation was that he now found himself in. Before he could speak though, the young lady across the table interrupted him.

"I need you to go through my things, Buddy. I need you to help me… to move on."

"What do you mean?"

"See, son… as you process your sense of loss and begin to let go, it makes it easier for me to continue on to what I have to do next. Do you understand?"

He nodded slowly and knew with certainty that she was right, that holding on to too many memories bound us to the things and to the people we love. Apparently, that was something that worked both ways, and he could see how those same ties could, in time, become shackles.

"There's so much I want to ask you about," he finally said.

"And yet, there's only so much I can tell you."

"Can I hug you?" he asked as his eyes found a new wellspring of tears.

She smiled and, for the first time, her smile seemed sad. "Isn't it enough for us to simply sit… and talk?"

He nodded, knowing that it was, and suddenly fearful that a touch might ruin everything.

"Is there anything you want me to do? I mean, other than go through the stuff in the box."

"Yes… be kind. To Naddy… to the people that you work with and the strangers you meet in your life. It really is the only thing that truly matters. Let go of your anger and bitterness. Abandon the dreams of how you thought your life would be. And instead, embrace it for what it is. People are all trying the best that they can, Bud, believe it or not. Even your sister. Life is hard. You've seen that, haven't you, Son. People make mistakes. Go easy on them… and on yourself."

He thought about what she'd said for a moment, and he knew in his heart that she was right—and how much of a fool he'd been in his life. The things he'd always thought were important in life—the acquisition of money, the success of the store, being well thought of by others in his field—simply weren't. In the end, it really was about how kind you were… and how kind could you could be.

He looked across the table at his mom and realized in that moment just how much of it he would give up just to have her back like this again.

"Is there anything I should know?"

"Only that time is precious and it oftentimes passes without us ever even noticing." She got a far off look in her eye. "You always think you'll have enough. Time, I mean, but…" She shrugged. "One day, it's all gone. And then…"

"Yeah?"

"Love is all that we have left to us."

The door to the dining room suddenly burst open and Nadine came in carrying a stack of plates for dinner. "Honey, can I get you to please set the tab…" She was brought up short by the sight of him and the anguished look on his face. Tears covered his cheeks, and his eyes were steaked with red. Clearly, he'd been crying, and was in some kind of distress. "Oh, God, Bill… what's wrong?"

Bill looked up and wasn't surprised at all to see his mother now gone.

"Nothing. I'm okay. I… it's just… this box." He looked up at her and his expression revealed the pain he was in. "It smells like her. I just… didn't expect…"

"Oh, I'm so sorry," she said as she set the plates onto the table. She knelt down to hug him. "Are you okay, Baby?"

He nodded, putting his arm around her, and resting his head on her shoulder.

"Hey, listen…" he said tentatively, "is it okay if we call Bob and Nancy and beg off tonight? I think I should probably go through this stuff as soon as possible, don't you?"

"Oh," she replied, trying to act like she understood, but it was clear that she was disappointed. She'd been working on the dinner for most of the afternoon, and he knew she'd been looking forward to it. "Okay, sure."

"Look, I just think I should do this as soon as possible, get it done now that I can. I've just been waiting for how long to get some kind of closure about her death. I think this may be the way I can do that."

She nodded, looking disappointed, but still trying not to show it. "I just wish it could wait until tomorrow…"

He suddenly caught the scent of his mother's Emeraude floating up from the still-opened box, and, in a flash, he understood.

"You know what?" He paused, and then nodded to himself, as if he'd made up his mind about something. "Never mind… It *can* wait. I've waited all these years to figure this stuff out, a few more hours won't hurt, right?"

"You sure?" she asked, her face brightening.

He nodded. "I am. I can always just go through it tomorrow, right? It's Sunday, after all."

She hugged him tighter and kissed the crown of his head. "Well, I love you, either way, Mister Potato Head. But thanks."

He smiled up at her and his heart spread warmth to his body.

"But, if that's the case," she said, reluctantly breaking the moment. "I need to you to help me with the silverware. They'll be here soon."

He smiled and nodded. "Deal."

And, with that, she stood up and walked out of the room, but not before casting one last concerned glance back at her husband. She loved him and knew he was going through a lot since the death of his mother. She loved him deeply but worried about him.

After she was gone, Bill carried his mom's box back to his study and left it sitting on his chair. Looking at it sitting there in the half-light, he smiled, and as he closed the door, he whispered to the empty room, "Thanks, mom. I love you."

COLLODI NO KIKAI

This piece came about pretty organically. I saw a photo online and the story—in its entirety—immediately popped into my head. The story itself is quite small in scope, but I feel like I left enough bread crumbs early on to make the landing stick. My only real problem was how and where to end it, where to cut away. Hopefully, you'll think I chose wisely…

A wave of cool, conditioned air flooded from the electric doors of The Yasuyado Hotel as they slowly slid themselves open. As if by magic, the two planes of glass moved aside, allowing the refreshing current of air to come pouring out like river water. Inside the hotel, the décor was distinctly Japanese: open space, pale bamboo, and shoji screens being the order of things.

Arthur Branson, an American man in his mid-fifties, yoga-thin and balding but for the nub of a ponytail that stuck out from the back of his head like a pot handle, got out of the hired car. He smiled appreciatively as he swam up the exhilarating stream of polar air.

Dressed casually in a Greenpeace tee and canvas slacks, Branson wasn't a man who felt the need to show off his wealth; although there was an awful lot of it. He'd always let his Amex Centurion, Chase Palladium, and Dubai First Royal cards do that for him. He felt like it had more impact that way.

He'd made his first fortune as a corporate lawyer.

He made his second as a property speculator and investor.

At one point, a few years ago, his accountant sat him down and basically said, "You're good," by which he meant that money wasn't something he'd ever have to worry about again.

As long as he didn't do anything crazy—like get married—his bottom line was pretty much covered until the day he died.

From that day on, the amount of money in his bank account didn't mean much to him. It generated itself without much effort or attention needed from him. His bills were covered, his most idle desires all within easy reach. And so, he was left to pursue his other variant preoccupations.

One such interest was spirituality, which he'd become fascinated by after his mother had died. Since money hadn't brought him happiness, he thought, surely this would. Or maybe it could.

In the beginning, it was him mostly just having a casual interest in astrology, tarot, and having his palm read by pretty girls at parties. It soon blossomed though to include meetings with modern mediums, some questionable holy men, and even some of the most respected religious leaders around the world.

As a result of all of this, and since he was, well… rich, he started traveling, looking for where he could for answers to his questions. First, he'd gone to hear these great people speak. And then, because he could afford to buy access, he would pay to meet with them in an effort to figure the world out for himself. All of which ultimately brought him here, to The Yasuyado and the Heiwana Basho, a temple in the Ishikara Mountains of Hokkaido, Japan.

He'd booked himself a couple of days here at the Yasuyado because of its proximity to the site of the temple. He didn't want to spend all of his time this trip in a car… like last time. He also picked it because it was the only *quality* hotel in the entire prefecture.

Branson had come to the Yasuyado because he'd scheduled time with the renowned psychic and religious deep thinker, Satotta Kyoshi. Reclusive and someone who usually only communicated with the outside world through his writing, Satotta Kyoshi was responsible for some of the most seismic changes to the Self Help and Personal Growth industries in the last thirty years. His humanity and innate understanding of what it was to be human spoke to people, like, *really* spoke to them.

As a result, his online congregation increased, and

international tax exemption status for him and his church came soon after. Then, about a year ago, it was announced that he would begin taking private audiences—such as the one Branson had paid for— with selected clients. To some people, people like Branson who were rich enough to afford it, it was like being able to sit and speak with the Dalai Lama, Gandhi, or, hell… even Jesus. The fifty-thousand-dollar entrance fee meant nothing to him if he could get the information—and the blissful feeling—he was looking for.

See, Branson thought of himself as something of a seeker, a man who sought greatness of character and excellence of thought. He'd been that way all of his life. At first, it had manifested itself in the search for material possessions: rare baseball cards, comics, luxury cars, art, that sort of thing.

Then, the money changed that, like it had changed him, and his interest became a passion for items of religious and historical significance, blessed by the highest positions in theological hierarchies. Soon though, it wasn't enough. He desired more, to understand more, and owning a few trinkets—no matter how rare and unaffordable—would not bring him any closer to God.

And so, he'd become a seeker of information instead; a hoarder of bits and pieces of data that were, in reality, puzzle pieces that he felt needed to be collected and compiled, so that the actual picture of his life could one day be revealed. He supposed it was what most people might called 'enlightenment.' For him though, it was like trying to scratch an itch he couldn't reach.

"Mr. Branson?" a voice heavy with a Japanese dialect interrupted, drawing the American up short and causing him stop walking.

"Yes?" Branson responded suspiciously. "Can I help you?"

Before him stood a young, well-dressed Japanese man in his early thirties. His manner of dress was not unlike many of the 'salarymen' Branson had seen in the country: black suit and tie, white button-up shirt, loafers. The man's expression was friendly, even accommodating, like his sole desire in Life was for someone to ask him for something.

"Sir," he chirped and bowed, remaining bent over as he spoke. "My name is Phillip Wada. I am the Concierge here at

The Yasuyado. I wish to welcome you to our humble hotel." He stood and smiled his winningest smile. "I trust your flight went well. I have taken the liberty of booking you a couple of hours at one of our spas, if that's acceptable."

Branson looked around, still trying to decide if the hotel met his standards, the sneer on his face obvious. So far, he liked what he was seeing, but he would never let this concierge know that. Not this early in their interaction. He just always thought it best to keep people on his toes.

"Or..." the Japanese man offered suddenly sounding nervous, his voice stammering slightly. He'd mistaken Branson's expression as a sign of him not being pleased with his spa suggestion, so he quickly offered up another. "Or, we can have a full team sent up to your room. 'Any *thing* you want. Any *way* you want it,' that's the motto here at The Yasuyado, Sir. Please give us the honor of being allowed to provide it for you."

Branson nodded and waved the man's concerns away with his hand. He'd decided to stay and he didn't want this guy saying or doing anything further to jeopardize that. And besides, he was here for one reason, and one reason alone, to meet with Satotta Kyoshi. If this concierge only knew the hovels Branson had stayed in over the years to get the information he wanted, he wouldn't have worried so much.

"No, no... It's fine. I'll visit your spa once I've been to see my room. It was a very long flight, and I'd honestly like to do nothing more than take myself a long bath, get a bite to eat, and go to bed. Your hotel is lovely, but I'm really only here for my visit tomorrow."

"Of course," Wada said, and with a gesture, he invited his guest to walk with him.

"My bags?"

"Will be brought up to your room, Sir. Everything's been arranged. We just have a bit of paperwork for you to sign first: the contract, of course, our Non-Disclosure... all standard stuff. I also have a printed receipt of your payment for your records as well, should you desire. We want you to relax here at The Yasuyado, though. You're in *our* hands now. You can leave your every comfort to us."

Branson smiled and made a note of the name on the man's nametag: Wada. If this trip went well, he'd see to it that the man got a nice bonus. If not, it was always nice to have a name on which to assign blame.

The next morning, just as the sun was poking its head above the edge of the horizon, a repeated chiming sound started ringing out in the silence of Branson's suite. He opened his eyes and looked around the semi-dark room to find its source. The room's décor was Spartan and continued with the hotel's Japanese motif of blonde bamboo paneling on the wall and pale cedar wood furniture. When he went to bed last night, Branson had been quite pleased by everything he'd seen so far during his stay.

That is… until now.

"What the good goddam hell?" Branson growled to the empty room.

The overhead light in the room slowly came on, starting low and almost indistinguishable, then becoming brighter and brighter in incremental stages. As the illumination increased, the soft sound of birds chirping filled the room.

Branson rubbed his eyes and sat up in bed annoyed.

"Good morning, Mr. Branson," a throaty, female voice whispered from the ceiling. "This… is your four a.m. wake-up call, sir."

"Okay, thank you!" he answered, suddenly remembering where he was, and why.

He swung his legs out of bed and, after a bit more grumbling, got himself dressed. He knew it was going to be hot out today after checking the weather online last night, so he'd set out a pair of linen pants and a white polo shirt before going to bed, hoping they wouldn't be too casual. He dressed quickly and left the room. It wasn't long before he was riding the elevator down to the lobby.

He found the concierge waiting for him at the front desk once he'd gotten off the elevator. He'd planned to have himself some breakfast before heading out for the day, so he looked around for a restaurant that opened early. He knew from past experience that he'd be doing a lot of hiking and standing today, no doubt in the sun. He wanted to not have to worry about needing to eat until the end of the day or at least not until he was done with his meeting.

Instead, his host informed him that a breakfast had been set out for him, and that a lunch would be provided after his meeting. As it turned out, 'breakfast' was nothing more than a lukewarm bowl of Miso Soup with a few blocks of flavored Tofu floating in the broth like icebergs. Branson ate it, but he did so begrudgingly. He knew he'd have trouble with his blood sugar later if he didn't have *something* in his stomach. This was just going to have to do.

His friend, Joe Franklin, who was an executive over at Microsoft, paid for a spot here six months or so ago, and he'd said that the only thing that hurt more than the cost of the trip was the physical toll it had taken on him climbing all the damn stairs.

The Heiwana Basho Temple sat at the top of a tall mountain and the only way to get up there was to walk up an inordinately long and breathtakingly steep stone staircase. According to the hotel's literature, the site had been here for centuries, and had been a Shinto monastery since the 16th Century. As a result of a request to the government from the Satotta Kyoshi himself, no helicopter or modern conveyance was allowed anywhere near the summit of the mountain. So, if you wanted a face-to-face with this guy, you better be prepared to walk or to climb.

After he managed to choke down as much as he could of his breakfast, the concierge—Wada—led him out a back entrance of the hotel. There, he took him to a trail that went into the forest that made up the majority of the hotel's property.

The Concierge led Branson down the path for some time until they finally came to a place where the path split, one trail heading off to the left, and the other circling back to the right, back to the hotel.

Around them, birds sang calmingly in the leafy branches of the trees.

"Proceed along this path, Mr. Branson. It is known as The Ascension of 10,000 Steps. You will soon see why. Satotta Kyoshi waits for you at the end of the path. Find the stairs, Sir… *that* is where your journey begins."

Then, without saying anything further, he turned and walked off down the path back to the hotel, leaving Branson alone amidst the silence of the trees. A tableau of Japanese maple, beech, and red cedar trees spread out around him, coming up out of the ground like stubble. Katsura, momiji, and azalea bushes cozied up to the tree bases as if huddling for warmth.

Branson stood by himself on the trail for a few minutes, breathing the fresh air and taking in the canopy of natural beauty around him. And it really *was* beautiful, probably some of the prettiest countryside he'd ever seen in the world.

Finally, he decided to get started, and headed down the path on the left.

Moving at a casual pace, he made his way down the path. He wanted to commit everything he was seeing to memory, wanted to be able to recount the experience back to his business associates at parties when he got back. Tree trunks rose up like Corinthian columns, creating a cathedral of natural serenity around him. And besides… no one seemed to be in much of a hurry here… and it was a pace, at least for the moment, to which he found himself now drawn.

Branson ambled along, finally beginning to feel a real sense of calm wash over him. He always felt depressed right before coming on one of these trips, especially if the meeting was with someone he respected, and last night was no different. It had taken him an extra Ambien to get to sleep.

He'd read everything Satotta Kyoshi had written, though, and held the man in his highest esteem. His philosophy was a fascinating amalgam of other, more classic, ideas that Branson was already familiar with: Freud, Kant, Schopenhauer, Wittgenstein, Descartes, Asimov… he even included quotes from some modern rappers in his essays, and that kind of open-mindedness made Branson like him even more. The idea that his perspective was open to ideals from across the spectrum really appealed to him. And everything he said confirmed so much of what Branson himself had always thought about the world.

He made his way around the next turn and finally came to the beginning of a long, stone stairway that followed the slope of the mountain up into the trees. A small sign had been mounted at the base with kanji carved into the wood. Below it, in English, an inscription read, 'The Ascension of 10,000 Steps.'

Branson hiked his trousers up and sighed. "Welp, this is it, I guess," and he began climbing.

Some time passed… how much, he couldn't really tell.

In this heat and growing humidity, it was impossible to get any idea of how long he'd been climbing. The only thing he knew was that he was hot, and now drenched in his own sweat. When he'd first started up the stairs, his quads had been on fire, their muscle fibers alight from the stress of the arduous climb. It was like being on a Stair Master times ten, he'd thought to himself. His legs warmed up though and he soon settled into his own rhythm.

The stairs themselves were flat, carved pieces of gray marble about a yard wide and a foot deep. The lip of each had a braided pattern carved into them that made Branson shake his head in amazement. Who made these? And how long ago? They were beautifully crafted, but there were literally *thousands* of them.

He looked up the mountain to see how far he still had to go, sweat beading across his forehead like dew. He sighed and shook his head when he saw the ribbon of stairs disappear into the trees in front of him.

Lowering his head, he continued climbing.

More time passed, and the sun slowly crawled its way across the clear blue sky. And still, Branson continued climbing, step by step, up the stone staircase. He thought back to his breakfast and wished he could have had time for those steak and eggs he'd dreamt of having instead of the saltwater and packing peanuts he'd ended up with.

"Goddam it," he cursed out loud, frustration finally rubbing against his last nerve. "I didn't pay fifty grand to go traipsing up and down this fuckin' mountain in the middle of Japan in a goddam heat wave."

He bitterly imagined that concierge—Wada—and a few friends watching him on a monitor and laughing in some Plebian break room. He spat onto the next stair, growing angrier with every footfall.

Despite his protestations though, he set his foot onto the next stone stair.

Just as Branson was about to give up and head back down the mountain to demand an explanation, he noticed that the slope of the staircase started to decrease. The angle of the stairs felt like it was flattening out and becoming more of a walkway. He felt the pressure on his legs decrease, dousing the fire in them.

At the very top of the mountain, he found a small, flat park about half the size of a football field, bountiful in its flora and fauna. A group of birds chirped contentedly in the boughs of the trees. Rabbits and sika deer roamed free, lazily feeding on the grass. A small, flat stone area lay at the space's center; in the middle of which, stood a white, stone pavilion.

Branson took a minute to catch his breath and stretch out tired muscles. Breathing in deep and strolling along the pathway, he gazed around at his environs, and even as physically exhausted as he felt, he was once again struck by the beauty of the garden.

"Mister Branson," a voice suddenly said from behind him.

Branson turned around, expecting to see a monk or some other temple employee. Instead, he was surprised to see a bald woman wearing a sky-blue robe standing in the path in front of him, looking completely refreshed and surprisingly happy.

The woman smiled and held up her hand to stop him before he spoke. "The climb is a part of the experience, Mister Branson. With each step, the Seeker sheds himself of thoughts of comfort and of ease. He becomes his more true self. Satotta Kyoshi desires that all who come here seeking knowledge be made to climb those same steps. Think of it as an act of humility."

Branson wasn't exactly please, but then he remembered the days he'd spent once upon a time standing in the lines in and around McLeod Ganj in Dharamshala, and he relaxed a bit. He fondly remembered being there for days, pissing in the street and trying in vain to sell his Rolex for something to eat.

"Lunch will be served back at the hotel once your audience with Satotta Kyoshi is complete. *He* will decide when your time with him is ended. You will speak only when questioned. Answer succinctly, but as quickly as you can. Other than that, it is advised that you keep your thoughts, and your opinions, to yourself… and *listen.* I doubt that you traveled all this way, and paid the kind of money that you have, to talk. Not if you're smart."

The woman presumptively reached over and adjusted the drape of Branson's shirt. She stepped back and looked at him appraisingly. "I hope you find what it is that you seek here, Mister Branson. And I hope Satotta Kyoshi is the one who will be able to help guide you."

She turned slightly, indicating that it was time for him to move along to the main pavilion. The American bowed and stepped passed her, out onto the open grassy plain.

Essentially, a large square, the meadow was carefully maintained in the meticulous style of Japanese topiary. The grass was closely cropped, and all the flowers and bushes were blooming and manicured to perfection. It was one of the most beautiful places he'd ever seen.

He approached the stone structure in the middle of the pasture in a way that he hoped showed reverence. The stone building was covered by a domed roof and looked old, but well kept. Ivy, small shrubs, and flowers bloomed from planter boxes set in the ground around it; a verdant island in the middle of a great, grassy sea.

Branson proceeded toward the structure, walking slowly in an effort to hide his growing excitement as he prepared himself for the encounter. His eye caught sight of a figure sitting on the ground in the center of the canopy. By its size, it appeared to be a man wearing the bright, orange robe of a Buddhist acolyte. From the distance Branson was away, the person's skin looked darkly tanned, but as he got closer, he saw that it was just the heavy shadows that blanketed him.

Branson was forced to look down toward his feet in order to not stumble as he climbed the steps up onto the platform. When he was once again on a flat surface, he looked up and got his first look at Satotta Kyoshi.

Sitting in the middle of a square bamboo mat sat what you might call a man in that he had two arms and two legs, a head, and torso. But his flesh appeared solid, not pliant and his skin looked like it was made of metal.

The man was thin beneath his twisted robes and sitting in the classic Lotus position. His hands were crossed over his lap, palms up, and his head hung down, making it look like he was sleeping or in deep meditation. But it was his face that intrigued Branson most.

Branson stepped closer, bending down to look curiously at the metal man sitting before him. Two round photo cells were located where his eyes should be. And the way his mouth was assembled, it made it appear like he had a wide, perpetual smile on his face. Where his ears should have been were recessed audio processors that would no doubt hear and record everything that took place around him.

The robot sat still, not moving.

Suddenly, the figure jerked and there was a whining, electric sound, like a photographer's flash going off, as he came online.

Branson stepped back to give the machine a respectful space. Suddenly, Satotta Kyoshi's head shimmied ever so slightly on the perch of his neck. The mechanical man's eyes flared with a deep, green light, and he turned to look up at Branson.

"Greetings. Traveler. Arthur Branson. I am. Satotta Kyoshi. I understand. You. Wished. For us. To talk."

SALA-AMPUJAR

Another quick one added at the last minute. As I type this, I am putting the finishing touches on stories as quickly as I can and adding them to the finished stack—creativity in real time. Anyway, as to the story below… it's based on another real guy named Simo "Simuna" Häyhäwho was a Finnish sniper in the Winter War in 1939-1940. His reported "kill count" is debated, but what is beyond question is that it is well over five hundred people. Some say it was as many as five hundred and fifty… with another reported two hundred submachine gun kills. After being shot in the face by another sniper, he recuperated for months and returned to civilian life, living to the ripe old age of 96 (although half of his face was visibly disfigured). His life is a crazy story. Here, I only tried to show a sliver of it. There are plenty of books out on Häyhä… and all are worth searching out. I just hope I did him justice here.

The dawn was cold, colder than the usual forty below he was used to. At this point, though, it didn't matter whether it was Celsius or Fahrenheit. Cold this cold… Once you got passed a certain point, it really didn't matter. It all became a searing, white numbness.

Simuna shifted his position slightly within the tight confines of his roost. He'd scouted a perfect spot for what he was here to do up on a ridge that overlooked a lone bit of road on the highway that ran between St. Petersburg in western-most Russia and Vilnius in neighboring Finland.

The road stretched across the landscape like a black python sunning itself on a bone-white rock. Snow-covered pine, spruce, and birch trees stuck up from the accumulated snow like tent poles, acres of them flanking the black ribbon of asphalt. And overhead, dark clouds silently brooded over the killing field he'd created.

Simuna had laid here for uncountable hours. He'd seen the sun rise like this twice now. Each time, each day, only brought him more waiting. His recon had confirmed that his target—Colonel General Sergey Gerasimov of the Russian Red Army—would be using the road in front of him to travel to a secret conference in Riga. With whom, they weren't sure, but Simuna was here to see to it that the Colonel General never made it there.

He reached down, moving his hand slowly, but inexorably, toward an itch near his groin. He'd been out in the cold like this for at least a couple of days now, waiting for his target to come, and he knew his hygiene was less than optimal. When he slept, and those times were rare, he had dreams of slowly immersing himself into the waters of a hot bath, relishing the feeling of the tropic bite of the water parboiling his frozen skin. When the demands of his itch were appeased, he slowly returned his hand to his rifle like a viper crawling through grass.

He'd buried the nose of the gun—a Mosin-Nagant M28/30—in the snow with only the tip of the barrel barely sticking out. Once it was set, he'd pulled the Spitz-ear sights back just a bit so that the snow would hide the muzzle flash when it came… just in case there was anyone else out on the mountain who might be watching.

For now, though, he had only to wait.

After another hour or so, he snatched up a few fingers full of snow and set it onto the flat of his tongue. Allowing the frigid water to run down his throat, he sighed, confident that the plume of his breath would pass unseen due to the arctic conditions created in his mouth. He stared down at the road and thought for a second that he'd seen something moving on the horizon, but it was only a lone moose crossing the roadway. Where it was heading was anybody's guess. It was rutting season, and therefore the animal was unpredictable, but he was confident it was far enough away that it wouldn't be a problem for him.

And so, with that bit of excitement passed, he returned to

his patient vigilance. He idly thought of home, and of the family he left behind when he went off to war. He smiled and the memories warmed him.

More time passed…

Simuna continued lying on his belly in his coffin-like igloo and did what he could to stay awake. Days and nights were passing by quickly and seemed to be flowing into one another. If the target didn't come soon, he'd be forced to abandon the blind and return to base. Or risk dying from exposure.

But Christ it was cold. The day had started to warm up, but now that night was falling, the temperature had once again begun to drop. He pulled his gray, wool coat tighter about him to conserve his body heat, thankful for the Long Johns his wife had insisted him bringing along. He had on his wool snow pants, and high leather boots, so he knew he was in no danger of becoming hypothermic, but… if he stayed out on the mountain for too long, that could all change quickly. He pressed the side of his face against the frozen birchwood stock of the Mosin and closed his eyes.

His mind slowed and his body began to rest and to replenish its energies. And in his own hyper-alert way, he dozed. His thoughts passed like clouds across the blue sky of his imagination; more memories of his home in Rautjarvi, of his friends and family there. It wasn't long before he found himself pining for a time when his country wasn't at war, when they had lived their lives in peace.

But then, the Russians came…

He smiled as he remembered himself as a boy, joining the Bicycle Battalion, and becoming one of the Finnish White Guard a year later. Of sniper school and the exhilaration and pride of being singled out as exceptional.

Rousing a bit, he reached his hand up to touch the small book that he had kept in his breast pocket since the beginning of the war. The book, a self-ordained talisman and 'list of his sins,' was something he'd had with him since the day he left home. His father gave it to him so that he could write his thoughts down during his tenure as a soldier. It soon became… something else.

Small, like a man's secret address book, and nondescript, the book had few pages left in it, and a stubby pencil nestled in its bindings. The pages were filled with small chalk marks, bundled like sticks into groups of five. He knew how many there were though without counting them, because each stood for a life—a *soul*—that he'd extinguished. And it was the knowledge of that number that he knew he would have to carry around with him forever.

"Five hundred… and one," he whispered softly to himself as if it were a confession.

Night fell quickly, like Mother Nature had had enough of the day, and she'd turned the lights off on her world in frustration. He settled in for the night, pulling his face shield aside now and then to munch on more clumps of snow.

When the moon had risen and was directly overhead, he pulled a bit of jerkied reindeer meat from his pocket. Using his short *puuka* knife, he carved off a piece of the hard material and returned the blade to its scabbard on his belt. Sliding the meat into his mouth, he replaced his face shield so that his flesh wouldn't be burned by the cold. He closed his eyes, and soon, retreated into the warmth of his thoughts as he methodically chewed.

What he wouldn't give for a bowl of Valkosipuli Soup, or some Lohikeitto. He imagined the taste of the hot broths on his tongue, warming him from the inside out and returning color to his frozen cheeks. He smiled beneath the fabric over his face and continued to chew on his cold meat. And, for the briefest moment, it tasted like his mother's Graavilohi.

A polar wind kicked up later that night, blowing even more of the loosely-packed snow that had been on the mountain over him. At this point, he was pretty confident that someone could walk right up next to him and not see him.

Confident in his invisibility, he continued to wait, dozing the night away.

When he finally woke, the first rays of the new day's sun were gently warming his inert body beneath its blanket of freshly fallen snow. His limbs felt stiff, so he flexed them, one by one, infusing their tissue with blood. Checking his fingers for signs of frostbite, he grinned sourly as he calculated how long he'd been out here. Any of the others in his unit would have packed it in and abandoned the mission a long time ago. But not him, he knew that the waiting was all a part of it.

He winced, abruptly feeling the first signs of needing to urinate. If the feeling persisted, he knew he'd have to either dig himself out or do it from this prone position. And, while he didn't relish the idea, the latter would probably be what he did. He'd hate to have to ruin a perfectly good blind for something so otherwise easily dealt with.

Just then, at the line of the horizon at the north end of the valley, his peripheral vision picked up movement. At first, he thought it might have been the moose from the day before on a return trip. But then, he recognized the linear movement of the object, and he knew it for what it was: the Colonel General.

He gazed down his gun sight and zeroed in on the moving vehicle. Once it got a little closer, he saw that it was a Sonderkraftfahrzeug, a treaded motorcycle/tank hybrid that was mostly used to transport personnel, mail, and light armory. The vehicle whisked along the roadway, kicking up loose snow and slush behind its thick, metal treads. There was a driver, but he sat low behind a windscreen to avoid the bracing wind, so it was difficult to see him. His head would bounce into view though, every time the vehicle hit a bump in the road.

Simuna once more sighted along the barrel and through the Spitz-eared gunsight of the Mosin. Closing one eye, he waited in the moment and breathed. Time slowed for him. The snowflakes themselves hung in the air like soap bubbles in his perception. It was as if reality was nothing more than a series of images that he alone could see and control, rifling through them until he could select the perfect one.

He drew the bolt back on the rifle like a lover pulling back a bit of lace. Easing it forward, he slowly drew in another breath… and let it out. He took another as his fingers caressed the knurling on the Mosin's trigger.

Then, he let the air out…

Colonel General Sergey Gerasimov huddled under the wool

blanket that had been provided for him, wincing against the bitter chill. Thankfully, it had stopped snowing just as they left St. Petersburg, and the morning's sun was already starting to bring the temperature up.

The Colonel General was still seething over the fact that he'd been roped into coming all the way out here by his superiors. Their idea was for him to meet with a group of local insurgents who they'd heard were sympathetic to their cause and to try and see if they were ripe for indoctrination. The group had little *real* strategic value to the war effort, but having them in the Red Army's pocket could prove helpful, for disinformation's sake alone.

The treaded transport hit an unexpected bump and Gerasimov felt the back end of the vehicle suddenly fish-tail on the snow. The lorry pitched forward abruptly, losing speed and power. Gerasimov was thrown forward into metal barricade that separated the driver's seat from the cargo compartment.

Fritz the driver sat silently still, his hands still tightly clutching the steering bar. Gerasimov righted himself and clumsily climbed up, thinking to warn the man of the importance of them getting to their destination quickly, but in one piece. He reached up and grabbed onto his shoulder, turning him around.

"Jesus, man," the Colonel General shouted over the wind. "Are you trying to get us killed?"

Fritz's body fell back into the bed of the Sonderkraftfahrzeug. His weight hit the flat, steel surface with a loud bang and the impact shook the vehicle violently. The fact that the man was now missing a good two-thirds of his head put an alarming answer to Gerasimov's posed question.

The Colonel General immediately dropped to the floor, hiding himself behind the metal rails of the truck and Fritz's rapidly cooling corpse. He slowly raised his head in an effort to try and ascertain where the shot had come from. Before him lay only an open valley that was hilled on both sides and stretched all the way to the other horizon. The roadway coursed through the icy landscape like an oily river. Snow-capped trees were everywhere, and each one was a potential hiding place for the sniper.

He waited and the wind howled forlornly around him.

Finally, Gerasimov decided that the only way out of this predicament was to go straight through it, and he began climbing over the divider and into the driver's seat. His plan was to keep low and barge his way straight through the snare. Hoping the inclement weather would hide his actions, he kept his body low. Looking at the thin piece of glass of the windscreen in front him, he was suspicious of his chances.

Still… it appeared to be the only way.

Straddling the seat, he bent to check the stalled engine. Nothing appeared damaged, so he sat up, and restarted the engine, slapping the vehicle into gear once it was running. Beneath him, he felt the engine roar to life. And for a brief moment, he imagined himself making it to the other side of the valley, and his heart beat faster in eager anticipation. Twisting the accelerator on the handlebar, the transport's treads bit into the snow, and the vehicle began to move forward on the ice.

Suddenly, from far off, the sound of a whip crack echoed across the valley. Unable to stop himself, Colonel General Sergey Gerasimov closed his eyes.

Simuna watched his target climb over the barricade, clambering into the driver's seat. The man momentarily fumbled with something under the fuel tank, bending low and out of sight. Then, a puff of white smoke was belched from the rear of the vehicle. Simuna surmised that the engine must have stalled when he took the driver.

He continued to watch silently as the man prepared himself for his last, desperate run. When it looked like he'd screwed his courage to its sticking point, he poked his head up above the windscreen to get a picture of the way ahead.

And Simuna once more pulled his trigger.

The head of Colonel General Sergey Gerasimov was slapped back violently as the 7.62 x 54mm bullet struck his cheek, just under the eye. The slug buckled in on itself creating a small flower of lead as it struck bone and continued on to exit out from behind his ear. Gerasimov's body was catapulted back by the force, and he fell to one side of the still-moving vehicle.

The empty transport slowed, veering off the road and into a snowbank.

Without giving it too much more thought, Simuna retrieved his two rifle casings cooling in the snow. Slipping them into one of his pockets, he slid his arm through the Mosin's strap, pulling the rifle across his back and securing it for travel.

Taking a moment, he retrieved his book from his pocket, turning to a blank spot on a page. Carefully, he scratched two new lines in it.

"Five hundred and … three," he said aloud, and his voice cracked like crystal from lack of use.

He set the pencil back in its hiding place and returned the book to his pocket. Taking a minute to appreciate the beauty of this, his Finnish homeland, he turned to get his bearings. Around him, the cold wind blew, stirring the snow that was piling up around his feet. When he was satisfied he knew the way back, he crawled off into the snow, disappearing into the white of the frozen landscape.

THE ESCORT

This is a story that I had been meaning to write for, well… ever. As a boy who'd grown up without a father, I searched for (and found) my father figures in things like books and movies… in Story. The tales of Robert E. Howard were fundamental to my growing up, though, as they helped me in my understanding of what it was to be a 'Man.' In a weird way, I got a lot of my moral core from those stories. Well, them… and things like THE GODFATHER and ENTER THE DRAGON. Anyway, I wanted to include one last tale with this batch, and I figured now was as good a time as any to finally jump in and do it. I took a few liberties with elements of this story, changed a thing or two to make it my own… y'know, so as to not get sued. And, in the end, I wound up getting a new character out of it! That's a win/win in my book.

The young girl's bare, bejeweled foot splashed loudly in the brackish water of a mud puddle as she fled along the foothills of the mountain. She'd lost her shoes at some point along the way; probably right after she'd dove into the brush and started her headlong sprint. Somehow, though, in all of her panic, she'd gotten herself turned around and had lost her sense of direction. She stopped running for a moment, leaning against a tree and panting heavily, as she tried to catch her elusive breath.

Frantically, she searched her immediate area. The mountain around her was steep, its peaks rising up grandly on all sides of her. Lodge Pole pines and red maple trees rose like palace columns around her, while witch hazel, wild azaleas, and giant ferns littered the ground with green at her feet.

Zara was the girl's name, and she was the firstborn daughter of the Count and Countess Von'El. And how she came to be alone on the mountain was a story that filled her very heart with horror. Her father worked in the city as the shipping magistrate for the Port of Palurmo. Rich in the way crossroads often were, Palurmo was a bustling hub that was located on the southernmost shore of the Stygian Sea. It was her father's job to see that shipping lanes remained open and free of libertines.

She'd been dispatched by her father to travel to the agricultural marketplace of Malurvia along with her most trusted handmaiden, Jatta. Her father had been insistent that she was now old enough to help handle some of the family's business, as well as do a few personal matters for him while in the city. Now that she was well into her seventeenth summer, he felt it was time for her to start taking on more of the responsibilities of an adult woman in her position. And that meant traveling to meet with important business clients in other cities. Knowing how dangerous road travel could be, The Count had possessed the foresight to commission a driver—a Neurog named B'Lith—and a bodyguard for her.

This man, B'Lith, was short, wide of body and of face, with black hair and beard like coarse wool. He'd been recommended to them by a friend of his father's who'd used him in the past. This friend said that the driver was both a good carriage man and adept with a blade, so they'd agreed.

The bodyguard had been another story. Tall, muscular, and lean in the way someone who lived perpetually outside could be, the man was handsome in a roguish kind of way, and he certainly *looked* dangerous. But it was his hair and skin that made him exceptional and seem to stand out in a crowd.

Pale as new snow, his skin was like bleached parchment. His hair—long and tied back—had the look of pulled cotton. B'Lith said he'd met the albino over a flagon of ale at a bar in one of the more disreputable parts of the city. The man—a Malakasian who'd said his name was Na'Nok—was on his way to Palurmo himself and was only too willing to take a job (and the gold) for sitting sentry on a wagon for some city-bred girl.

Zara and Jatta hadn't been completely sure whether the man was safe, but B'Lith told her confidentially that he'd insisted on him riding up top in the co-driver's seat rather than inside the carriage with her as a condition of their agreement.

And, since the hour was rapidly growing late, she'd agreed.

They wound up leaving Malurvia at sundown, far later than desired, traveling through the cold of the night. The way had been bumpy, but not entirely unpleasant. During the night, cicadas chirped in the fields and they even caught a glimpse of a small herd of white-tailed deer eating berries by the side of the road.

Then, just after dawn, she'd heard a shrill cry erupt from the trees above them. The howl was high-pitched and strained and its sound echoed through the forest. Instantly, the forest around them fell silent. At first, Zara thought the cry was merely a cock crowing to welcome the new day. But then, the howl was answered behind them by a series of deep, guttural whoops. The albino's upside-down face suddenly appeared at the side window like a ghost.

"Hold on to something," he said, and his eyes burned with the fire of impending battle. "Those were Kr'Longi war cries. I would know those dog's howls anywhere."

And then, he was gone, disappeared from the window, his moon-white face replaced by the blur of the rapidly passing landscape.

She didn't remember much after that. Something heavy crashed into the side of the carriage knocking it off its wheels and making it veer wildly toward the side of the road. The horses broke free of their harnesses and the long arm of the wagon's tongue struck the ground and dug in, catapulting the coach end over end.

When everything finally settled, Zara found herself on her back on the inside roof of the compartment. She noticed the lifeless body of Jatta lying on the floor under a heavy bench, her head hanging at an odd angle on her neck. She wanted to stop and mourn her friend; they'd been together since they were children, but she had no idea what was happening outside, or if she was in any danger. Regretfully, she was forced to set her grief for the girl aside until later, when she was back home and safe.

She dragged herself from the carriage and struggled to get

to her feet. Around the wreckage, several half-naked men in buckskin leggings cautiously moved in and out of the shadows, sniffing at the air like hounds. She watched as the flames of their torches flickered in their dark eyes as she stealthily moved toward the shadows at the edge of their firelight.

Just as she was about to duck into the anonymity of the darkness, she saw that the—what had the albino called them?—Kr'Longi had encircled B'Lith and were shouting and demanding something from him. One of them, the one giving all the orders who as presumably their leader, shouted for quiet and he approached the short Neurog menacingly.

Mysteriously, the albino bodyguard, or his body, was nowhere to be seen.

"Bracka! Neoph ta metlurgi!! METLURGI!!!" the Kr'Longi leader shouted at the driver, spittle flying from his lips. He struck the short man across the mouth, and angrily pointed back at the ruined wagon.

The Neurog was now bleeding from his lip and he looked genuinely frightened. He plaintively held up his hands and shook his head to show that he didn't understand what was being said.

Zara edged closer to the shadows, knowing there was little a young girl like her could do for the man. And as she dove into the trees, the last thing she heard was the sound of a Kr'Longi battle axe strike something soft and wet. Without looking back, she ran as fast and as hard as she as able through the brush. It wasn't long before she heard the now familiar war cry of her pursuers giving chase.

And so, she ran…

Zara tried as best she could to not make too much noise as she rapidly moved through the forest. But there, in the darkness, her fear soon blossomed into a raging fire within her breast and caution was left behind. Imagining savages at every turn in the dark, the girl plunged headlong ever deeper into the slowly awakening forest.

Na'Nok the White awoke with the feeling of a terrible pressure on his chest. His sternum barked sharply in pain as he tried to move, his breath coming in short, painful gasps. He pushed what turned out to be a thick branch off him, levering it to the side. He set his great hand onto his chest and pressed to see if anything inside had been broken. When his probing brought no additional pain, he sat up, groaning like a drunk having a particularly bad morning.

The last thing he was able to remember was hearing the Kr'Longi war cries in the trees and its response. He'd warned the driver and the passengers of his suspicions and was only just beginning to visually search the area around them, when there was the sudden sound of a branch breaking high overhead. In the next instant, the limb—having been suspended by a single rope—swung like a pendulum toward the carriage. The log came up high, missing the vehicle entirely, but striking him across the chest and knocking him from the top of the stampeding wagon.

After that, his mind remembered only blackness… and the sensation of tumbling.

He slowly got to his feet and tried to calculate which way the wagon had gone by its tracks in the road. From up ahead of him, he heard some sudden shouting in the forest. He quickly searched around him to see if he might have somehow taken anything with him from the wagon with which to defend himself. Finding nothing, he took off running in the direction of the yelling.

A few short seconds later, he arrived at the crash site, but found no one. The wagon was on its back, splinters of wood lay like matchsticks everywhere on the ground. He noticed with sorrow the body of the handmaiden of the girl who'd hired him lying inside the carriage, beneath some shattered planks of wood. Further away, he saw the newly-gutted body of the man who'd hired him. Blood was splashed over his legs and across the ground.

Suddenly, off in the forest, he heard a girl scream.

Still weaponless, but not exactly caring, he sprinted through the trees to find the girl.

Zara paused, hiding herself as best she could behind a tree. The dawn was only now starting to peek its head up over the mountain tops and the sun's rays brought to her some much-needed warmth. She listened and looked around furtively. Birds had only just started to raise their voices to greet the new day with their song. Around her, bushes of trillium and fern nestled against the tree trunks and thankfully helped hide her from view.

She'd heard the Kr'Longi men frantically searching up and down the mountainside for her an hour or so ago, but nothing recently. She'd noticed that they seemed to communicate like coyotes, letting one another know where they were on the mountain by those frightening animal-like calls.

She scanned the area around her, searching for someplace better to hide. She was well-aware of how exposed she was out in the open forest like this and how desperately she needed to change that. She glanced down at the fabric of her sky-blue dress and imagined how easy it would be to see from a long way off. Feeling more and more anxious, she searched to find herself sanctuary.

Another whoop erupted to her right, and the sudden sound made her nearly jump out of her skin. She had to go. She wouldn't allow herself to consider what might happen to her should she be caught. The only thing she kept focused on was getting away.

Her eyes drifted over the forest's tapestry. She saw only the expansive panorama of foliage, her mind creating dark, malignant figures amidst the tree trunks. Then, a short distance away, she noticed what looked like the mouth of a cave or the opening to a culvert. A tattered hedge of greenery half-hid it from view, but she could see how the rock wall behind the brush opened up.

She listened intently for any sound of movement nearby. Hearing none, she sprinted for the opening, crashing into the brush. She clawed her way through the brambles, finally breaking free on the other side. Just then, an excited shouting from one of the Kr'Longi, who was searching for her a short distance away, broke the silence of the forest. A chorus of yips and more wolf-like howls soon answered him.

Terrified, Zara ran into the break in the mountain wall, hoping the hedge would slow them down long enough for her to make her escape. As it turned out, the space beyond the hedge was not a cave, but an open passageway that led through the stone. She noticed that the path jogged to the left a short distance away. With hope rising in her breast, she ran on, even as she heard the men coming to the blind behind her.

Rounding the curve, she was horrified to see the passage come to a blind end. An imposing stone wall rose up in front of her, offering no way to climb it, nor any place for her to hide. Desperate, she turned to escape the blockade, but came face to face with her savage pursuers instead.

There were six of them, spread out loosely across the flat, open area. Shirtless and red of skin, the brutes circled her menacingly, brandishing their weapons. The one who'd been the leader back at the wagon's wreckage approached her and bared his teeth. His pate, like all of his brethren, was shaved on the sides with a top knot that stuck out from his head like the stem of an apple. Another man came up to flank him. The other four were loosely spread out behind them, anxiously edging closer.

"Kanta ta metlurgi!" the leader grunted to his compatriots as he nodded to her.

The savage near him only stared at her intently as he massaged the front of his breeches with his hand, eyeing her lustfully. "Satta va…" he shrugged. "Vas nottala pugi."

"Kasak flavia!" the leader responded snidely.

All six of men chuckled darkly. The second one though continued staring at her and rubbing at himself. The leader slapped him sharply across the back of the head, pushing him away. He turned toward the girl and leered at her. He thought a second, and then turned slowly back to look at his tribesman.

"*Ma* kasak flavia!" he shouted at them, grabbing the girl roughly by the arm.

His grip hurt her, and she cried out in pain. The Kr'Longi leader gazed at her hungrily, clearly excited by her terror, as he slowly started unfastening the front of his pants.

Zara screamed out in protest, but the man was too strong for her and he pulled her roughly to her knees. The men all drew closer, angling to get a better view, and to take their place in line. The girl sobbed sorrowfully and closed her eyes.

Then… one of the savages spoke.

"Oklawana," he said, as if in awe. He slapped the leader on the back and directed him to look to the skies. "Oklawana."

The group looked up into the boughs of the trees as one, and to their consternation, they saw the form of a great snowy bird descending through the forest's canopy. Its broad, wide wings were fully extended as it fell from the sky like a great, white stone. Confused, the Kr'Longi leader squinted into the sun to get a better look, his mouth hanging open like a fish pulled from the water.

"Oklawana," he whispered in wonder.

Na'Nok plunged through the tree branches, his arms and legs splayed, after having leapt from the cliff side above the culvert. He'd heard the crashing of the Kr'Longi tearing their way into the stone wash as they searched for the girl and ran toward it. Hearing her screams only pushed the Malakasian warrior to move quicker, and to act with more rashness than usual.

He'd leapt from the rock without thinking. It was only after he'd left the safety of the ground that he realized how high up he was. The tree's branches reached out to grab him, but their boughs were not enough to support his weight, and they only succeeded in slowing his descent and helping to break his fall. At the last second before hitting the dirt, he saw one of the Kr'Longi, the one closest to the girl, look up gape-mouthed and point at him.

After that, time got choppy.

The great pale warrior landed on the ground in the middle of the first four Kr'Longi fighters. Their surprise at his sudden appearance was immediately evident on their brown mongoloid faces. Na'Nok's right hand landed in the dirt near a rock roughly the size of a large piece of fruit. Thinking quickly, he took it in his vice-like grip.

As he rose to his feet on the bounce, Na'Nok swung the rock up in a violent uppercut. The stone connected with the underside of the Kr'Longi leader's jaw, clapping it shut and severing his tongue. The plug of flesh tumbled to the sand like a slug. Blood splashed from his mouth as his head was rocked back brutally. His jaw, having been shattered to splinters by the blow, drove bone shards into his throat; killing him before he ever really knew what had happened. His body toppled to the ground like felled timber, but not before the albino helped himself to the axe the man was carrying in his hand.

The albino turned at the waist and, using his thickly-muscled frame and a good bit of torque, swung the heavy weapon in a powerful overhand arc. The thick, stone cudgel of the axe split the Kr'Longi's skull like a melon. Once again finding himself unarmed, Na'Nok plucked the dead man's sword from the scabbard on his belt.

And then, he was moving across the dirt toward the others.

He struck the next man, deflecting his sword, and gutting him as he raced passed. The pale warrior's blade bit deep into the meat of the Kr'Longi's exposed belly, spilling his intestines onto the ground in a squiggling heap. On a whim, the albino claimed the dead man's sword from his hand in a backhanded, dagger-like grip. Moving on, he came at the next man in a cyclone of shimmering death, carving the savage before him into pieces.

The pale killer turned to address the last two Kr'Longi who looked at each other nervously, as if trying to bolster one another's courage. Finally, one of them nodded, and they both rushed toward him blindly. Na'Nok absorbed the brunt of the first man's attack, catching his initial blow against his sword and falling back. He then severed the man's arm at the elbow with a powerful downward stroke, and the Kr'Longi fell to his knees screaming, his life's blood pouring out from the stump of his arm like wine.

The ghostly mercenary suddenly felt the hot slash of a sword on the left side of his waist and he turned to quell this last threat. He quickly checked the wound, but found that it was superficial, so he ignored it. It would bleed a bit, but it wasn't anything to worry about. He glared at the savage in front of him and chuckled darkly, thinking he'd cut himself worse whilst shaving.

The last Kr'Longi put up a valiant fight, even landing a few blows against the Malakasian's steel. But, in the end, the pale warrior's overwhelming strength and the ardency of his attack won the day, and he killed the man by severing his head from his neck.

The girl pressed herself against the far rock wall. Her knees were drawn up close to her chest, her arms hugging them tightly. Her face lay buried deep in her chest. Her mind still reeled at the last few hours, terror coursing through her blood like acid. She'd thought she was doomed—cornered and destined to die at the hands of savages.

Or worse.

But then, in an instant, her tormentors were gone, torn away and ravaged by some large, unknown animal that the Kr'Longi had called, 'Oklawana.' She had no idea what the beast was as she was so petrified she was unable—or unwilling—to open her eyes.

But suddenly, the world had gone silent, and a new terror took hold of her.

This beast? Where was it?

Then, she heard the sounds of the great animal moving closer. She could hear the creature's breath coming in short, hot pants; its sound accompanied only by some low, pained grunting. Her imagination caught fire and she conjured a monster with giant jaws and teeth like knives in her mind as the sound of its approach came ever closer. She clenched her eyes tighter and silently prayed to her gods that her death would be quick.

But nothing came; just a heavy feeling of anticipation that settled over the space like a doused blanket. And in that moment, she could hear birds calling out again in the boughs of the trees above and the gentle rushing of the wind.

Maybe the beast left, she thought hopefully. Maybe the creature's appetite had been satisfied with the meat that it had, and so, it had left her. Even as she thought it though, a part of her knew that it wasn't the true. That it was, in fact, impossible.

She heard the creature come ever closer.

Finally, unable to bear it any longer, the girl tentatively

opened her eyes, half expecting to be staring into the face of a monster. Instead, though, she saw only the pale, tired eyes of the Malakasian bodyguard she'd paid to protect her back in Malurvia, the one she'd thought long dead like her dear Jatta and the driver back in the crash of the wagon.

"I can only offer my apologies, Miss. I was... delayed," he said, grinning roguishly and extending his hand. "Come, there may be more of those dogs about. Let's get you home."

SALAMAT!!

As always, I thank my wife, Cat, who saved me.

My kids… Jhustin / Alesia & Connor / Taylor: You make me so proud. It is an honor to have watched you all grow up.

My best pal, Ripley… your light gave me hope.

To the person who listened: Heather Strbiak. You're help is beyond beneficial… as is your friendship. Thank you!

To TJ Tranchell & CK Burch … for simply being. Buy their books!

To Django & Jeffrey @ A Comics Place… thank you for the help

To Julie Marletto and the staff at KMRE… thank you for giving me a chance.

To David Wilson and Crossroad Press… thank you for still believing.

This book, as always, was written and edited to certain folk's podcasts:

Doug Benson, Kevin Smith, Marc Bernardin, Gilbert Gottfried, Frank Santopadre, Paul Scheer, June Diane Raphael, Jason Mantzoukas, Tony Hinchliffe, Brian Redban, Jeremiah

Watkins, Joel "Joelberg" Jimenez, Chroma Chris, Jessie "Jetski" Johnson, Dana Gould, Erik Griffin Gaming, and, of course, The Mommies… thank you!

All praise to Crom
Mom… I miss you and I love you.
To Jun Fan… again, thank you for the example. I'm trying…

And finally, to my friend (and dog), Rocko… here we are again, buddy.

Thanks for listening.

ABOUT THE AUTHOR

Thom Carnell. As a journalist, his interviews and profiles can be found in *Carpe Noctem Magazine* (for which he served as Head Writer and Creative Consultant), *Fangoria Magazine,* Dread Central.com and Twitchfilm.com. Carnell's fiction has been featured in *Carpe Noctem 20,* the Pill Hill Press anthology *Bloody Carnival, Swank Magazine,* in his novels *No Flesh Shall Be Spared,* and *No Flesh Shall Be Spared: Don't Look Back,* and in his short story collections *Moonlight Serenades* and *A String of Pearls.*

www.thomcarnell.com

Made in the USA
Monee, IL
18 October 2026

66035058R00142